# Nissus

## Carl Sorenson

Cover art by cheriefox.com

The text of this book is set in 11 point Constantia

First edition published by Phoenix Unchained

ISBNs

979-8-9881694-3-7 (eBook)

979-8-9881694-0-6 (paperback)

979-8-9881694-1-3 (hardcover)

979-8-9881694-2-0 (audiobook)

nissusnovel.com

Acknowledgments

This book would not have been possible without the encouragement and patience of my wife, Lala, and my children over the years of writing and revising. Lala's different perspectives were invaluable to fleshing out several characters. And I'll always fondly remember introducing the premise to my then six-year-old girls, only to be surprised at the instant game of "Bionics" they invented.

I found my small army of beta readers, sensitivity readers, editors, and people acting as sounding boards to be indispensable. I owe much of the quality of this work to, among others, Mike Waitz, Joshua Powell, Elissa Richter, Ritika, Nicole Neuman, and of course my parents, Frank and Ellen Sorenson.

Agnes knew it was practically a miracle they had escaped detection so far, not to mention the fact that they had managed to find passageways through the city that were sufficiently hidden from their pursuers' view.

Unfortunately, they were certain that a manhunt was underway. Twice they had heard people discussing the "security breach" while the two of them were hiding, and once, they were sure a search party had passed within shouting distance. Perhaps worse, Agnes could see that Willym was reaching the end of his strength—he'd been wobbly to start with, and hours of frantic scrambling to escape Nissus had left him gasping and near collapse.

Time for some hard choices.

Contents

# Chapter 1

# Absence

*You are a traitor,* Agnes thought, watching Mr. Marks warily. *Or at the very least, you're a fool. A dupe. You're just a puppet doing the work of the Bionics. In fact, what if they....*

Her thoughts trailed off. With abrupt self-awareness, Agnes glanced around the classroom. Forcing herself to be calm, she set aside her paranoid train of thought. The other students were showing different levels of interest or boredom, but nothing like her suspicious intensity. *What's wrong with me lately?* she thought. Her feelings had been so jumbled up for the past few months, ever since Elaina had left, and even more so since the recent trouble with her dad. But she shouldn't be irrational like this.

Letting out her breath in a measured way, Agnes tried to think logically. *Mr. Marks is just a bit* overly enthusiastic *about the Bionics,* she decided, *that's all. The Bionics are certainly not secretly using my social studies teacher—why would they? If I keep feeling paranoid like this, I'll need to see a psychiatrist.* She smiled to herself wryly.  Plenty of those among the Bionics—and good ones. Only problem was, that was who she was most afraid of.

Time to participate in the discussion. Agnes raised her hand and was called on.  "I think you're missing the point, though. Regardless of whatever other...virtues the Bion—I mean the Factus—might have, as long as they're a threat, you have to keep that in focus. Does humanity have a future or not? We can't get all buddy-buddy with them if our survival is at stake."

Mr. Marks looked like he was dismissing her comment before she'd even finished. "Right, you see the Factus as an existential threat to the Traditionalists. You've made that argument before. Most people, if they're concerned at all, would say that Petram is the answer. If we can keep doing things our own way here in Petram, and keep the Factus out, we'll be fine."

While he took the discussion in another direction, Agnes glared at him. She wanted to shout, "I don't have to make any argument! You can see the empty seat right there!" She looked over at the forlorn chair next to her, where Elaina had sat, but the teacher had already moved on.

Seething, Agnes continued the argument in her mind. She could almost hear Mr. Marks saying impatiently, absurdly, "People move, Agnes. We all know she wasn't really happy here in Petram."

For the second time in a minute, Agnes calmed herself. *I shouldn't be surprised that my comment went nowhere.* Absently retying her straight blonde hair in a ponytail, she tried to listen to the class, but failed. "If they're concerned at all," the teacher had said. Exactly. Most people were content living on the reservation—not that they called it that—and venturing out as tourists sometimes. If the gods are kind, what's to complain about?

Well, for one thing, most people didn't have their father kidnapped by the Bionics like hers had just been.

***

Today marked one week since her father—"Willym" to his colleagues, "Dad" to her—had been taken. One week of frustration, with the Petram government—*her* government—giving no answers. They simply reported that the Bionics had escorted him from his lab in the middle of the day, "relocating" him along with his team and some of his equipment, and they were sure he would be in contact soon. Even as a seventeen-year-old, Agnes could tell that they knew more than they were saying.

It was obvious that the Bionics—the Factus—had acted right after Willym had started on some new research, something important. Normally talkative and open about his work, her father had suddenly grown more serious, tense even, the week before he vanished.

*First Elaina, and now Dad.*

At the bell, Agnes slung her bookbag over her shoulder and joined the flow of students leaving the room. A few short months ago, she had been like all of these other chatting high school students, blissfully unworried about friends and family. But Elaina had been her best friend. Achingly lonely, Agnes walked silently through the crowd of people.

She paused in a stairwell, where the large glass windows presented a view of the nearby mountains, marked now by November snows. Somewhere past those trees and hills was her father. Though she had no idea which direction he was, she gazed out anyway, as if there might be some clue in the scene.

For the twentieth time in a week, Agnes thought back to what he had said the night before he was taken away. *"I had it all wrong. Hale's going to be a hero—he's going to save Petram. Trust me."*

Agnes had been surprised. *"The prime minister? But I thought you and Mom didn't like Hale. You even called him 'loony,' I remember."*

Willym's eyes had burned with an unfamiliar, fearsome intensity. *"That was before he gave us this project. I see now what it's going to take to really protect Petram from the Factus."*

Agnes tore her eyes from the window and continued down the stairs. Well, he may have thought he knew how to protect Petram, but that didn't stop the Bionics from snatching him up anyway. He really must have found a weakness, if they were that desperate to stop him. It was beyond strange— she'd never heard of the Factus interfering inside the city like this before.

As she slid onto her physics lab stool, Agnes made a mental effort to set aside her concerns. *I just need to make it through this lab, and then I can head home. I can't keep brooding about the Bionics.*

She felt her spirits lift measurably as she began thinking about this new class. Physics made for a nice distraction—a hands-on lab experiment that had nothing to do with the

Factus or their interference. And on top of that, some of her classmates here were genuine friends.

Agnes and her lab partner, Cara, walked through the steps of setting up their experiment together, winding a thin wire in a coil around a rod of iron and connecting various devices. However, when they flipped the switch to their power supply, nothing happened.

Cara looked back at the instructions. "We're supposed to hook it up like *this*, but the magnetometer isn't registering anything. I think you wound the wires correctly, and the sensor is definitely on...." She paused to look at the schematic displayed on the surface of her table, rotating it and enlarging it with some finger commands.

Agnes traced the connections back to where the leads for the power supply disappeared into a small jumble of wires and transformer boxes. Poking around, she suddenly smiled. "Yo, Emil! You unplugged our power!"

Across the table, Emil regarded her dismissively, looking down his long nose at her. This wasn't hard for him to do, given that he was nearly a full head taller. "Look here, Agnes Barker. I've had just about enough of you blaming me for your own screw-ups. Good thing you have a lab partner there to carry your weight or you'd probably be frying all of my equipment right now."

Laughing, Agnes picked up some electrodes and held them up threateningly, with Cara smiling to herself off to the side. "Oh, really? How about I come over there and see what I can fry...maybe I'll start with your face...."

Emil grinned and dismissed her with a wave. "Nah, you wouldn't want to fry me. I might think it's an improvement."

Agnes wagged an electrode at him and agreed pensively. "That's probably true..."

Emil was rather good-looking, most people would agree. His dark, curly hair contrasted sharply with Agnes's straw-colored blonde. Regardless, he was in fact casually dating one of her other friends, Catteryn—which pleased Agnes, as the two of them were a good match.

With the electrodes finally in their proper places and the power supply plugged back in, Cara and Agnes ran through a series of tests, measuring the magnetic field coming from their wire coil. Entering the numbers into a spreadsheet on their table, they soon had enough data to plot a graph showing the results: The magnetic field varied as a simple function of the electric current in the wire and the distance from the coil. Cara sent the graph to the teacher shortly after Emil and his partner finished their own experiment, leaving the group with just enough time to pack up their things before the bell rang.

"Are we all coming over this afternoon, Agnes?" Emil asked. Agnes paused before answering, but just for a moment. She nodded yes, and then headed outside to the walkway with him.

She could still feel a bit of the paranoia from earlier, and she wasn't sure if having friends over would be a welcome distraction, or if they would all just end up dwelling on her problems together. *Well, they say misery loves company, so either way, I'll probably be glad to have them there. And who knows, maybe we'll even get some studying done!*

On the school sidewalk, she and Emil met Catteryn and exchanged greetings, and as usual, the three of them chatted while waiting for their other friend, Jonnan, to be let out from his school across the street. Once the group was complete, they would all walk to her house together, where they could get their homework done while socializing.

The one glaring problem with the setup was the hole that Elaina's absence left—and even though it had been nearly two months since she had abruptly disappeared, the group dynamics still had not really recovered. Not least of the drama was that Jonnan sometimes seemed to assume that, with Emil and Catteryn dating, he and Agnes must be an item, too. *Problems, problems.* Absently, she batted away a dragonfly that had flown close by her head. It flailed momentarily before landing on a nearby wall, iridescent in the sun.

Agnes was just starting to wonder what a dragonfly was doing, flying around in the November cold, when she saw Jonnan approaching. "Hey, Emil, Agnes," he called as he approached.

A soft *ping* sounded. "Hang on, guys," Agnes called out. "I just got a note from my mom. Maybe she has some news...." Rather than pulling out her handheld, Agnes used some finger commands to direct the message to display on the wall next to her. She and her friends crowded around to watch.

In the video, Zusana Barker bore a fair resemblance to her daughter—light-complexioned like most people in Petram, nice-looking but not glamorous. Agnes had always been happy to wear her face, so to speak. Of course, people who were *not* satisfied with their appearance often left Petram, to go live among the Bionics. There, they had more options for changing how they looked.

Zusana seemed fractionally less tense than she had been this morning, and it didn't take long to find out why. The message was quite short but significant. "Agnes, I've gotten a message from your father. He isn't being released yet, but we're starting to get some more information. Come on home and I'll show you."

The four friends gave a brief cheer and began racing toward Agnes's home.

***

The Barkers' house was neat and well-cared-for, a two-story white frame with dark green trim, perhaps nicer than average for Petram. Zusana had a respected position directing a large greenhouse producing heritage crops for export—a job from which she was currently on leave, given the family crisis—and Willym was at least as important in his role as a government scientist. Sharp and very focused, Willym surely earned every cent he made, Agnes knew. His work was arguably too advanced for their home in Petram. If her suspicions were right, he had even begun to investigate the Bionics themselves—though being a proper scientist, he always used the more appropriate term "Factus."

The teenagers hurriedly came through the door, greeting Mrs. Barker inside, barely pausing to take off their shoes. Familiar with the family and the house—practically family members themselves—they settled on a couch and chairs to watch the message.

Projected on the wall, Willym appeared to be nervous, and a bit fatigued. He was accompanied by a rather tall, Nordic-looking man in what appeared to be a conference room. "Hi, Zusana, Agnes. I'm sure you are terribly worried about what's been going on. Mainly there's been a disagreement with the

Factus about the research my team is undertaking. They think...well...actually they'd rather we just shut it all down."

For a brief moment, Willym gazed, silently contemplating something unknowable to them, before shifting back to the camera and the current moment. "I'm trying to work with Erik here on a way forward. I can't really discuss anything about the research. I'm here with two others from Petram, but the Factus blocked all of our communications with the rest of the team back home. That's why I haven't been reachable."

He looked over to Erik, who now spoke with an authoritative voice. "The situation is somewhat more complicated than Willym just indicated, but he is essentially correct. There are some safety and ethical concerns that I cannot appropriately discuss with you right now. Please know that we were reluctant to restrain your husband and father and restrict his communication.

"We did not do this lightly, and we have been in continuous contact with the authorities in Petram, trying to negotiate a resolution to the problem. I understand that they have not been very forthcoming toward you." At this, Erik looked a bit angry. "However, I have been assured that they will be more cooperative going forward and should be in contact with you shortly."

Erik paused. Eyes fixed on the camera, he continued intently. "We are quite concerned for your family—more than you can know at this point—and we are trying to arrange for a way to make up for what has happened. We will talk again soon, one way or another."

After the video ended, Agnes silently processed what she had heard. While watching the video, she hadn't realized immediately that Erik was one of the Bionics, and when she did realize it, she again felt the visceral paranoia and the unsettled feeling she had experienced that morning. It took a moment for her to get her feelings back under control.

*Bionics.* More formally, species *Homo factus.* The term meant "made or constructed man," and though she wouldn't have known there was anything artificial about Erik by looking at him, she knew he must not be quite human, no longer *Homo sapiens.*

Apparently, she was the only one without something to say about the message. Catteryn pointed out, "They didn't even say where he was."

Zusana nodded at this and murmured, "Oh, Willym, what have you gotten yourself into?"

Jonnan said, "They said they're trying to make up for what happened. How about just let him go? It's not that complicated."

Zusana said, "I *had* felt like the science ministry was stonewalling me when I tried talking to them about what's going on, and this video confirms it." She gave a resigned sigh. "I'll have to try again tomorrow."

Emil said, "What I don't get is why *our* government is stonewalling you. You'd think they would be yelling and screaming about this, especially with Hale in charge now. It goes right to the heart of our relationship with the Factus. Are they controlling us after all? What about our rights? Is it even safe to leave Petram now, if people are being detained?"

At this, Agnes dismissively said, "We all know half of Petram thinks the Bionics are just fabulous. I'm sure they've convinced themselves the Bionics had a good reason to kidnap someone. Somehow."

Zusana got up from her chair and headed out of the room. "Well, I've already watched Willym's message half a dozen times. Since there's nothing much I can do about it right now, I should go ahead and start preparing dinner." When Emil offered to help, she declined the offer. "Thanks, Emil, but no, you guys should get started on your homework and studying. You've got some tests this week, right?"

Emil glanced forlornly at his study materials. "Yeah, we do have a bunch of tests to study for. Guess I just need to suck it up and do it."

Agnes empathized with his wish to put it off. School was about to go on hiatus for five full weeks, and they were in the midst of a veritable academic storm before the five-week calm.

It was after dinner, with homework largely completed and friends sent home, when Erik's promise of more cooperation from the Petram authorities was fulfilled. Agnes didn't hear the call come through, since it was directed to her mother, but Zusana let her know about it as soon as she was finished.

"I have an appointment tomorrow morning to talk to our diplomatic mission!" she told her. "They didn't make any promises but at least *something* is happening."

***

Willym stared at the blank wall across the room in front of him, not talking to Tomas or Edmon, his two companions sitting to either side of him at the small, round table. He had already said everything important, in whispered conversations drowned out by loud music. He couldn't be sure there were no microphones in this room—a kitchen— but the three of them had disassembled everything they could access, trying to check. Certainly, other areas of the laboratory suite were being surveilled.

As if to emphasize that fact, a chime sounded in the lounge nearby. All three got up and marched over to the display wall.

Erik spoke from the display. "Good news, Mr. Barker. We've just had a breakthrough in our talks with Petram. How would you like to have a visit from your wife in a few days?"

Willym didn't try to hide his entirely genuine smile. He glanced at Tomas, silent understanding passing between them. *Perfect. Now we just need to find a way for her to pass a message to our asset outside the lab once she gets here.*

He gestured a command to turn on the music once again. *Time to get busy. We have preparations to make.*

# Chapter 2

# Fear

Agnes found it difficult to focus at school the next day, knowing that her mother was off doing hostage negotiations—or at least that was how Agnes thought of it. She kept wanting to check for messages during the day, even though she knew quite well that anything sent to her would probably be embargoed until after school.

There wasn't anything in her calculus class that should have made her think about the Bionics or her father, but she managed to feel distracted anyway. The discussion in her literature class was another matter. One of the other students was explaining his take on the book they had read:

"The story is about adapting to change. The main character, Okonkwo, can't bring himself to adapt to the colonists. He just keeps insisting that things should stay the same. If he really paid attention to what was happening around him, he'd see that he needed to adapt."

Another student raised his hand and countered, "Oh, I think he was paying attention. He just didn't like it. Why should he have to adapt and change? That was his home, his culture, and he wanted to keep things the way they were. He had a right to do that."

"But he couldn't win. He should've been able to see that."

Agnes piped up. "He *could* have won if his people had been willing to stick with him, though. That's the real tragedy here. He was all alone in his fight to save his culture." *It's more than a little like us here in Petram. Don't you see what the Bionics are doing to us?* But of course, they did see. People were simply too much like the Igbo of the novel—they didn't fight back, not hard enough.

The teacher responded, "They had to make a decision between trying to maintain control and allowing things to change, didn't they? But the question is not just, 'What is worth fighting for?' They had to decide, 'What kinds of things can we even influence?' Even before the colonizers came, there was great conflict for him. Even someone as driven and strong as Okonkwo was forced by circumstances into exile. And later, even as the toughest and strongest leader, he couldn't make his people be what he wanted them to be."

*Depressing*, Agnes thought. *And way too much like my life. "Live on a reservation." "Go to school." "No, you can't have your father back." When did anyone let* me *make my own decisions about my life?*

Agnes was beginning to feel her paranoia creeping back when the class mercifully ended, and she could move on to less treacherous topics.

***

After school, Agnes hurried home without her friends—they all had other plans and wouldn't be going to her house today. Agnes didn't want to wait even a moment for them anyway, since she wanted to hear how her mom's meeting had gone.

The moment Agnes opened the door and saw her, she could tell that it must have been good. Zusana looked unequivocally upbeat. "They're going to release him?" Agnes asked hopefully.

At that, Zusana deflated fractionally. "No, they haven't said that, not yet. But we can go visit him! We've been invited to go to Nissus!"

Stunned, Agnes dropped her backpack on the floor and walked over to a chair to sit. "Wait. They're not releasing Dad, and now you want to go to the Bionics that kidnapped him? With me? Three hostages instead of one?" After waiting all day, and getting her hopes so high, Agnes wasn't sure now if she wanted to cry or punch someone.

Zusana was taken aback. "No, not as hostages. He's not really a hostage. He's there because of something to do with his work—you heard him in the message he sent yesterday. This is just a way to help us be together as a family while they resolve whatever the problem is. They're trying to do something nice for us. We can see Nissus!" She looked at her daughter placatingly.

Agnes felt her frustration surge toward anger. "Nissus! I've never even heard of Nissus. What's it got to do with anything? The Bionics kidnap Dad and you forgive them because they say you can go be a tourist somewhere?"

"Agnes, Nissus is the city where they took him to continue his research. It's in Greenland, about a day's journey by rail." She sat to face her daughter. "That's where he's been this whole time. I've heard it's spectacular. I think the Factus are making a peace offering here. You heard Erik last night. I don't think they're trying to be evil or trick us or anything." Zusana smiled. "We'll get to visit Dad! Just think of that!"

Agnes looked at her mother levelly. "I don't like the Bionics! Have you ever heard me say I want to go to some city of theirs? In *Greenland*, of all places? After what they've done, don't tell me you've gotten all excited about them like everyone else in Petram! They got to you, too! I'm going to be the last real human left, I think! It's not safe, Mom!" She could feel her pulse pounding, her face flushing.

Zusana frowned at her daughter. "Safe. Actually, I think it would be safer than leaving you here—no, don't interrupt. I know you're 17 and can take care of yourself. I'm not talking about that. See, I talked to your father a couple of weeks ago about how to keep us all safe. He said he was nervous about this new assignment from the prime minister. He told me that he actually trusts the Factus more than Hale, and—"

Agnes cut her off. "You heard what he said last week! He said he was wrong about the prime minister. He knows how dangerous the Bionics are, now."

"I know what he said. But I know some things about the Factus, too. I talk to them every day for work. Trust me. I don't know what exactly is going on, but I know it's not as simple as you think. We need to take this trip to Nissus."

With a cry of frustration, Agnes got up and stormed upstairs to her room, her face burning with anger, worry gnawing at her. *Even Mom wants to leave Petram?* she thought furiously, trying to find a persuasive way to explain why this was such a betrayal. *Clearly, the Bionics are trying to entice us out of Petram, dazzle us with Nissus, and make us forget their one giant sin.* The kidnapping of Willym Barker was one stain that could not be erased by any number of tourist packages. Agnes would not forget.

She heard a knock at the door. "I'm not going!" she shouted without opening it.

"I'm not going to decline the invitation, and I'm not going to leave you here. We're both going. We leave early Saturday. It'll be educational for both of us, I think. We'll talk about it later when you're ready to come out." She could hear footsteps walking away from her door.

One frustration after another. Her father held against his will. Her mother apparently determined to take her to the kidnappers, like it or not.

And now, when Agnes tried to search online for material about Nissus, there was little information available—the Petram censors blocked most of it. Literally *everyone* was trying to control her.

Only the most basic information about the city was accessible. *Nissus is in southern Greenland. The Arctic.* Huh. That wasn't exactly close to anything, except it meant the city was on the rail line between North America and Europe. So that must be what kept Nissus going—lots of people passing through all the time.

Heading east from Petram, it would take quite a few hours to get to Chicago, where they could pick up the vactrain. It might be a long day before they got to their destination.

It was hard to see why her mother thought Nissus would be so interesting and "spectacular." From what little she could gather, it was a planned city, one of the most densely populated in the world. Nearly everything about living there was artificial, from the sunlight to, presumably, the people. Bionics. *Sounds like loads of fun.*

***

"So let me get this straight," Catteryn said, sitting on the floor of the bedroom Friday evening as Agnes packed for the trip. "You ditched school this morning, took the trolley all the way to the other side of Petram with a backpack full of food, snuck into an empty vacation cabin to hide out, and were there for hours before your mom and the police found you and marched you back here?"

"Pretty much, yep," Agnes said as she zipped up the suitcase, sitting on it to squeeze it shut. "Turns out the government can be motivated to find *me*, just not my dad."

"You really don't want to go with her to Nissus, do you?" Catteryn said.

"No, and my mom really doesn't want to leave me behind. She said, and I quote, 'I think we'll take our chances with the Factus over Hale for now.'"

The last few days of school had passed in a dreamlike blur—*if the dreams were nightmares*, Agnes figured. She had tried to focus on tests and schoolwork but was completely distracted, dreading the upcoming departure. She had barely spoken to her mother, and there was no question her grades would be bad after her poor performance on these tests and especially after missing school entirely today.

Now, with Agnes safely back home and the school term ended, Agnes's friends had come by her house to commiserate with her as she packed, and to wish her well on the trip. The four teens made for a crowded room.

As usual, Emil tried to be a voice of moderation.

"I think your mom has a point, Ag. What do we really know about the Factus? It probably *would* be educational. And it doesn't sound like they're trying to do anything against *you*. It really could be as simple as their way of trying to make up for what happened with your dad. At least be happy you'll get to see him."

Jonnan retorted, "Oh, sure, absolutely they're using this as a way of getting on your good side. Don't forget, these guys are master manipulators. But the minute you're out there, away from Petram, they can do anything to you. Anything. Once you get some nanobots inside, they can mess with your brain, read your thoughts, and make you think whatever they want."

Agnes groaned, huddled on her bed with her knees pulled up. "That's not helping, Jonnan."

"Hey, it's the truth." He shrugged helplessly. "Better to go in knowing what's at stake."

Catteryn was skeptical. "I'm not sure they can really do all that. I don't think the Factus really want to mess with us that badly. It's not like we could stop them here in Petram if they wanted to do something to us. They control literally the whole world, other than a few Traditionalist communities like ours.  The fact that Petram exists means that they're willing to leave us alone."

Emil had another take. "Your Dad traveled out of Petram before, right? He knows as much as anyone here about the Factus and what they can do. Lots of people leave Petram on vacation trips all the time. I really don't think this is such a big deal."

Jonnan gave a sly smile and countered, "Yeah, if Petram's best scientist could misjudge them so badly, what chance does anyone else have? Agnes will come back saying she was wrong, and the Bionics are actually fantastic. Just wait."

Emil frowned at him, while Agnes groaned again and dropped her forehead onto her knees. But after a quick moment, she raised her head again and said, "I don't know what to believe about the Factus. It's hard to explain what I'm so upset about. I'm just...so scared for some reason. And I just hate them. I think the best explanation I have is it just...feels like regular people are in danger. That we're going to be extinct. Because everyone will want to join the Bionics."

"And that's why what Jonnan says is not helping," Catteryn offered gently. "You're afraid they will make you want to abandon your 'self', your identity. That you won't be able to make your own choice."

Agnes nodded tentatively. "Yes, a bit...but mostly I'm just afraid. Probably because I'm being dragged out on this trip and there's nothing I can do about it. Just like my dad is being held and there's nothing he can do about it."

The friends offered a few more words of encouragement, but eventually there was nothing more to say. Agnes and her mother were going to have an early start in the morning, so it was soon time for everyone else to go home and for her to get some rest. They left her with a few quick hugs and well wishes, and then she was alone with her fears.

Petram was nearly the only place in the world safe from the Factus, and tomorrow she was leaving it.

***

Willym rubbed his temples, watching Edmon. In a whisper, he said, "But can we send enough information that way? The number of bits we need...."

Edmon glanced around the room again, for the third time in two minutes, as if trying to make sure the Factus still couldn't see or hear their plotting. He had been doing that all day. "Yes, I think so. See, we have two different things to work with here...."

Willym worried while he listened. *Everything will have to go just right for this to work.* But what choice did he have? The future of the world—his world, anyway—was riding on this.

Chapter 3

# Meltdown

Considering this was Agnes's first-ever time to step outside Petram, the actual departure was a bit anticlimactic. For one thing, her sleep had been both quite poor and much too short; consequently, she couldn't stop yawning and her thoughts seemed to be stuck in syrup. For another, she couldn't really tell when the train had officially left Petram—it wasn't like they had a big sign reading, "Welcome to Factus territory!" as they sped along. And if they had, it would have been too dark to see the sign unless they had put lights on it. Agnes and her mother may have been up, but the sun wasn't.

They simply accelerated through some of Petram's urban nightglow for a while, then raced past some scattered houses and neighborhoods, and finally out onto farmland before winding through the mountains, heading east.

Forehead against the glass, Agnes could see occasional lights in the pre-dawn darkness, but got little sense of what was out there. The train car was dim inside, too, so she couldn't very well make out who her fellow passengers were, either. But she knew they must be Factus, and therefore unnatural.

As Agnes and Zusana had boarded the train, a few lights had come on momentarily and she had seen some other passengers stirring in their sleep. Most had blankets pulled up around them, seats reclined to nearly horizontal. No one else had boarded or gotten off the train at the Petram station, so the stop was merely seconds long. Thus, Agnes did not get a very good look at her fellow travelers.

From what she did see, they had seemed normal enough...mostly. She wasn't sure, but she had thought for a moment that one man a few rows in front had horns on his head. *Horns?!* That creepy thought did nothing to loosen the knot of anxiety she could feel in her stomach.

"Agnes, honey," her mother said, and tried to pull her away from the window. "Please try to sleep while it's still dark. I can tell you're exhausted."

Agnes gritted her teeth and retorted with a little more venom than she knew she should, "Well, if I'm exhausted, that's your fault. It wasn't my idea to get up in the middle of the night and go to some horrible huge city."

Zusana sighed and gave up for the time being, pulling out her own small blanket and reclining her chair.

*I really do need sleep,* Agnes thought, *but we'll be traveling all day. I'm sure once we've been traveling for a few hours, I'll be bored enough to sleep.* For now, just the thought of where she was and where she was headed filled her with fear and made sleep impossible.

Soon they were really flying across the countryside, though their carriage gave them a smooth ride, quieter than Agnes had expected. Before very long, she realized that the night was easing into dawn, and she could begin to make out the form of the landscape outside her window. As the train approached a shallow curve, the track ahead of them came into view, and Agnes could see the overhead catenary wires with their support posts extending into the distance.

For some reason, thinking of the electricity coursing through the wires and into her train made Agnes think about the school science experiment she had performed a few days before. She almost smiled at the contrast between the little tabletop setup she had used, and the massive force pushing her train across the continent. But then she remembered everything that was happening in her life, and the moment was lost.

Agnes moved little in the hours of traveling toward Chicago, where they would transfer. Still uneasy about being among Bionics, she had no desire to get up and walk around the train. Each station stop after Petram saw a number of people get on or off, and she no longer needed the lights to come on in order to see her fellow passengers. This did nothing to ease her fears, as she could now clearly see, when the man a few rows in front of her stood, that he did indeed have a pair of short horns curving upward from the sides of his head.

"Mom..." she nudged.

Zusana looked at where she had gestured. "The man with the horns?" she asked quietly. Agnes nodded. Her mother shrugged. "I guess some people like to grow horns. Must be a fashion thing."

Agnes just stared at her, willing her to acknowledge that this was bizarre. "Look, Agnes, we're probably going to be seeing a lot of new things on this trip. He's not doing anything to you, so just ease up and let this be a chance to see the world a bit."

"People don't have horns, mom."

"*Homo sapiens* people don't. Apparently, *Homo factus* people sometimes do."

Agnes gave a little shiver and looked around herself. "There must be nanobots everywhere."

"They're not *viruses*. You're not going to catch horn-growing bots from someone you meet on a train. They don't work that way."

"How would you know?" But even as she said it, Agnes knew the answer that was coming.

"Your father has worked with them in his research in the past! He knows how they're programmed, what they can do. He doesn't want nanobots inside him any more than you do, but he's been outside Petram lots of times. They're not dangerous."

Frustrated, Agnes sank farther into her chair and stared out the window again. Rationally, she knew her mom was right, that the bots were not going to infect her like a disease. But *knowing* they were there on the train with her, active and unseen, made her want to run. *But there's nowhere to run. I'll be surrounded by Bionics and their nanobots for this whole trip.*

Somehow, through her swirling fear and anxiety, sleepiness finally asserted itself and Agnes managed to doze a bit. The window did not make a comfortable pillow, but the ride was surprisingly smooth, and it was not until the train was about to pull into the station in Chicago that she fully awoke.

***

Zusana hurried Agnes off the train, and after checking some overhead signs, began heading down a long concourse full of other travelers. "I want to make sure we can make our connection. It leaves at fourteen hundred."

Agnes struggled to keep up while dragging one of the suitcases. "We have nearly an hour, mom. I'm hungry."

"I think we need to be boarded a few minutes early. We can eat some of the food we packed once we're on the train."

The busy, crowded conditions in the station made for slow progress, despite their attempts to hurry. Even Agnes was beginning to worry that they would not make their connection, when at last they found the boarding area for their vactrain.

Waiting in the line, Agnes finally found a moment to truly look at the people around her. Most of them looked fairly normal to her. They could have blended in among the people of Petram without anyone being the wiser, except there was so much more diversity here. Previously, nearly everyone Agnes had met was of European descent, but here that was a distinct minority. It seemed that this line she was in contained people from every corner of the world.

And here and there she saw people who would not have fit in at all in Petram. One woman had electric blue skin. A young man had eyes that seemed to glow red, and a wild mane of dark hair. Come to think of it, a lot of the people had green or blue eyes, more than she suspected should be likely. Agnes was startled to realize that a pair of children right in front of her had pointed, elfish ears to go with blond, nearly translucent hair.

For some reason, the sight of these unnatural variations provoked a strong disgust in Agnes. Before they reached the front of the boarding line, she was keeping her eyes on the floor. It was a relief to walk through the gate, out of the waiting room, and toward their train.

Zusana commented as they walked along, finding the right car to board, "I'm pretty excited to take a vactrain. Can you believe I've never been on one before?"

"Yeah, I can believe it. We don't exactly travel much."

Zusana looked a bit wistful. "That's true. Before your father and I got married, I actually *did* do some traveling, though. I'm not sure I've ever told you much about it."

Agnes frowned. Was Petram not good enough for her mom that she wanted to see other places? Apparently, that was the case, since here they were, on their way to Nissus.

"Dad's most recent 'trip' was being kidnapped by the Bionics. I think travel is overrated."

A tall, dark-skinned woman walking just ahead of them turned her head and gave a quick, confused glance at Agnes, but then looked away again and boarded the train.

"Agnes, I think you're going to need to get in the habit of saying 'Factus'. If you need to say it at all. You can just treat them like regular people."

Agnes hissed, "They're *not* regular people, Mom. Even if they hadn't kidnapped Dad, they're not us."

Her mother said nothing in response, and they were soon at their car. As they boarded, Agnes noticed how the vactrain differed from their train of that morning. This new train was a long cylinder sitting inside its vacuum tube, and she knew that the tube extended all the way to their destination at Nissus. The doors of the train lined up with hatches in the tube, so that people could board the train while keeping the tube air-free.

They had just enough time to stow their belongings and pull out some sandwiches before the doors were sealed and the train began moving. Whereas the vactrain's tube was clear and transparent at the station, they soon entered a stretch where the walls of the tube were opaque. Nothing was visible in the blackness outside Agnes's window for a time.

If the train this morning had been a smooth ride, the vactrain was even more so—like soft silk. For a while, the only way Agnes could even tell that they were moving was the gentle pressure from her seat that said they were still speeding up. Then, while they were in Michigan, there was a long section where the tube was clear, and she could see the countryside passing in a blur.

Zusana fiddled with her handheld, and remarked, "Ok, so we're going about twelve hundred. Not bad, about airplane speed. We're on an express train, so we'll skip Detroit and Toronto. But we'll make a stop in Montreal, which is apparently a big transfer point for everyone coming up the East Coast. After that, it's a long, straight shot to Greenland and we should get up to *several times* as fast as this. I hope we can see out the window for some of that."

Agnes tried to ignore her.

Doing some mental estimates of the distances, Agnes realized that the whole vactrain portion of their trip must only be a few hours, given how fast they could move. *Only a few hours to Nissus.* Agnes tried to think about how that meant seeing her father soon, but Nissus seemed to be a focus of everything she didn't like about the trip. It loomed in her mind, crowding out the adventure her mother said she should enjoy.

After the brief stop in Montreal, Zusana suggested they go get some food from the café car. "We should eat while we can—we know where to get food here on the train, but we don't know Nissus at all. And we only have a little while before we'll be there."

"No. I just want to sit here." Agnes pulled her feet up on her seat and put her head on her knees, trying to calm her pounding heart. *Breathe.*

"At least let me bring you something. Honestly, no sleep and no food, you're going to make yourself sick."

"Fine. But I did get a little sleep earlier, and I ate one of the sandwiches when we got on the train," she replied, though she knew it hadn't been enough.

As soon as her mother left their car to get the food, Agnes felt very exposed. She was alone on a train flying at breakneck speed toward a Bionic metropolis. All alone, surrounded by the creatures she feared. Clenching her eyes shut, she tried to calm her mind, but instead sensed a growing dread, seeming to feel the presence of the Bionics on every side. Tense, she groaned softly and rocked a little as the world seemed to spin around her.

A woman seated a few rows away glanced up at the sound, then stood in surprise at seeing Agnes.

"Hey, there. Are you feeling ok?"

Agnes lifted her head and met the pair of green eyes with her own, before quickly shutting hers again. *She has both green eyes* and *horns!* The fear and anxiety boiled over into panic. *Where's Mom? They're right here! The Bionics!*

A man joined the concerned woman looking at Agnes. "Something's wrong here. I think she's got a medical problem."

Agnes slumped over onto her mother's vacant seat and shook violently, eyes tightly shut.

The woman nodded. "I think her mother went to the café car toward the front of the train. You go run and get her and I'll see if I can help her." She knelt by Agnes and asked, "Can you tell me your name?"

Another passenger stood up from the seat behind. "I'll alert the conductor and see if we can find a doctor," he offered.

Agnes trembled uncontrollably as she opened her eyes and saw the woman with the green eyes. She tried to say her name, but all that came out was a croak. Her throat and lungs felt like they were being squeezed. She gasped for breath.

The woman tried again. "Hey, what's wrong? Can you tell me what's going on?" Agnes simply folded tightly, struggling to breathe.

Moments later, a young woman with dark features popped through the door to the following train car, took one look at the small knot of people gathered around Agnes, and ran up the aisle. "Excuse me, please, I'm a doctor, I got the summons."

Everyone stepped out of the way for her. Just as she knelt beside Agnes, Zusana came running back from the forward car, trailed by the man who had run to notify her of the problem.

"Agnes! What's wrong?"

Agnes lay curled up across two seats, trembling and breathing hard. The doctor reached out for her. "Agnes, I'm Doctor Marshanda. Can you tell me what you're feeling?" When the doctor's hand touched her, she jerked and groaned again.

Dr. Marshanda looked up at Zusana while opening a small bag and setting a display tablet on the seat. "Does she have any known medical conditions that could be causing this, ma'am?" Zusana shook her head. The doctor frowned at the tablet. "I can't get any connection to her mites."

"Mites?" It took a fraction of a second for Zusana to process this, before what the doctor had said registered. "Oh, you mean nanobots? Yeah, she doesn't have any. We're not Factus, we're from a traditional community called Petram."

Dr. Marshanda set the tablet aside and looked up at Zusana briefly while fishing in her bag for equipment. "Ok, that makes more sense. Right, well, normally what we'd do here is use the mites' diagnostics to see what's going on. With your permission, I'll start an IV and give her a dose of mites, and probably also a sedative. We should start getting some data in seconds."

Zusana, kneeling on the floor, staring at her stricken daughter, hesitated. "What are our options? I know she doesn't want mites."

Dr. Marshanda asked, "You are her guardian?" Zusana said that she was.

"And when she said she did not want the mites, was she in a position to make informed medical decisions about them?"

Zusana shook her head. "Certainly not."

The doctor looked intently at Zusana, and said seriously, "Then you must choose what is best for her. Without the mites, I could still administer the sedative, but I can assure you she would be vastly safer with the mites right now than she would be without them. Especially here on a moving train where we only have this emergency kit. We need to find out what's wrong before we can know how to help her. And when we're done, we can deactivate all of the mites easily enough."

Zusana said, "Yeah, from what I know about the nanobots, I believe you. Let's do it, then."

Zusana held one of Agnes's shaking hands, while Doctor Marshanda took the other and quickly inserted a needle, taping it in place. She directed one of the bystanders to hold the IV bag above her head, while Zusana held her and tried to calm her.

As they waited for the diagnostic data, Dr. Marshanda asked for Zusana's name, and she gave it. The woman with the green eyes introduced herself to Zusana as well, "My name is Faylen. I saw your daughter when she started groaning and shaking and sort of fell over. She looked at me but didn't say anything, and I could see she was in distress."

"Thank you for getting help. This is Agnes's first time out of Petram among the Factus. She was very nervous and didn't want to come." She stroked Agnes's hair.

Dr. Marshanda, peering at her tablet, put in, "I can corroborate the nervousness. Her heart and lungs seem ok so far, but she has very high levels of stress hormones and…yes, it looks like she has some very high anxiety right now. Some sort of panic attack."

She frowned at what she was seeing. "She's never had mites before? I'm not sure how to interpret this."

Zusana shook her head firmly. "No, we don't use them at all in Petram. So, should we stop the train and take her to a hospital?"

A man in the scrum spoke, and Zusana realized that it was the conductor. "No, the fastest way to a hospital, the only way, really, is to continue to Nissus. In a few minutes, we're going to be hundreds of meters below the sea anyway. I've arranged for us to delay our deceleration as long as possible, so we'll be there pretty soon."

Dr. Marshanda spoke up again. "Mrs. Barker? I still don't understand why exactly she's having this attack, but I can counteract some of what's occurring." She used her tablet to display a diagram of the brain, along with several graphs and indicators. "These brain centers are overactive. It's almost like a seizure, but not quite. With the mites, I can selectively dampen the activity here, which should calm her down."

Zusana hesitated. "Oh, she's not going to like this."

Dr. Marshanda explained, "We're not causing any significant permanent changes if we use the mites this way. In this case, all we are doing is administering a very targeted dose of medicine, which will wear off eventually. You use medicine in Petram, yes?"

"We do use medicine, yes. You can turn the mites off as soon as she's ok?"

"Yes, once she's stabilized, I can put them in standby or I can even zap them—that's a technical term," she added with a smile, "—so they are all deactivated. I'd recommend we keep them, of course, since that will allow me to give her the best care."

Zusana nodded, still holding her daughter's hand. "Let's use the mites to give the medicine, but then zap them as soon as it looks like she's doing better and doesn't need them anymore. I'm so sorry, Agnes. I know this isn't what you wanted."

"Very well. I'll increase the sedation, too, since that seems to be helping a bit." She stared at the tablet for a moment, where several of the indicators slowly adjusted. Everyone waited, watching Agnes and the tablet display.

Almost immediately, Agnes's trembling began to subside. It only took a minute before her breathing was fully peaceful once again.

Seeing the improvement, Zusana gave a sigh of relief. "Oh, thank goodness! That was so quick!"

She waited a minute to make sure Agnes was fully calmed down, and then began lifting her so she could sit cradling her daughter.

As she got settled, Agnes began to cry softly. Alarmed, Zusana looked over at Dr. Marshanda, who reassured her. "I think that's a pretty natural reaction to what she's just been through. I'm turning off the last of the mites now—we can probably zap them if you're ready."

Zusana indicated her assent, and Dr. Marshanda held a small device up to Agnes's head and pushed a button. Nothing happened that anyone could see, but she glanced between Agnes and her handheld for a few moments, and declared, "That's it, then. They're all destroyed."

As Dr. Marshanda stood up, the tension of the crisis broke, and those in the little scrum surrounding them congratulated her on successfully getting the situation under control. She shared a few grins with her supporters, and then took over the job of holding the IV bag, where she could keep an eye on her patient while they approached Nissus.

Zusana held Agnes and spoke to her comfortingly. The sedatives seemed to be strong, since Agnes only mumbled confusedly, and then yawned. Her mother stroked her hair and spoke some quiet words of reassurance as the train began braking for their arrival in Nissus.

Chapter 4

# Factus

Drifting awake, Agnes tried to make sense of her disordered memories. *I was on a train, going to Nissus—is that where I am now?* She seemed to be in a bed, and soft light filled the room. Thinking, she vaguely remembered being hustled off the train and being taken past rows of people looking at her. On a hospital gurney?

One particular memory stood out: A nighttime view of a busy city square, with a vivid, orange-red sculpture of some sort. With her first clear, lucid thought, she hoped that the memory was real, and that she could find the sculpture again.

Sitting up, Agnes yawned and rubbed her eyes. She was definitely in a hospital room, and seated near her bed was a woman she didn't recognize immediately. The woman looked up from something and smiled at her. From the other side of the bed, Agnes heard her mother say, "Hey there, you're awake! How are you feeling?"

Agnes turned and saw the concerned expression on her mother's face. "Uh. Ok." Her mouth felt dry. "Thirsty. Where am I?"

"You're in a hospital, in Nissus. Here, let's get you some water."

"What happened? Why am I in the hospital?"

Zusana got some water and ice from a dispenser in the room and handed it to Agnes, who took it shakily. "You had some kind of episode, like a bad panic attack. A doctor on the train took care of you and they brought you here as soon as we arrived in Nissus. You were sedated for a little while, and then I think you were just tired and needed some sleep."

"How long was I asleep?"

"About nine hours."

Agnes glanced over at the other woman. "You were on the train, weren't you?" She was starting to feel steadier and more awake.

The woman nodded. "Yes, I was the one who noticed you were in distress, and I asked someone to get your mother. My name is Faylen." Gesturing toward Zusana, she continued, "We've been talking for a while. Since you two don't know Nissus, I've offered to help you get settled."

"Ok, well, thanks then, I guess." Agnes stared at the woman. She remembered looking into those green eyes on the train, and she remembered the terror she felt then. She couldn't quite understand why she had been so panicky and scared. Even the fact that Faylen had horns...well, they were more like knobs or bumps poking through the light brown hair, rather than horns. Weird, certainly, but she hardly felt the need to run away at this point.

In fact, if one could look past the horns, Faylen was rather beautiful in a willowy, delicate way.

Agnes turned to her mother. "Why did I have a panic attack, Mom?"

"The doctors don't really know, but you were pretty upset about leaving Petram, weren't you? Do you still feel anxious? We're in Nissus now, after all."

"No. I feel...fine. I don't know why I was acting so weird on the train. I'm starving, though."

A food menu appeared on a nearby display screen for Agnes to see, and Faylen said, "These are the hospital's options. If they're not suitable, we can find something else nearby."

Agnes looked at her uncertainly. "Did you just make that happen? You made that display show something using your mind?"

Faylen gave a little smile. "I asked for a menu using my interface with my mites, yes. Doing things like that is pretty normal, outside Petram."

*Maybe Jonnan was right about the nanobots,* Agnes thought, but decided to set the issue aside for the moment. Faylen was using mites, not telling *her* to do so, and Agnes *was* very hungry. She perused the menu and ordered a split pea and ham soup, with toast, and citrus fruit juice to drink.

While she was waiting for the food to arrive, a doctor stopped by to check on her. This doctor was an older man, and it wasn't obvious to Agnes that he was Factus.

"Hello, Agnes, I'm Dr. Wallace," he introduced himself with a bit of a rumbly voice. "It's good to see you're up and feeling ok, and I can finally get to talk with you. I'm afraid we don't really know why you had your problem on the train. Without any mites to provide a window into what was going on inside you, we've just been keeping you under observation and letting you rest."

At Agnes's confused look, Zusana said, "Mites are what people in Nissus call the nanobots. They use them for diagnosing and monitoring what's going on inside their bodies." With an apprehensive expression, she hesitated before going on. "Agnes, there's something I need to tell you. I know you're not going to like to hear this, but when we were on the train, I was really concerned about you. The main tool the doctor had for figuring out what was wrong was the mites. So, we gave you some of them in an IV."

Agnes felt her breath catch. "I've got nanobots now? Did you just make me into a Bionic? *Me?*" *All week I've been terrified of the Bionics, and the moment I leave Petram, my own mother does this to me?!*

Dr. Wallace said, "No, no, you don't have any mites inside you anymore. Dr. Marshanda destroyed them all within a few minutes at your mother's request. I've reviewed the records from the train, and I can assure you that she didn't do anything that should permanently affect you."

Agnes sat back in the bed with a huff and shot an accusatory glance at her mother. The doctor went on, "The mites *were* quite useful to Dr. Marshanda for dealing with a very scary crisis. They showed which parts of your brain were at the center of the panic. She used the mites to nudge those brain centers to a lower activity level and calm you down."

Agnes threw up her hands in exasperation, and practically shouted, "Less than one day out among the Bionics and they're already literally messing with my brain and turning me into one of them? Jonnan was right! I can't believe this!"

Zusana looked unhappy. "Honey, I was really scared for you. I wanted you to have the best, safest treatment possible. I do think the doctor on the train did what she could for you. The doctor explained that all the mites did was administer some medicine and that it wouldn't do anything permanent."

Dr. Wallace nodded and agreed. "It's better than most medicines, really, because mites can target specific areas, and not your whole body. Agnes, I think you're going to have to just trust us that we have a pretty good idea of what we're doing, and we didn't hurt you with the mites. At any rate, they've been gone for many hours now."

Agnes glared from him to her mother, not speaking.

Faylen jumped into the conversation, saying, "You said they turned you into a Bionic. A Factus. I don't think so." Agnes let her continue. "All they did was try to address a medical crisis. That doesn't make you Factus. Factus is when you use the mites to start enhancing things. Changing genes. Building something different from *Homo sapiens*. But that's not what they did—you're still the same girl you were yesterday."

Agnes stared at her hands for a moment, thinking. Quietly she spoke, more calmly than she felt. "I'm not sure that's true. I don't really trust the Factus." She raised her head to look Faylen in the eye. "Your people kidnapped my dad, for one thing. And it seems like the mites did affect me more than the doctor says. I've been pretty afraid of the Factus for a while, but it seems like when the mites messed with my brain, they killed the fear. Numbed it. I don't feel quite the same as I did yesterday or the day before."

Dr. Wallace frowned as she spoke. "I'm not sure how I can address that concern. I stand by what I said earlier: There should be no significant permanent changes from the mites. Perhaps you had simply worked yourself up and just needed the sedation and some rest. But at any rate, I think we can remove that IV and discharge you from the hospital as soon as you feel up for it."

He excused himself and left the room as Agnes's food was arriving. She ate while her mother talked, and Agnes found that getting some food in her seemed to take some of the edge off her anger.

Zusana said, "The main reason we're here in Nissus is to see Dad, of course, and try to find out what we can do for him. The people that are holding him are with the Nissus Security Group, the NSG. They had a liaison waiting to meet our train as it came in, but of course we came straight here to the hospital. The liaison stopped by, and I talked to him once we got you settled, while you were sleeping.

"It turns out that Faylen, here, is a good fit to help out with the liaison role. She has a background in cross-cultural communication and counseling, so it's really kind of perfect, actually."

Agnes looked at the woman with a bit of surprise. "Wow, and you just happened to be sitting near us on the train?" she asked.

Faylen smiled. "It's not as unlikely as you might think. There are a lot of people like me, for starters—there were probably several others just on that one train. That's because

Nissus is extremely culturally diverse. And as for counseling, well, people who immigrate to Nissus are probably looking for something in their life. They want a purpose, and they want balance. So, counselors help them design a lifestyle to meet their goals."

Agnes digested this. "You're kind of like a psychiatrist?" she asked, remembering how just this past week she had thought about how she might need such help if she kept feeling paranoid about the Factus.

"I don't have training in clinical psychiatry or neuroengineering or anything like that, no. I'm just good at helping people evaluate and design their lifestyle options. My own academic background is in anthropology, which does make me pretty excited to talk to some people from Petram, I must admit." Faylen did look eager.

Agnes had to smile at the thought of a Factus considering her to be exotic, but then her smile faded at the sad implication. "Are *Homo sapiens* so rare that we're exotic, now?"

Faylen's face registered surprise at the unexpected question. "Oh! I...didn't realize that's how you might view it." She seemed embarrassed. "I'm sorry if I made it sound like you are a research subject or something. I had just never met someone from your community, and I *am* very interested in cultures and lifestyles."

Agnes nodded her acknowledgment while Faylen paused to gather her next thoughts. "And I'm not sure that I agree with calling us *Homo factus* and calling you *Homo sapiens*, even if that is the popular and convenient terminology. Quite likely, you and I are genetically more similar than I am to half of the other Nissians."

Agnes had a ready answer—she had talked to her friends about this topic, after all. "I agree with calling you a different species because, to me, Petram represents pure humanity, people without any tinkering. I want to make sure we can survive. Isn't that what anyone should want for their own people?" Despite her calm words, Agnes wasn't ready to forget the recent tinkering she had just received from the mites on the train.

Faylen considered this, then carefully replied, "First of all, I would say that I welcome your goal and wish all of you success in keeping Petram independent and 'pure,' as you said, if that's what you wish.

"Second, I do talk to lots of people. They want to survive, yes, but most of them are not interested in trying to keep things static. They want to give their children a better life, whatever they decide 'better' might mean. For most of us, that does include mites and genetic engineering."

Agnes glanced uncomfortably at Faylen's strange skull protrusions. "I can kind of understand wanting to fix diseases, but why horns?"

Faylen let out a light laugh and put a hand against her head. "Oh, these? They're just for fun. They were all the rage a few years back. Kind of gave an exotic air. Or a virile air, for men, perhaps. I'm actually in the process of reabsorbing the bone of the horn, but it will take a few more months before they're gone. I may regrow them again sometime, who knows?"

Seeing Agnes's discomfort, she continued. "Agnes, I know the idea of growing horns for fun is pretty foreign to you, coming from Petram. It's just simply the way of most of the world. Nissians especially are quite comfortable with change, experimentation, and differences." She thought for a moment. "Actually, we value differences so much that we think it's important to have places like Petram. I certainly think the world is a richer place because your community exists, don't you?"

Sensing an olive branch, Agnes decided to accept it. *I still think I shouldn't feel this calm about the mites they gave me, but there's no reason to take it out on Faylen.* She smiled and said, "Yes, that's one thing I can definitely agree with. The world should have places like Petram."

Finished with her food, she got up from the bed and began gathering her regular clothes so that she could change out of the hospital garb she had been given. Faylen stepped out of the room to give her some privacy, and then reentered so that they could discuss plans.

Zusana explained, "Agnes, while you have just had a good night's sleep, I'm really quite exhausted, and I bet Faylen is, too. The NSG, the Nissus Security Group, arranged an apartment for us to use while we're here, so we're going to head over there, and I'll try to get a nap. It may not help me get on the right sleep schedule, but it's what I need right now. We're going to see Dad tomorrow morning, after we've had some rest and some time to get settled."

***

Deep inside the Nissus Security Group compound, Tomas padded into the kitchen of the isolation unit where he and his Petram colleagues were being held. He took one look at Willym, and said, "You look terrible. Have you had any sleep at all?"

Willym regarded him, annoyed. "No. And you should have stayed up to help."

Tomas shrugged. "You guys were taking care of it."

"Yes, we have been. And we've just about got the encoding figured out. You can start setting up the fabrication while I take a turn to rest."

Edmon, who had been watching the other two, now set a small box on the table with a smile. "Thank goodness the Factus didn't confiscate the raw materials we need."

Willym barely glanced at the box as he turned and left, seeking his own room and his bed.

Chapter 5

# Nissus

Once Agnes was ready to leave the hospital room, she grabbed the handles of their suitcases and began to walk out of the room with them. Faylen stopped her. "We don't want to carry that luggage around. We'll just have a carrier take it to the apartment." She showed her guests how to use their handhelds to request a carrier.

Moments later, a metal luggage cart rolled down the hallway and came to a stop outside their room. "See? You can just put your luggage in the carrier, and it will meet you there."

Zusana was hesitant. "This doesn't look very secure. What if someone takes our luggage?"

Faylen was working on putting the bags inside the cart, but she looked up at that. "Why would someone take it? You mean theft? You don't need to worry about theft in Nissus. Your things will be fine."

Zusana gave a concerned frown as she watched the carrier trundle off on its own.

As the trio began walking toward the hospital exit, Agnes realized that there had been so much to talk about, she hadn't even thought to look through the window blinds in her room to see what Nissus looked like. Well, she would get to see it now.

To her surprise, there didn't seem to be any doors—the hallway just opened onto a small, tree-shaded walkway between two buildings, both of which appeared to be a part of the hospital campus. Quite a few patients and visitors were walking or resting on benches by the walkway. Looking around, Agnes could see a busy roadway in the middle distance to her right. To her left, there was a scene so beautiful and surprising that she stopped abruptly to stare at it.

The sun was rising over a peaceful lake stretching far into the distance, where white-tipped mountains were faintly visible. A few wisps of clouds in the morning sky emphasized the fair weather. Birds whirled in the air over the water, their cries faintly audible.

Irresistibly drawn to the scene, Agnes walked up to a stone balustrade at the end of the walkway, joining several other people looking out over the lake. The waist-high ledge marked a steep drop-off, with the shore being some dozen meters out from where they stood. She breathed in the cool, invigorating air; the freshness seemed to clear her mind and sharpen her senses.

As the others joined her, Zusana remarked, "So beautiful, isn't it? I came out here for a few minutes earlier to stretch my legs while you were sleeping. I still can't get over it."

Agnes looked around her again, and then at Faylen. "I don't understand, Faylen. I thought Nissus was supposed to be an extremely big and crowded city. How far are we from the downtown?"

Faylen shared a look with Zusana that said they knew something that Agnes didn't. She gave Agnes a mischievous and knowing smile. "Oh, we're in Nissus alright. This is the heart of the city. There are probably five or ten million people within one kilometer of here."

Agnes couldn't help sputtering a bit at this preposterous statement. "But I don't see a single skyscraper! And there's a huge lake on one side of us!" She looked at Faylen in a way that suggested she might start running away from her after all.

Faylen nodded that she had heard, then stooped down and picked up a couple of small stones. "Here, throw this rock into the water. Throw it high." Bewildered, Agnes took the stone she was offered, and threw it as hard as she could out over the water.

The rock didn't make it. Barely an arm's length past the balustrade, it bounced off an invisible barrier.

"What—," she exclaimed, flinching as the rock sailed high over her head to land behind her with a faint rattle. Recovering, she peered at the point where the rock had bounced off the barrier. It seemed the rock had left a smudgy mark hanging in the air just out of reach. "Did they put a glass wall in front of the lake or something?" she asked, looking more closely to try to detect the glass.

Faylen shook her head and explained, "There's a wall, yes, but...there's no lake. Not here anyway—it's probably a recording of a lake somewhere, though. It might be a composite view."

Agnes looked at her for a moment, then turned back to the view in front of her. "There's no lake? But...I can hear the birds and feel the wind coming off the lake and..." She paused and sniffed. "And I can even smell the water. I can see it right there!"

Zusana put in, "Apparently in Nissus, they have displays that can do more than show a flat picture. This display sends a slightly different image to each of your eyes, making the picture appear three-dimensional. Your eyes get the exact same input they would get if they looked at a physical lake in front of you, so that's what it looks like."

Faylen agreed. "And if you move your head, the perspective changes just like it would if you were looking at any other lake."

Agnes could only stare and try to make sense of it all. Seeing the lake right in front of her, feeling the light breeze...she got another small rock and tossed it more gently this time. Again, the rock struck a barrier and dropped. This time the stone appeared to lie motionless in the air, hovering over the sloping ground beyond the railing.

"How can they fake all the other parts of it? The wind, the birds, the smell?" she asked.

Faylen gave a little shrug. "Playing the bird sounds is easy, and for the lake scent, all you need to do is figure out what molecules to fabricate, then release them. We need to have sophisticated air handling anyway, to keep the city smelling fresh and clean. Now, getting the breezes right, that's the tricky part. The wall's display must be permeable or something; I'm not sure of the details."

Zusana pointed to the place where the first rock had left a mark, and asked, "So Agnes damaged the wall display with the rock?"

Faylen nodded in the affirmative. "Sure, but it's ok. Some maintenance bots will be along in a while to repair it. Tomorrow it should be good as new. Anyway, let's get moving on so we can go sleep."

As they walked back in the direction of the buildings, Agnes peppered Faylen with questions. "Why would they do all of that, even faking the smell of the lake? Don't people resent living in a fake environment? How much of this is fake?"

Faylen objected. "I don't think of any of it as 'fake.' The lake is real enough for its purpose—we have a real lake view here. We just don't need to leave water sitting there to make it happen. We manufacture the experience we want."

She continued, "And why did we do it? So we can have a beautiful lake to enjoy, of course. We want a lake, so let's put a lake there. It's great."

"You can't call it a real lake if there's no water," Agnes said.

Faylen frowned, thinking. "You've probably had a picture of a natural scene on the wall of your home at some point. Or even an artificial plant, right? It's not really so different from that. You don't want to live in an actual forest or meadow, so you bring a little of that into your home."

"An artificial plant is one thing, but this is a whole fake landscape. I wouldn't want to live with a pretend lake. I want my world to be real."

Faylen raised her eyebrows a bit. "You live with a lot of 'fake' things. Remember the soup you had in the hospital? It had ham, right?"

"Yeah, what about it?"

"Well, you know what 'real' ham would be, right?"

"What do you mean?" Agnes was momentarily confused, before realizing what Faylen meant. "Wait, you mean like from an animal? A pig? I certainly hope it wasn't from a pig! That would be barbaric!"

"Exactly. You accept a lot of artificial things in your life. Things that are made, rather than natural. They seem normal. You're used to them. If you see a garden or a lawn in Petram, you don't say, 'This is a fake wilderness!', but it's still artificial compared to a truly wild place. In Nissus, we just do more of it."

They had walked past a few hospital buildings and were reaching the edge of the campus, near the brightly labeled emergency entrance at the main road she had seen. Here, people strode every which way, some coming to or going from the hospital, many passing by, and not a few heading to what looked like an elevator bank right next to the hospital emergency entrance.

Agnes looked at the building housing the elevators, thinking about what Faylen had said, and idly wondering where these elevators would lead. Were they about to get on a subway? She figured that must be the case, since the elevators clearly went down from street level. There was nothing but sky above them.

Faylen instructed them to pull out their handhelds again. "Now, you don't *need* to do it this way, but since you're new to Nissus, I'll show you how you can always find directions to where you want to go. Right now, we're going to your apartment. All you need to do is put in the coordinates like *this*, ask for an itinerary, and it will just work with all of the default options. No, we're not in a super hurry, and no we don't mind walking a bit, et cetera. It is assuming we're all going together."

Agnes fiddled with the handheld, and soon it displayed a purple symbol like a P inside a hexagon. Faylen said they would follow that symbol to find the apartment. She mentioned offhandedly that the P probably stood for Petram, since sometimes the computer came up with mnemonics for the symbols. Looking up from the handheld, Agnes saw that one of the elevators now showed the same glowing purple symbol next to some additional marks.

Curious and a bit apprehensive about what they would find when the elevator stopped, Agnes crowded in with the others in her group, joined by several strangers. To her surprise, their elevator car began rising, not descending. *If I saw sky above the elevator building, does that mean that the sky outside was faked, too?*

She didn't have long to wait to see where the elevator led—in almost no time, the doors opened again, and she was swept with the group out into an enormous hall. Clutching her mother's arm, she stared around agape at the streams of people crisscrossing the hall, mixing and dividing as people sought various destinations.

Zusana turned to Agnes and commented, "I'm not sure if you were really aware of it last night, but we passed through this station to get to the hospital. We got off the train over that way," and she pointed toward the other side of the room. Agnes caught a glimpse of what looked like a city outside, through an entranceway. It appeared to be nighttime out in the city. *That's odd. It was morning outside the hospital building, but night here outside this train station?* She only had a moment to look, though, as the others were eager to get going.

Faylen pointed to the floor. "See the purple line with the Petram symbol? We just follow that. It's only visible for us and for anyone in the same line of sight as us." As she and Zusana began heading off following the line, Agnes spared a last curious glance toward the city. She remembered seeing the orange and red sculpture the night before—was this the place? She thought she could see a splash of color outside, but before she could investigate, she had to turn and hurry after her mother and Faylen.

The guide line led them down a short hall and to a station platform, where a train was waiting. She could get glimpses of a few other travelers' guide lines on the floor, one of which joined theirs, leading toward the same train. They boarded—Agnes managed to get a seat by a window—and within a minute of sitting down, the doors closed, and the train pulled out.

Faylen described a bit of how the guide system functioned: "Since the computer knew where we're going, it could put us on a train that's not making any local stops in this area. It can get all of the passengers pretty close to where we're transferring before we start making stops. It's all dynamic, scheduling people and trains minute-by-minute."

Nose to the glass, Agnes tried to take in the view as they sped out of the station: a nighttime cityscape that reminded her of the fuzzy memories from when they had rushed to the hospital. From what little she could see, the city was indeed busy and vast. Bright lights, crowds, skyscrapers—it was intimidating to one who had never been out of Petram.

Shortly, however, they entered a tunnel, and as they came back out, the view had completely changed—the train was now charging through an ancient forest. Widely spaced trees, some with the diameter of a house, created a canopy high above them. While the city had been lit up against the night, here the trees shaded the forest understory from what appeared to be the morning sun.

Agnes knew that this must be another simulated view, like the lake, but she still found it interesting to watch. Once, she saw a small herd of elk browsing. Shortly afterward, the tree cover broke and they could see a dizzyingly high waterfall sparkling in the sunlight to their left, cascading into a pool that the train raced across on a truss bridge, with the window on the right showing a limitless valley extending into the distance.

It felt like only five or ten minutes into the trip when the train began slowing as it approached an enormous stone wall. Passing through an aperture in the wall, she could see that they were now in a place with people again. This looked like a small town, with modest buildings and narrow, quiet streets. The train slowed, and Agnes could see into some shops and restaurants, which looked lively enough but nothing like the bustling city of a few minutes earlier.

"Faylen, I know the forest scene was fake, but how do I know if this is, too? I don't like not knowing what's real. What about the city that we saw? Was that real?" she asked.

Faylen acknowledged her concern. "I can see how it's a bit disorienting at first. Once you get more familiar with the city, you'll have a better sense of what's decoration and what's actually out there that you can touch. Until then, there's a command you can use on your handheld to see what's simulated."

She waved toward the window. "This is all unsimulated. The city we saw earlier, that wasn't a projection, either. For the rest of the trip to the apartment, most of what you see should be the true view, except of course the sky."

As the train stopped to let some people off, Agnes glanced through the open doors at the fake sky. A few puffy clouds floated in the distance, and, despite everything, Agnes found it hard to believe that they were simply projections and illusions. She could not see anything that indicated the sky was simulated...except, now that she thought about it, the sun wasn't as bright as a real sun would be.

*Hang on*, she thought, realizing something. "The sky at the hospital was fake, because we went *up* in the elevator to another level. If *this* sky is fake, too, does that mean there's another level above this place, too?"

Faylen smiled. "Now do you see how we can have millions of people packed in a small space, and it doesn't even seem crowded?"

Agnes couldn't help feeling a bit uneasy about knowing there was another tier of city above her head, people with their own buildings and streets and fake sky. *How many levels are there? How high up does Nissus go?*

# Chapter 6

# **Friends**

The little group got off at the next stop, again took a short elevator ride up to a new level, and stepped out onto a busy street scene. In this section of Nissus, the buildings appeared to be no more than three or four stories, and Agnes could see an obvious residential aspect to the neighborhood. While the street was busy, it was clearly not high-speed. There was a mix of pedestrians, cyclists, and a few long "trolley" vehicles that were familiar to Agnes—they were similar to ones she used in Petram, though these were newer and shinier.

The purple guide line led to a raised curb at the side of the road, where a trolley pulled up at just the moment Agnes walked to the edge. The doors opened, and they stepped on, grabbing for a handhold as the vehicle promptly started off again. Agnes found the trolley to be roomy and open, with poles and straps to hold on to, plus a few benches on the sides and at the front. She made her way to one of these.

Agnes was a bit surprised to see that the trolley had no glass in its windows, and the roof was not solid but only consisted of a few metal crossbars over their heads. *Of course, I keep forgetting that the sky is not real, and it's not going to rain here unless they make it rain. And I guess they don't have to worry about winter.*

Sitting on a bench at the front of the trolley as it eased down the road, Agnes watched the dance between vehicle and pedestrian play out in front of them. The trolley steered itself within designated, painted lanes, occasionally slowing as a youth or a cyclist crossed too close in front of the vehicle. A few times, they stopped while passengers got on or off, and soon the purple P symbol appeared over the doors to indicate that it was their turn to get off. The whole trip, from the hospital to their destination, couldn't have taken more than about twenty minutes.

Once again, the guide line showed the way, taking them off the main street and under an archway. Faylen said, "So, this area of Nissus, on this level, is called New Canberra, or just Canberra for short. This little neighborhood is Ward F-142. I don't know anyone in here, but we'll meet some people soon enough—in New Canberra, they give a bit of a family flavor to each ward. They cook up a big breakfast and dinner, and whoever wants to eat with the group can do so. Or you can take some food over to your apartment if you want."

The neighborhood was a cluster of closely spaced apartment buildings, centered on a long and narrow outdoor common area. Agnes found that her new temporary home was on the second floor of a building near the road, overlooking the eating area Faylen had mentioned.

At the stairs to the apartment, Faylen stopped and turned to Agnes and Zusana. "I'm going to leave you here for now. I'm borrowing a visitor's den right there on the other side of the commons. I'll sleep for a few hours, since my body needs it. I can get my body to match Canberra's clock pretty easily—since I'm Factus, I have control over my sleep cycle—but Zusana, you'll probably have a rough few days adjusting. Just ping me when you need me, or I'll ping you tonight, either way."

Zusana thanked her for her help, and Faylen disappeared across the commons.

Zusana and Agnes climbed the steps to their apartment, and at the top of the stairs they found the carrier with their luggage waiting for them. "How did the carrier get up the steps with those wheels?" Agnes wondered aloud. But Zusana was apparently too tired to care, as she just waved her indifference and carried her things in.

The apartment was quite small and narrow—a front living room, then behind it a tiny kitchen, and finally a bathroom and two little bedrooms. But, small or not, Agnes could see that her mother was happy for the place to rest—Zusana gave her a quick hug and, like Faylen had done moments earlier, disappeared into her room to take her nap.

***

Suddenly alone, Agnes finally had a moment that wasn't a whirlwind of new information or rushing around. *What a crazy morning!* Waking up in a hospital bed in a strange city that was far stranger than she had expected or initially realized, hustling across it so they could get to their temporary home and let her mom rest. Not to mention learning about her swoon on the train yesterday, the mites, and the concern about what they'd done to her. Come to think of it, she was almost glad to have a day to rest and adjust before they went to see her father.

She dropped off her luggage in her bedroom, and, still not tired, kicked off her shoes and padded to the front room. Outside the window was a small veranda overlooking the commons. She could see a few small children out playing, but at the moment it seemed pretty quiet. *I'll go explore the neighborhood in a little while. It's going to be hours before Mom is awake, and I can't just sit around here the whole time.*

Sitting down on the couch, Agnes checked to see if there were any messages from her friends back home. There were a few, but nothing of great significance. She hesitated instead of replying. *What can I even say to my friends at this point? 'Yeah, Jonnan, you may have been right about the Bionics. And by the way, I had an embarrassing meltdown on the train before I even got here, and I ended up in the hospital. And Nissus is bizarre. I can't trust what I see or hear or even what my brain is thinking, now that they put the nanobots in me.' Yeah, let's hold off on sending that for now.*

By her estimates, it was early Sunday morning back home in Petram—still dark—so there was no point sending anything right now anyway. No wonder her mother was so exhausted—she must have been awake for a full twenty-four hours.

She idly wondered if Elaina had found a place like Nissus. All she knew was that her former best friend must be out among the Factus, but that could be anywhere in the world.

Agnes got up and unpacked some of her clothes. Taking a quick shower and brushing her teeth left her feeling immensely refreshed. She was even beginning to feel a bit more confident about facing Nissus now that she was rested and cleaned up. She might be tainted by the mites, but she actually felt pretty upbeat.

She opened the apartment door and stepped out onto the veranda, wondering briefly if she needed to take a key, before realizing there was no lock on the door. At the railing, she looked out at the neighborhood. It was well-kept, clean, and quiet, though a bit compact. Off to her left, she could see the entrance to their ward, and on the right, past a few more apartment buildings, there was forest.

Just as Agnes was about to head down the stairs, she noticed a small group of youths sitting at a table near her building. They looked to be about her age, and when they saw that she noticed them, one of them gave her a wave.

"Hi there," said one boy with dark brown skin, unruly hair, and a narrow, pointed nose. Indian, Agnes judged. He said, "Did you get all settled in?"

Agnes nodded as she warily descended the stairs. The boy waved her over, and she came to their table and sat. He said, "We're the welcoming committee, so, welcome to our ward. I'm Sahil."

Beside Sahil sat a girl, who chuckled at that. Agnes saw that she, too, looked Indian. Looking at him, the girl said, "I guess we *are* the welcoming committee, aren't we?"

To Agnes, she smiled, though a bit stiffly, and said, "Sahil's father works for the NSG, and he said you'd be staying here as their guest. He told us to make sure you feel welcome. My name is Pari."

Agnes said hi to Pari but sensed something, a wariness beneath the surface of their interaction. It was as if Pari was on her guard, or not entirely happy to have Agnes there. *Hmm, she needn't worry about* me. *I wouldn't be a threat to her—she's beautiful.*

In fact, it seemed difficult to look away from that striking face—and not just because she had never met someone from India.

Agnes looked over at the third person at their table, an Asian girl, who gave a little wave and introduced herself in perfect English. "Hi, I'm Jinjing. I'm a visitor to New Canberra, like you. I'm from Nissian Anhui—that's a Chinese community. I'm staying here to visit Sahil and Pari for a few days—we met on a cultural exchange last year."

Agnes glanced around at her new acquaintances. Jinjing was certainly pretty enough, and somehow conveyed more friendliness than Pari.

Agnes said, "Ok, well, I'm Agnes...." She wasn't sure how much they knew about her already. "I'm here with my mom to try to visit my dad. I don't know how much Sahil told you about it...."

Sahil shook his head and explained, "All I know is there's some kind of security concern that has something to do with your father, or he wouldn't be mixed up with the Nissus Security Group. Honestly, they barely even told me your name. I just got a ping a few minutes ago that you were here and could use a friendly face. We were about to go knock on your door, when you came out."

"Oh! Well, I'm fine, we just got in to Nissus last night and my mom is resting. I was just going to look around the neighborhood a bit while she sleeps. I'm sure I don't need to take up your time."

Jinjing lightly countered, "Well, at least can we get to know you a bit, Agnes? I should meet the ward's visitors, if I'm going to be on the welcoming committee." She shot an amused look at Sahil before continuing. "What do you think of Nissus so far? It's your first time here, right?"

Agnes let herself relax a bit. Obviously, this group wasn't about to rob her, and she doubted they were going to try to inject her with nanobots, so she may as well reciprocate their friendliness. "Yes, but really it's my first time anywhere. I'm from a traditional community called Petram. I'm not Factus; I never even met one until yesterday, since we...uh, don't allow Factus to visit Petram." She felt a little embarrassed admitting this, as *she* was a guest in Nissus.

All three of her hosts expressed surprise, and Jinjing remarked, "Well, this is another cultural exchange, then! Tell us about Petram."

Agnes fumbled a bit. "I'm not sure what to say about it. Petram is a small city, in a valley in the Rocky Mountains near Yellowstone. We've got a bunch of farms and greenhouses and we're pretty independent. I'm in high school...."

Seeing Agnes's obvious discomfort with the questioning, Sahil spoke up. "From Petram to Nissus—that must be a bit of a shock for you. Small town to big city."

Agnes nodded. "I've got to admit I'm not very comfortable with seeing a fake sky and things. I guess there are more people and buildings and things above us and below us right now? It feels a bit claustrophobic."

Pari knit her brows. "I don't like that word, 'fake'. I guess we're just used to it and don't really think about the sky being a projection. I've never felt claustrophobic, but then I did grow up here."

"But why?" Agnes queried. "Why stack neighborhoods and buildings on top of each other, and go to all the trouble of projecting a view of a sky from the ceiling?"

Sahil grinned. "Well, that's an easy question. Everything is nearby this way."

"And that's only half of it," Pari pointed out. "Having a constructed reality means that anyone can have whichever features they want. So, you can have the lifestyle you choose, but you're right next to everyone else and can easily visit *their* reality."

Agnes frowned in confusion and appraised the other youths anew. She wasn't expecting teens to talk like this. "Constructed reality? Lifestyle? I'm not sure I follow."

"I think I can explain with an example," Jinjing offered. "My family in Anhui lives in a small village of about five hundred people. It's arranged a bit like an old-fashioned rural Chinese village, with traditional courtyard houses and ancestor hall. We have recreated a clan structure like the Chinese had in prior times, and we speak a dialect similar to standard Mandarin. But everyone knows English or other languages, too, and we're all educated and usually have jobs outside the village. We don't do agriculture, like a traditional village would, not much anyway. But we get the best of both worlds—some traditional culture and lifestyle, plus modern education and social life."

Pari continued. "And they get it because they've constructed those villages and designed the environment they want: weather, landscape, architecture. It's not so much that the sky is fake—it's constructed. Designed and built."

Jinjing nodded. "Since we're in Nissus, it means it's a short walk from one village to any of fifty others. And we're near other, completely different communities, so if my brother decides he'd rather live, say, in a high-rise in an English-speaking city, he can still stop by for lunch any time he wants. It's not far away. Whatever reality you want, whatever lifestyle you want, someone has built it in Nissus."

Agnes mulled this and acknowledged, "Ok, I can see how that makes sense if you want to keep some of your traditions. So, they've built a community for every major language?"

Sahil chuckled. "Why stop at just the major languages? Let's see what I can find in the directory," he said. His eyes had a faraway look for a moment, and the table surface suddenly lit up with an interface. After selecting some options and peering at the table for a moment, Sahil said, "Looks like we have over a thousand languages, including a couple that had been extinct and some other invented ones. Huh, a few kilometers over that way is a group of fifty speakers of a language that was designed specifically for writing beautiful poetry." He thought for a moment, staring into the distance. "Wow, that might be pretty interesting to hear, actually."

Agnes couldn't hide her surprise. "They have a thousand different languages in Nissus? That's...a lot of languages."

"Oh, that's only the beginning," Pari replied. "If you are constructing a reality and a community, there are a lot more variables than language that you need to decide on. Like, what climate do you want? Do you want both winter and summer? How long should the day be? What kind of housing?"

Sahil continued the thread, "You could live in a small university town on a quiet campus in the mountains. Or maybe you want to be allowed to blast music late at night, and party with your friends. It's all about choices and options. Whatever you want, if you can find a few other people to share it with you, you can have that lifestyle."

Jinjing commented, "I heard of a village where everyone has to sleep on the grass under the trees or the stars—no buildings or tents are allowed."

"There are a bunch of nudist districts, too, of course," Sahil added with a mischievous grin, speaking to no one in particular.

Agnes couldn't help but laugh at what she was hearing. "You can fit all of that in one city, in Nissus? Just how big is this place, anyway? I haven't found out yet how high up it goes, how many levels there are."

The three friends glanced at each other, and Pari spoke. "You didn't see the view from Phoenix Square, when you came in on the vactrain?"

Agnes shook her head. "No, I, ah, missed it." She didn't want to mention how she had been rushed to the hospital the night before.

Jinjing spoke to the others. "I think we need to take her to the Phoenix. Just telling her won't do it justice." The others nodded. "Agnes, let's go do some sightseeing. We can talk about Nissus, but really you should see it for yourself. You're already in the city, anyway."

A little apprehensive about heading out with three teens she didn't really know, Agnes glanced up at her apartment, where her mother was sleeping. Pari offered to let her mother come along, too, but Agnes explained she wouldn't be awake for a while.

"Well, all the more reason to go explore now. No point in waiting around for hours, unless you want to rest. We can leave a message for her, but we can be back in less than an hour if you want."

Agnes hesitated for a moment longer, but finally, her curiosity won out. That, plus the fact that she was beginning to realize just how much she didn't know about the world outside Petram. If she was to protect *Homo sapiens* from the lure of the Factus, she would need to have a better idea of what she was up against.

"Ok, let's go." *Wow*, she thought, *the mites really did clobber my fear*. She wasn't sure how much to be worried about that.

***

Tomas typed furiously, stared at his screen, and typed some more. "We don't have the right software for this. If I had all of my tools back in Petram, this would be easy."

Edmon shook his head. "If we were back in Petram, it wouldn't be necessary."

"True. I can't believe how quickly the NSG figured out what we were up to and made a move against us. We had a special project from Hale himself—no one else should have even known about it!" He stopped typing to think, tapping his fingers nervously.

"Well, we're definitely in trouble. We've had no contact at all from the prime minister's office, or anyone else from Petram for that matter."

Tomas rubbed his head. "I've never been under so much pressure. And if this doesn't work, I have no idea what to do next."

Chapter 7

# **Phoenix**

As the four teenagers got up from the table, Agnes saw that Sahil was a bit shorter than she had expected—perhaps not quite her height—and yet he was the tallest of her new acquaintances. Together, they walked out toward the archway that led to the street. Before crossing under it, though, they showed Agnes where they could find some bicycles. "Just grab whichever one you want; they're for everyone," Pari explained. Agnes examined a few and chose one that looked to be about the right size.

They pedaled out of the ward and onto the street. Pari led them a short distance through New Canberra, past restaurants, shops, and offices, as well as numerous other residential wards. Soon enough, they turned off the main road onto a pathway, joining a sparse flow of other cyclists.

Apparently, this pathway was dedicated to bikes, as there were no pedestrians that Agnes could see.

After passing a few residential buildings and a playground, the pathway became steeper, leading downhill. It wound through a green meadow with scattered clumps of trees, the grass as high as her bike's wheels and dotted with wildflowers shining in the sun. Agnes assumed that much of this must be another projected view, but the air was fresh and cool, and the wind generated by the bicycle's speed felt entirely natural. It was impossible not to enjoy the ride, regardless of her misgivings about the Factus and the episode with the mites.

She commented to Sahil, who was biking next to her, "So, let me guess: in Nissus you probably never have to bike uphill. Just take an elevator up, and then roll downhill, right?"

He grinned. "You got it."

At length, another neighborhood came into view ahead of them. They followed the pathway down to a small trailhead at the edge of the neighborhood, where the four of them finally stopped and dismounted. They dropped off the bikes and walked over to a train that was boarding in the middle of the street.

As the train rolled down the road, Agnes asked about the Phoenix that Pari had mentioned. Jinjing explained, "The Phoenix is an art sculpture, the most famous one in Nissus, or possibly the world. That's partly because it's in the main square that people walk through when they get to the city. And partly it's because the whole thing is a single diamond crystal, and even here there aren't *that* many diamond statues. It's really pretty cool.

"But we're going there to see more than just the sculpture. In the square, you can look up and down to see all the way to the top of Nissus and all the way down to the bottom. I don't think there's anywhere else that you can see the full scale of the city that well."

Sahil nodded his agreement about that.

*Maybe the Phoenix is the sculpture I remember seeing last night*, Agnes thought. She hoped so.

After passing through a number of neighborhoods of varying styles, the train entered what looked like a tunnel, and immediately came out into a bustling city. It looked like it was the same city Agnes had seen on the way to New Canberra from the hospital a short time ago that morning. As before, the city was full of skyscrapers shining in the night.

"This place is called Nachtstadt, which is German for Night City," Sahil explained. "Phoenix Square is part of it. As you might guess from the name, this city is always night, always busy, and of course it has a lot of Germans."

Agnes peered at the buildings and activity through the train window. "Just one of those buildings might fit all of Petram's population," she commented to Pari.

"It might," she agreed. "But a building might not actually have a lot of people. You sometimes can't tell from the outside what the building is. Some of them are going to be air or water processing plants or have other mechanical systems. Some of the buildings are entertainment venues, or museums, or even food storage space."

The breadth and scale of the city was making Agnes feel small, and she hadn't even gotten to Phoenix Square to see Nissus's true extent yet.

In minutes, they were arriving at the central station, the train pulling up to a platform not far from where she had departed with Faylen and her mother earlier.

Phoenix Square was crowded, with some people hustling between trains, but quite a few were clearly there to see the sights. Agnes could tell pretty quickly that they were at the right place to see the sculpture she had been wondering about. Over the sea of heads, she could make out the orange-red color she remembered. *Is that the Phoenix?* It looked too big to be something made out of diamond, even for Nissus. But as she approached and the view opened up, she could see that it was in fact the square's namesake monument.

The statue depicted a flaming, orange-red phoenix taking flight. It was immense, as tall as her house back home, yet with a delicate grace. Light sparkled from wings fashioned from frozen flame. Eyes radiant, the phoenix seemed to be reaching, lunging into the air, its feet breaking free of dark manacles that were falling, shattered, to the ground. The manacles were on chains that led deep into a cracked, opened sphere, which, Agnes realized with a start, appeared to be the Earth, complete with blue waters, green and brown continents, and a snowy white ice cap on Antarctica.

The whole work glowed with internal light. Agnes's breath caught as she gazed at the wondrous monument, astounded. "You said this was a single diamond crystal? How?"

"How did they make it? Not easily. It's quite the engineering marvel," Pari expressed, staring at the Phoenix with undisguised admiration. "It's really the perfect work of art for Nissus. It shows the diamond-working technology that makes the city possible, and it symbolizes so much about Nissus."

"What's the symbolism?"

"Well, lots of statues commemorate something from the past. A war hero, usually. The Phoenix shows that we look to the future. The Earth is like an egg, see, giving life to the Phoenix. But once it hatches, it doesn't need its egg anymore. It is bursting through the chains that are trying to hold it back from soaring."

Surprised, Agnes finally took her eyes off the statue to glance at Pari. "You don't think we need the Earth?"

Pari shrugged. "Well, obviously *we* do, but one of the great works of the modern age will be to finally reach out beyond Earth. We don't just want to sit around on one planet until it dies. That would be like visiting Nissus and never leaving your apartment," she said drolly.

Jinjing put in, "The fact that we managed to build Nissus before we got to the stars tells you just how hard it will be."

Pari agreed, and continued, "But there's other symbolism in having the Phoenix break the chains. The whole idea of becoming Factus means that we aren't bound by the old limitations of *Homo sapiens* anymore."

Agnes was surprised to hear Pari so openly acknowledge the abandonment of their humanity. At least that was what Agnes heard in those words. She opened her mouth to reply, then hesitated, unsure of how or whether to challenge Pari. At that moment, Sahil called to them and waved them over to a large patch of light on the ground.

"Agnes, come take a look through here," he directed, pointing.

Walking toward Sahil, Agnes could see that he was standing on a glass—or perhaps diamond?—square several meters across. One look through the glass was enough to make her recoil. Getting down on her knees to peek over the edge, she peered through the glass to see the expanse of the city beneath Phoenix Square. Distant, far below them, she could barely make out miniature-looking trolleys and buildings. She could barely even perceive that there were people on the streetscape—they were too small from the distance.

"That must be...I don't know, more than a thousand meters down!" she exclaimed.

Sahil smiled. "It's about two thousand. And look up."

There seemed to be more glass windows set in metal frames far above their heads, and beyond the glass, the skyscrapers rose, and rose, and rose. She looked over at Sahil, incredulity on her face.

He began explaining, "Nissus is over four kilometers tall at this spot. That sounds like a lot, and it is. Think of this. Imagine an old, built-out place like, say, Manhattan. Most of its skyscrapers are two or three hundred meters tall, some a bit more. So Nissus is like a *dozen* Manhattans all stacked on top of each other. Maybe twenty Manhattans. Or if you think of Jinjing's village where she's from, it's like stacking the villages maybe six hundred on top of each other. Now *that's* a city!" he finished proudly.

Agnes stared agape at the sights below and above her, and at Sahil. "But, how?" she finally managed to get out. "How can they possibly make something so tall?"

Sahil gave a knowledgeable air. "With diamond fiber, of course. I guess you don't use diamond fiber in Petram?"

Agnes shook her head.

Pari corrected him. "People call it diamond fiber, but it's really a more complicated material than diamond. It incorporates other elements besides carbon, and it isn't just a simple crystal. Pure diamond wouldn't really be very good as a building material, and it's more difficult to fabricate than the diamond fiber. And this stuff is actually stronger than pure diamond—about a thousand times stronger than steel, as I understand."

Sahil pointed at the glass above them. "See that glass ceiling way up there? The city is tall enough that different levels need to be pressurized separately, so that people have enough oxygen. A lot of the elevator shafts actually have airlocks, depending on if they cross a pressurization boundary."

He turned to Pari and said with a chuckle, "Ok, here's an engineering question for you. What fraction of the load on Nissus's foundation comes from the weight of the air in the pressurized sections?" To Agnes, he commented with a wink, "Pari's on an engineering and materials science track. She's probably already answered that in one of her classes."

"Yeah, I think I have done something like that." Pari smirked.

Agnes stood and took a moment to gaze around—at the Phoenix, at the lights and bustle of Nachtstadt, at the impossibly distant top and bottom of Nissus. At this focal point of the city, where its immense scale was on full display, where the Phoenix soared, Agnes felt how insignificant and provincial Petram must really be.

The founders of Petram had chosen its name from the Latin *petra*, meaning "rock." Agnes had always known that her home was to be a fortress, a refuge from the changes happening on the outside. But here, with the capabilities and sheer might of the Factus paraded before her, she realized that both of her friends Jonnan and Catteryn had been right. Jonnan, because surely the Factus could do anything they chose to Petram and its people. Catteryn, because clearly Petram was being allowed to exist, apart from the Factus, clinging to the past.

*How can I fight the Factus and get Dad back if they can do all of this? I can't fight them head-on, certainly.*

Even as the differentness of Nissus induced a pang of homesickness in Agnes, she wondered how her home would look to her when she returned. While she was sure that she would never abandon Petram, the way so many others were doing, it still seemed impossible that this trip would not affect how she thought of it. Petram would always look smaller and weaker, less relevant to a world that had moved on in a different direction.

*Petram is a relic.*

Chapter 8

# Control

Prime Minister Hale watched the door of his office close as his assistant exited the room, leaving him alone.

*What will become of Petram?* he pondered.

The truth was that for all his bluster and rhetoric against the Bionics, the Bionics were winning. People were leaving every day. This was not sustainable, and he needed to change the rules of the game.

*Willym Barker,* he thought with a chuckle, *you poor fool. You've given me the opportunity I was looking for. After what you did, after I tell people my version of it, they will be begging me to do what I need to do!*

A different man than Prime Minister Hale might have felt uneasy or chagrined about what he was about to do to

Willym Barker and his family. But a different man could not save Petram from the Bionics, he knew. As it was, Hale had a smile on his lips as he began formulating his next speech.

Soon, the Bionics would not be drawing any of his citizens away. No, not a single one.

***

Agnes was still looking at the city and mulling her thoughts of home, when Jinjing suggested they find something to eat before heading back to New Canberra. She prodded Sahil, "You said we're the welcoming committee, so we should do more than just show her Phoenix Square and dump her back at the ward! Besides, it's probably about time for lunch anyway."

As the friends conferred about what to get for lunch, Agnes spoke up tentatively. "How much would lunch in Nachtstadt cost? I haven't really talked to my mom about our budget for our trip."

Jinjing reassured her, "Oh, you don't need to worry about paying for it."

"Are you sure?" Agnes asked uncomfortably. "I don't want you to treat me to lunch if it's coming out of your account...you guys are still in school and don't have jobs yet, right?"

Jinjing shared a look with Sahil, and then said, "Agnes, no one pays money for food in Nissus, not usually."

Agnes looked at her with surprise. "Food is free? Really? How does that work—who pays for it, then?"

Sahil gave a little sigh, and said, "You haven't had anyone explain to you what Nissus is all about, have you?"

Agnes could feel herself getting frustrated and a little defensive. "I don't know, it seems like it's been one surprise after another all morning. All I really know is that my dad is stuck here because your NSG won't let him go, and Nissus is so huge and full of Factus that it makes Petram look like nothing...."

Sahil backpedaled. "Hey, I know, I'm sorry, that didn't come out right...."

Pari said, "We can explain it all, get you up to speed, whenever you're ready to learn more. We're the welcoming committee, after all," she finished with a somewhat forced laugh.

Jinjing asked, "Are you still up for a bit of lunch? Looks like I can order some spicy black beans and rice. Comes mixed with veggies and chicken if you want."

Agnes nodded her assent, and said, "Yes, that would be good, thanks. Sorry, I just keep thinking I know what I'm dealing with here in Nissus, and I keep being reminded that I really don't, yet. Ha, I thought it was pretty simple when I was back in Petram."

A glowing guide line appeared on the ground, green this time, and Jinjing began leading the quartet away from Phoenix Square, down a people-filled city street toward where they would eat.

Agnes said, "For a long time I've figured that the Factus, or the Bionics as I would sometimes call you, were a threat to Petram, to what's left of *Homo sapiens*. People have been leaving Petram to join you. My best friend, Elaina, moved out suddenly a few months ago. Then suddenly my dad is kidnapped, or at least that's how it looks to me. Honestly, I was pretty scared about coming to Nissus, and angry with, well, all of you. All of the Factus. And my mom, for making me come." *Should I tell them about what the mites seem to have done to me?* She looked up at the night sky, full of looming buildings, and pondered what she felt inside, troubled.

Sahil had been looking over at Agnes with a serious expression as they walked and talked. Now that she had finished, he replied, "I can see where you're coming from. Strange city, very different from home. Potentially hostile people, who may not even really be people as you would define it, yes?"

Agnes smiled uncomfortably. "Yeah. And there's more, too...." *The mites. The nanobots.*

Pari said something teasing to Sahil, partially audible to Agnes, but he protested. "No, it makes sense—from her perspective, we really are a threat to Petram and its community, even if we're not *trying* to hurt them. I mean, just look at history, with colonialism, and assimilation, you could draw some pretty clear parallels...."

Pari remarked to Agnes, "See, now we've found his area of interest."

"History?"

Sahil shook his head. "Not specifically. I mean, I've studied a lot of history, philosophy, sociology, and psychology, which all seems to be leading me toward being an ethicist. It ties in pretty well to my family's history with the Nissus Security Group."

"It does?" Agnes didn't see the connection.

"Sure, there are ethical minefields everywhere. Do you know how many murders have been committed in the name of 'security' throughout history? What kind of horrible things have been stopped by groups like the NSG? I'm sure you can imagine what people did as soon as they invented the mites."

"Umm...." Agnes wasn't sure that she wanted to imagine.

Pari bluntly laid it out for her anyway. "The mites can allow control over someone's brain—their feelings and desires and beliefs. It didn't take long for someone to create a bunch of slaves to open a brothel."

Agnes flushed, but Sahil quickly added, "And they got arrested and we shut it down, because slavery isn't ethical of course. Most questions aren't that obvious, but they can still be really important."

*So again, Jonnan was right...they really can use the mites to control someone.* Yes, Sahil said they put a stop to it, but still Agnes gave a bit of a shiver at the thought that she had had the mites tinkering with her brain just the day before.

***

The group hopped on a trolley for a minute, then hopped off again several blocks farther from Phoenix Square. Jinjing pointed to one of the skyscrapers, and they all followed her inside and around a corner, leaving the night behind. After so many unusual experiences and sights that morning, Agnes almost wasn't surprised by what she found within. From the outside, it had appeared to be a rather ordinary, if quite large, office building. But Agnes was sure that, even in Nissus, office buildings were not filled with the towering trees that she was now viewing from a wooden platform. She decided that it must be a true view and not a projection, since a leaf-strewn boardwalk led in among the tree trunks and branches, and she could see a few people coming and going on the walkway.

Peering over the railing of the platform, Agnes found that the view downward was lost among the leafy canopy, so that it was impossible to tell how high they were from the "ground." Likewise, she could not see any glimpse of the sky. Despite that, the ambient light in this forest was fairly bright.

Jinjing was handing her an umbrella at just the moment that a fat drop hit Agnes in the face, making her blink. *Ok, so it's raining in here.* And apparently, the umbrellas were supplied for anyone to use, just as the bikes had been back in New Canberra.

Pari pointed to a spot in the trees, calling to the others, "Let's eat up there." Agnes couldn't quite tell where that was, with all of the leaves and branches obscuring the view, but the group tromped up a few wooden staircases, down a walkway, and around a huge tree trunk, until they were at a secluded deck that featured a large fabric awning to keep the rain off.

It wasn't raining very hard, but Agnes was glad for the umbrella anyway. Once she reached the awning, she shook out the umbrella and set it down, then looked around at the forest. She could make out several other walkways snaking through the branches, but at any rate, it felt quite private here. Looking up from this vantage point, she thought she could perhaps see a break in the tree crown in one spot, and gray clouds in the sky beyond.

Jinjing sat on a bench and said, "Two minutes until lunch is here."

The others sat down with her, and Jinjing restarted their conversation from earlier. "Agnes, Sahil said that no one had told you what Nissus is all about."

Agnes nodded, curious. "Well, I know it's a very big and strange city...."

Jinjing replied, "It is that, but that's not really what it's all *about*. Nissus is named after the word 'nisus,' that's N-I-S-U-S, from Latin, meaning effort or work to achieve some goal. You know there are Factus all over the world, doing all sorts of things, but Nissus has a certain...ah...unity that you might not find in other places. It was founded with a particular set of ideals. We are each working to achieve some sort of purpose."

Agnes remembered what Pari had said earlier at Phoenix Square. "You mean about reaching out to the stars?"

"Well, yes," Jinjing said, "some Nissians are working on that. But there are so many more. You've seen around the city what we've accomplished with engineering and design. We are trying to preserve traditional cultures, like we're doing in my home of Anhui. We're also designing meaningful lifestyles and new ways of living for people to try."

Agnes mentally made a connection. "Oh, like the group of people that invented a language for poetry?"

"Yeah, that's an example. See what you can do with art if you throw out all the rules and design a language from scratch. We've also built more effective...politics, I guess you could call it. And, of course, we're always trying to improve ourselves, with the mites and gene modifications."

Agnes had a bit of a sinking feeling at the mention of the mites and genetic engineering, but she was distracted as several food carts wheeled to a stop in front of the group. Jinjing opened the lid of her cart, and inside was a steaming bowl of rice and black beans, mixed with chicken and vegetables, as she had said earlier.

Agnes opened her cart, as well, and found with her meal a set of silverware to use, as well as a cup, with a water dispenser built into the cart, and a pastry of some kind that she did not recognize.

"Wow...how can they possibly give this away for free?" she asked as she began to dig in to the food.

"Well, everyone needs to eat, right?" Jinjing began. "So, we don't charge money for it. Just like how everyone needs clothes and a place to sleep. If we charge money for those kinds of things, it's like we're saying you don't automatically have a right to them."

Agnes shook her head. "But someone needs to make all of those things!"

Sahil agreed, "Sure, and we've got hundreds of millions of people here who can work, most of them very smart and capable, plus plenty of automation."

"Well, who pays them, then?"

Sahil frowned slightly. "You're still thinking in terms of money. Working to earn money to buy food. A lot of what goes on in Nissus just isn't transactional like that."

Now it was Agnes's turn to frown. "It sounds like you're talking about Communism or something."

Sahil agreed brightly, "Sure, you could call it that, I suppose, if you strip away the baggage of the way the word was used in the past. Dictators and stuff—that's nothing to do with Nissus, obviously."

"But Communism doesn't work!"

"Why not?"

"You can't expect people to work, and make things just to be helpful, without getting paid, and you can't just give away stuff for free!" When Sahil just looked at her, questioningly, Agnes continued. "People would take advantage of the system. It's human nature...."

Even as she said it, Agnes realized with dismay how Sahil would respond. "Who says we can't change human nature?"

Agnes set her fork down and stared around at the other three with alarm. "But...but you just said you want to be an ethicist! And you go and turn millions of people into obedient sheep, to just go happily work for the greater good?" *That must have happened to me! The mites took away my fear and made me more trusting, and here I am hanging out with Bionics!*

Seeing her reaction, Sahil dropped his fork to gesture with his hands and appeal for calm. "Hold on, hold on. Let me rephrase that. No one is turning people into sheep here."

Agnes eyed him warily as he tried again to explain.

"What I should have said is, people can choose to adjust their own personalities and attitudes, using the mites. Obviously, that kind of thing is dangerous, tweaking the brain that way, and we have to build in lots of safeguards and protocols around it. But we do it all the time as Factus. It's not just a Nissus thing, actually.

"Now, keep in mind that we can also *observe* people's minds, again with safeguards and protocols. So, if someone wants to be a freeloader here, we'll know it and ask them to either choose differently or go somewhere else. Nissus is for work, for doing something important. People only live here if they have a purpose."

"So, Nissus is one big happy family, then? Utopia?"

Sahil stared off at the trees, a look of concentration on his face. "*I* don't think of it as a utopia—I know too much about the disagreements and differences we have here, problems we're working on solving."

Jinjing said, "You know, if you tried to explain *your* city to someone from ancient times, they might think *you're* describing a utopia. No one dying of war or hunger. Petram is a big improvement from what people had in the past—and so is Nissus."

Pari, still eating, had been watching the exchange dispassionately. Twirling her fork, she commented, "Back to the whole 'turning people into sheep' thing, it just goes to show that Sahil's ethics stuff isn't theoretical. Everything we do with the mites has to be ethically cleared one way or another. And there are so many scenarios to consider, like what do you do if someone wants to be more focused on their work, but you think that wouldn't be healthy, and they should have a more balanced life? Do you respect their choice and approve the request, or do you say, 'Sorry, I don't think that's a good idea to use mites to make that adjustment?' What if someone is just not very social, but they're ok with that—how hard do you push them to open up so they can be more successful in their relationships?"

Sahil continued, "Right, see, we're very careful to respect people's autonomy. We're only going to use mites to intervene against a person's will if they are mentally ill or if they might be violent or something."

"Or if you think it's an emergency," Agnes added.

The three looked at her, a bit surprised by the interjection, and waited for her to continue.

Agnes sighed. *I guess this is as good a time to tell them as any.* "Ok, so there's something I guess you should know if we're talking about this." Briefly, she described the meltdown she had experienced on the train, the doctor's use of the mites, and her subsequent worries about how they had affected her. "Everyone is telling me the mites shouldn't have permanently changed my brain, but I'm telling you, I feel different now. Something's wrong with me—my fear and anxiety have been deadened."

After a moment when everyone sat thoughtfully, Jinjing said, "Ok, here's an idea. Let me ask you a question. Imagine climbing onto that railing and trying to stand on it, balancing so you don't fall over the edge. Now imagine someone pushes you and you lose your balance—does thinking about that feel scary to you? Does your fear feel normal to you when you imagine that?"

Glancing at the railing and the drop-off into the tree branches beyond, Agnes replied, "Yes, that does feel scary."

"Well, if you still have normal feelings like that, maybe your anxiety was just rebooted or recalibrated or something. Because what you describe about your panic attack on the train certainly doesn't sound very healthy."

Agnes picked her fork back up and began glumly eating again. "I don't know. Now that I've had the mites do whatever they did, it feels like I'm tainted so I don't know if I can trust anything I think at this point."

Jinjing smiled and offered another idea. "You know, you don't have to use mites to influence a person's brain. People were already trying to change you and turn you into an obedient and hard-working member of society before you left Petram. It's called parenting and schooling. What happens if you lie to your parents in Petram? You probably have some kind of consequences, right? I'd say that whatever taint you got from the mites has to be less than the taint you've already gotten from all the people in your life so far."

Contemplating that, Agnes didn't have a ready response.

"Something to think about," Jinjing said.

***

Tomas bent over his worktable, carefully pouring the molten metal into a small formwork, where it would cool in the proper shape.

Watching, Edmon asked, "So why did the Factus let us keep this equipment, anyway?"

Tomas didn't look up. "There was a lot of pressure from the Petram government. You know how since Prime Minister Hale was elected, he's been going on about 'Factus interference!' and 'Indigenous rights!' and all that. Well, even though the NSG doesn't trust us, they did try to make a show of giving us independence."

Edmon scoffed. "Well, I think we can all agree that's all it was—a show."

Tomas straightened up. "Well, if they want a show, a show is what they're about to get," he said with a smirk.

Chapter 9

# Home

As Agnes quietly finished her meal, she found herself enjoying the rich flavors despite her worries. Likewise, the gentle rain on the awning overhead was peaceful, even if it was artificial. *I can enjoy the rain and the trees, can't I? It's not mites messing with my brain, it's just rain and leaves.*

Agnes saw some motion in the foliage some distance below them and pointed it out. "Is that a monkey down there?" The others got up to peer over the railing.

"Looks like it," Sahil said. "Wherever Nissus has anything like nature, you're probably going to see some animals. That way we can use the space for people, for animal habitat, and for zoo all at once. Lots of animals are extinct in their original environment and might only live here."

Agnes watched the monkey swing into view, climbing closer. "It's not behind a fence or something, though?"

"Of course not," Pari said flatly. "Why would we need those if we have mites? We can just program the mites to tell the animals where they're allowed to go and what they can eat. Keeps them safe, keeps us safe, and they can have a huge living space that way." She seemed to be bored, or deliberately controlling her impatience.

Agnes felt Pari's annoyance rubbing off on her, and she made an effort to keep her voice neutral. "But is it nice to control the animals that way? They're not really free."

Sahil looked puzzled. "I'm sure it's a whole lot nicer for animals to simply know where they're allowed to go instead of being stuck in a cage or something. Besides, with the mites, we can see how an animal is feeling. We know they're not in distress from anything we're doing."

*If you say so,* Agnes thought skeptically.

Once everyone was finished eating, the teens sent the meal carts off to wherever such things went, and retrieved their umbrellas to head back into the rain. Up another set of stairs, down a few walkways, and curving around through the foliage, they eventually came to a landing much like the one they had used to enter the forest. Tired, and ready to be back at the apartment, Agnes let the others show the way back to their ward in New Canberra.

Agnes found that the common area outside her apartment was now busier and noisier than it had been when they left, mostly due to a dozen or so children running around and climbing on the playground equipment. Sahil said, "Looks like your mom hasn't gotten my message, so she must still be asleep."

"Maybe I should wake her up soon."

"Will you and your mom be at the ward dinner tonight?"

Agnes shrugged. "Probably, but I guess it's up to my mom. I should be around."

Jinjing said, "You're welcome to sit with us if you do come. We'll see you later!"

Agnes thanked them for taking her to see Phoenix Square and headed up to her temporary home.

***

For the second time that day, Agnes was left with a few quiet moments to rest and think about all that she had seen. The sights had been spectacular, as her mom had said, and the friends had been nice, but she was no more at ease about the mites or the future of Petram.

She lay on the sofa for a minute. *Tomorrow we'll see Dad, finally.* Could she and her mother help mediate whatever dispute or misunderstanding had kept him here, or would the stalemate continue to drag on indefinitely? Maybe she could use some of Sahil's "ethics" rhetoric against Dad's captors.

Sitting up, Agnes decided she ought to respond to her friends' messages. She waved the command to call them with a video chat, but then frowned as the call failed to go through. *Hmm. Calls to Petram are blocked? It looks like I can still send offline messages, though.* Briefly, she recorded a short message for her friends.

"Hi guys, it's me. I'm safe here in Nissus. I mean...." *Well, not safe exactly.* "I made it here, anyway. We're going to go see my dad tomorrow." Skipping over the incident on the train, she mentioned that she'd been around the city a little bit, and explained how Nissus was composed of many stacked layers of city, each with its own artificial sky and unique character. "I can see why my mom said it would be impressive. But this really is a Bionic city, I mean Factus city. They're pretty open about using nanobots on themselves. Mites, they call them. It's kind of disturbing; they admit they're not *Homo sapiens* and they're fine with that."

Agnes was just finishing the message and sending it off when she heard her mother moving in the back room. When Zusana came out, she looked a bit rumpled but rested.

She greeted Agnes cheerfully, "Hi, honey! I sure needed that nap. How are you feeling?" Behind her cheeriness, though, Agnes could see her concern. She reminded herself that her mother had been resting because she had been up all night at a hospital. Watching over *her*. Even if Agnes felt none of the panic from earlier, she couldn't blame her mother for worrying a bit.

"I'm fine, Mom, though I still think the mites did too much while they were working on me. Umm, actually, while you were asleep, I went out for a while. Some...friends, I guess, took me out to see some of the city."

Zusana had been getting some water at the sink but turned to look at Agnes at this news. "Really?" Sounding surprised and worried, she sat at the kitchen table. "Ok, I've got to hear about this. You just got out of the hospital, and went off with some strangers?"

Feeling a bit defensive, Agnes sat across from her. "Well, I knew you were going to be asleep for a while, and it seemed safe. I needed to learn more about what's going on here and why they have Dad." She began recounting her meeting the three friends, their jaunt into Nachtstadt, the splendor of the Phoenix and the sheer scale of Nissus, and their treetop lunch. "Oh, my goodness, Mom, you're going to need to go see the Phoenix for yourself at some point. I can't even describe it, or what it feels like to be able to see all the way to the top and the bottom of Nissus."

Zusana chuckled. "Yes, it sounds like I do need to go take the tour. But I'll admit, I'm just as amazed by your recovery as I am by Nissus. You managed to make some friends and go on a tour of the city, without any of that anxiety you were feeling? I don't think I've seen you this relaxed and confident for weeks."

"You mean since before Dad was taken? Well, like I said, I don't think my 'recovery' is really natural. I'm worried about the mites. But...." Zusana waited for her to go on. "But I *am* glad that I went out and saw some more of Nissus. There's so much to learn about the Factus."

Agnes remembered with a touch of embarrassment that her mother had insisted their trip to Nissus would be educational, and she wondered how much "I told you so" was behind that satisfied smile she saw on her face.

*She needs to hear the disturbing things I learned, too,* Agnes thought, slightly piqued. "Um, well, speaking of the mites, I'm not being paranoid to worry about what they can do to me. Sahil confirmed they can—and do—use the mites to make people do what they want, even change their personalities."

Zusana frowned. "That doesn't sound right...."

"Ok, I guess he said that's what they do if people *want* to have their personalities changed. He said they try to do it all ethically, and the Nissus Security Group makes sure people don't go make slaves out of anyone. Which *has* happened in the past, apparently."

"Right, I'm sure the mites have been abused at some point, but that's not the same as saying they 'make people do what they want' in Nissus. I haven't been to this particular city before, but I do know a bit about what goes on among the Factus. And you know Dad was concerned about the mites, too, but he did believe Nissus would be safe for us."

"Well," Agnes said as she pulled her feet up onto her seat and wrapped her arms around her knees, "no matter what, there's a lot to worry about. And not just about the mites I had in my brain yesterday. I can see why some people have been leaving Petram, if they're...dazzled by places like Nissus. And we *still* have no idea when Dad can come home."

Zusana sighed. "Yes. I've been counting down the hours until we can meet. Our appointment is scheduled for first thing in the morning." She swiveled her head, looking around the kitchen. "Although I might not survive that long if I don't get some food. I'm absolutely starving."

Agnes pulled up a display and began trying to find the ordering system that she knew must be there. "So, apparently, food is something we *don't* need to worry about in Nissus." Zusana watched what she was doing, offered some suggestions, and between the two of them they soon had a meal on its way to their apartment.

***

Prime Minister Hale sighed audibly as his fool of a minister sputtered and stammered across the table from him. *He doesn't get it yet. I can't allow this. And I won't.* He tented his fingers and waited a moment longer for the other man to grow even more uncomfortable.

*Enough.* "Secretary Walton, I don't understand. I've laid out the facts. We are dealing with a crisis, here—the Bionics have attempted to subvert Petram's independence. We need to protect ourselves. We need to prepare the public. Are you willing to do that, willing to support this proposal, or not? Speak clearly, for once."

The prime minister coolly watched as Secretary Walton affirmed that yes, he did support the emergency measures. It would have been painful to watch, if he had cared about the man's discomfort and fear. As it was, Hale was happy that everyone could see he was beaten.

There was ample reason for Walton to be afraid of Hale. Walton was one of the few who had known about the special research project that Hale had assigned to Willym Barker. It would be best if he decided to forget what he knew about that disaster. All he *really* needed to know was the story that Hale was now telling everyone—and it appeared that Walton was smart enough to understand that, finally.

Walton finished speaking. And as Hale looked around the room at the intimidated cabinet officials, he knew that he had won.

***

Tomas handed the small box to Willym, who set aside the caulking gun he'd been using. He peered inside the box and gave a short nod. "Good, you did it. Now, help me get my quarters set up. Edmon, I think it's time you smash the last cameras in the front room. The longer it takes them to know what happened, the better."

Edmon said, "Once we're all ready, we should ask the Factus for some bubbly. Have a toast to celebrate."

Willym scoffed. "Don't be ridiculous. We don't have time for nonsense like that. Got to focus on our mission."

Tomas just nodded in agreement. The mission was the only thing that mattered, of course.

Chapter 10

# Children

While Zusana ate, Agnes took some time to look around their apartment and put some of her things away. Compared with the sights she had seen earlier, this place was refreshingly mundane—this could have been an apartment in Petram.

Afterward, the two of them walked down the steps outside their door to have a look at their surroundings. The ward consisted of a row of low apartment buildings with a tree-lined, grassy common area in the middle. The—simulated—sun was past zenith but still high in the sky, and just a touch of breeze made the shade cool and pleasant.

Agnes walked with her mother past the empty cooking and eating area close to their building, over toward the playground. About a dozen small children were climbing on the equipment or running around, while in the open lawn just beyond, it appeared that some slightly older kids were playing soccer.

"They sure look like they're having fun," Zusana commented as they strolled by.

"They do." Agnes watched the children with a touch of wistfulness. *Did I ever have that many people to play with when I was little?* Their innocent fun seemed to be out of Agnes's reach, with the weight of so many problems on her mind.

Continuing toward the back of the ward, opposite the exit to the street outside, they encountered the edge of the forest Agnes had seen earlier. "Is that a stream?" she asked, as she caught a glimpse of water through the branches.

"Looks like it!" Zusana said, and she led them onto a path into the trees. Crossing the stream via a small wooden bridge, the trail continued up a rise. "It looks like there's a whole trail system back here," she pointed out, gesturing to a posted sign that seemed to be a map.

Agnes peered at it. "This connects to some of the other wards in New Canberra, and even to some other Nissian communities. In fact, right over there is our neighbor, uh, KandaNorth." She pulled out her handheld and fiddled with it for a moment. "Let's see...says here, 'For Pashtuns, KandaNorth mixes a touch of tradition with generous helpings of modernity...housing options include neo-industrial communal and Western-style tower apartments...dogs prohibited except for two soundproofed dog-friendly wards...Pashto-speaking.' And then it links to a bunch of other communities with different options for language, culture, and housing types."

Zusana had been peering around at the trees while Agnes read the information. "Ok, I think we can skip that one."

"Yep."

Zusana strolled a short way down a path, while Agnes stepped into the trees to look more carefully at the branches above her. *Ok, from what I saw in the other forest this morning, I bet I could find...there!* High in the top of a nearby tree, something gray and furry was moving.

Agnes called to her mother, who joined her in peering upward. "Is that...a koala?" Zusana asked.

"Looks like it."

"These must be eucalyptus trees, then."

The two of them began working their way through the undergrowth to get a better view of the koala, but almost immediately discovered a display wall blocking them. Agnes found that unless she was directly next to the wall, the forest looked vastly larger than it really was—virtual trees stretching away with no end in sight.

After watching the koala for a few minutes and then poking around the trails for a while longer, Agnes and her mother headed back in the direction of their apartment. Crossing back over the stream, Agnes noticed that a young girl was now playing a short distance away among the trees, poking at the water with a stick.

Agnes hesitated, then stepped off the path to go talk to the girl. "Hi there. What did you find?"

The girl, about eight or nine, dark of skin and hair, looked up at her as she approached. "I think I saw a crab, a little one. But it's hiding."

Agnes crouched to look at the water. "That's cool. My mom and I saw a koala over that way."

The girl nodded. "I've seen them. Yesterday I found a salamander." Sitting up and looking at Agnes, she continued, "There aren't any fish in this stream because it's too small, but there are a ton of fish in Warao. You've been there, right?"

Agnes shook her head. "Is that in Nissus?"

The girl giggled, "Yeah. You've never heard of Warao?"

It was hard to be offended by the cute little face grinning at her. "No, we're just visiting Nissus—everything here is new to us. My name is Agnes. What's your name?"

"Vaishnavi. You like animals?"

"I guess so. It sounds like I haven't seen as many animals as you have."

"You should see Warao."

"Hmm, maybe so." Agnes stood up again. "Hope you find your crab again! See you at dinner."

"See you."

Agnes and her mother walked back to the pathway and out into the sunshine of their New Canberran ward. Children were still playing and running around.

Zusana pointed to a bench in the shade, facing the playground, and suggested, "Let's rest here for a minute." Agnes agreed, and together they watched the youthful commotion.

Presently, a young man walked up to the soccer players and called out, "Dingoes! Over here! Wallabies go with Miss Nora over there." Most of the kids gathered and followed one or the other of the leaders, going into one of the buildings nearby. Some small children remained, playing in a sandy area.

While turning to watch the kids go, Agnes caught sight of Faylen coming their way. They waved to each other, and Zusana stood to say hi.

Looking much refreshed from the morning, Faylen greeted them, and asked, "You got some rest, Zusana?"

"Yes, just a couple of hours to keep me going until tonight."

"Good. Me too."

Zusana went on. "The two of us explored the little forest over there just now, but earlier, when I was sleeping, Agnes went to visit a place called the Phoenix with some friends she made."

Faylen looked quite surprised. "Oh! Well, that was a quick job of making friends!"

A bit self-conscious, Agnes replied, "They said they were told to talk to me because I'm a visitor. The boy, um, Sahil, actually said they were the 'welcoming committee'."

Faylen looked a bit amused. "Whatever works, right? Did you like Phoenix Square?"

Agnes equivocated. "It *was* pretty amazing, but it's intimidating, too. It makes Petram seem so small and, uh," she thought for a moment, "powerless, I guess, by comparison. No wonder we haven't been able to get my dad released yet."

Zusana squeezed her daughter's shoulder, comforting her. "Tomorrow, hon. We'll find out what's going on."

Lost in her thoughts for a moment, Agnes idly watched the children playing and didn't really listen as the women sat on her bench and talked for a moment longer. Suddenly, a question that had been lurking in Agnes's mind pushed itself to the fore.

"Faylen? I'm confused. It seems like New Canberra has an Australian theme because it has koalas and eucalyptus and stuff, but all of the people here seem to be *Indian* and have Indian names. And...they're speaking English."

If Faylen was thrown off by the abrupt change in subject, she didn't show it. "Yes, this ward has people with an Indian background and with a little bit of Indian culture, but other wards are different. New Canberra tends to be a mishmash of different ethnicities. Some districts in Nissus try to protect a particular culture or language, but that's not what New Canberra is trying to do."

"What *are* they trying to do, then?"

"Well, it's kind of a 'default' district, a place where anyone can go and find a welcome, like you did. You don't have any particular ties to any subgroups in Nissus; you just need a place to stay. New Canberra is good for that."

That made sense to Agnes, but Zusana said, "That sounds like living here would be a bit rootless—don't people want to be a part of a community that is more *community* than that? Some kind of shared culture or values?"

"People want all sorts of different things," Faylen replied calmly. "A few people want to feel like they are actually in, say, India, and forget about the larger world most of the time—to them, that's home, and nothing could make them happier. They can find that in Nissus if they want. But other people would go crazy in a district like that. For me, I'm energized by meeting people, by hearing a dozen different languages in a day, traveling, being challenged by something new all the time."

Zusana laughed a bit. "I don't think that's really us, is it, Agnes?"

Agnes shook her head in agreement.

Faylen continued, "But on the other hand, just look around the ward here. These kids *do* have a community—it may not be as insular or homogenous as some districts are, but they've got enough stability. They've got family and friends. It's home for them."

One of the smaller children, a toddler, had wandered close to where they were sitting, and Agnes smiled at the boy and waved. *At least I have a chance to talk to some children here,* Agnes thought. She walked over to the boy and sat next to him on the grass. "What did you find there?" she asked, pointing.

"Big leaf, little leaf!" He held them up to show her.

"Oh, I see." Agnes glanced at her mother, who gave an encouraging wave. "Is this one from this tree here?"

"Maybe," the boy answered, and then said some more in a different language.

The boy handed one of the leaves to her and began collecting some more.

Zusana called out, "You're making all sorts of friends today, Agnes!"

She grinned back at her, and then turned to the boy, who had taken the leaf back out of her hand and traded it for a different one.

***

Making friends with a number of the children turned out to be easier than Agnes would have thought. She was content to play with them for a while, unwinding after a morning of seeing strange sights and learning disturbing things. Meanwhile, Faylen took Zusana out to show her around Nissus.

When she saw that people were gathering and starting to get food, Agnes headed over to the eating area and found her three friends from before. Sahil, Pari, and Jinjing were eating at a table with several other youths, but they made a spot for her. Agnes sat next to Jinjing, who had a small boy between her and Pari. She couldn't help noticing that he was the only light-skinned and blond boy at the whole table. *He looks like he could be my brother*, she thought. Pari and the others were helping him with his food.

The dinner turned out to be some sort of spicy Indian food—Pari called it "aloo gobi"—that Agnes sampled but couldn't really stomach. Fortunately, there were some alternate food options, and she ended up with a blessedly normal, familiar sandwich.

On the other side of the table, Sahil was lost in some discussion with another boy, and it sounded like they were getting a bit animated. Jinjing filled Agnes in on the context. "They've been working on a project for school. Apparently, it's not going very well." Pari told the boys to talk more quietly.

Agnes smiled to herself at hearing that. *School projects? Problems? How refreshingly ordinary.* They may be Factus and not technically human, but how different could they really be if they worried about school projects like anyone else? Aloud, she replied, "That sounds familiar."

Jinjing prodded for more. "Oh? What kind of projects have you worked on?"

"Actually, I was mostly thinking about all the tests and assignments I had last week. It was the end of term, and I had to review everything, write a paper, and then on top of it all, the whole situation with my dad and leaving to come here, to Nissus." Agnes stared distantly for a moment, remembering the awful turmoil of a few days before. "I don't think I did very well. My grades will definitely be bad for last term. I'll have to work really hard to pull them back up."

Jinjing was sympathetic. "That does sound pretty stressful."

"What's Sahil's project?"

"He said it's a Michelson-Morley experiment." At Agnes's blank look, she continued. "You know, measuring the speed of light, disproving the ether?"

"Oh...." Agnes wasn't sure what that meant exactly, but it sounded like it would be a lot more complicated than the magnetic field experiment she did at school last week. "You do that in high school here?"

Jinjing made a little dismissive wave. "*I* didn't do that experiment, but everyone needs to do *some* kind of lab work if they're going to really study science. It's a whole different skill set from just reading a book and solving equations." She made a face. "But relativity's not really an interesting subject for me. Pari and Sahil have both gotten deep into it, right, Pari?"

Pari smiled as she helped the blond boy with his food. "Yeah, if I'm going into materials science, I'm going to need QED, and if I want to understand *that*, then I certainly need to understand all of the classical theories. Maxwell's equations, deriving the Lorentz transformations, all that good stuff." She gave a quick sideways glance at Agnes that made her feel like she was being measured, somehow.

Once again, Agnes thought, *these are teenagers?* Trying to dismiss her feeling of intimidation, she turned her attention back to Jinjing. "So, if you're not interested in...that stuff...then what *are* you interested in?"

"I think I'm going to be a teacher," she said.

Agnes brightened at that. "Oh, for young kids?"

"Not sure yet. Maybe."

Agnes confided, "At some point I'm going to take some child development classes, do some babysitting. I'm an only child, so I haven't really been around kids much. I've always wanted to, though. Maybe there's a career in there somewhere for me."

Jinjing looked pleased. "I've always thought that talking about atoms or photons or whatever is boring compared to working with people."

"No argument here."

"Actually, my studies are part of why I'm visiting New Canberra again—I wanted to see how Sahil's brother is doing." She nodded toward her other side. "He's actually slightly famous."

Agnes, who had just started to relax talking with Jinjing, was suddenly confused. "Sahil's...brother?" She scanned the line of people along the table, unsure who she meant. The little blond boy, next to Jinjing, looked up and met Agnes's eyes.

Jinjing spoke to the boy. "Rachit, this is Agnes. She's new to Nissus—never been here before!"

He didn't seem particularly shy, but neither was he talkative. Agnes had a hard time estimating his age, since she had so little experience with kids, but she figured he must be around six. That was probably why he was quiet—he was not around kids his own age.

"Are you going to say hi to Agnes, Rachit?"

"Hi."

"You're Sahil's brother?" Agnes realized her tone might have been a bit impolite, but Rachit just nodded. At Agnes's questioning look, Jinjing leaned down and suggested to the boy, "I think your friends are here now. Do you want to sit with them?"

He nodded, and the girls helped him move his plate and cup to a nearby table. Agnes noticed that he did, in fact, seem to open up and talk once he was with kids his age.

When they returned to their seats, Jinjing answered Agnes's unasked question. "Sahil and Rachit both have the ability to consciously control their skin color, hair color, and hair type. For some reason lately, Rachit really likes to be white and blond. I haven't been able to figure out if he just wants to be different from his brother, or he actually likes how it looks, or what. But," she gave a shrug, "it *is* his skin, so it's up to him. Honestly, it's probably just a phase he's going through."

Agnes looked back and forth between the two boys. *Ok, now that I know to look past the skin and hair, they do kind of look like brothers.* "So, Rachit controls his mites to change how light or dark his skin is? You said he can *consciously* control them, like, just with his thoughts?"

Jinjing began to shake her head but ended up with a noncommittal expression. "Yes and no. Or, I guess *no*, he doesn't use mites for it. It's a genetic enhancement, so it's an inborn ability. Even if Sahil and Rachit removed all their mites, they could change their skin pigmentation and hair color however they want. I guess you could say with their thoughts. It would take weeks or longer, of course, to fully darken or lighten."

Agnes tried to wrap her head around this strange ability. "But *why* would someone give them that ability? What's the point of being able to change your skin color?"

Jinjing gave a look that made Agnes feel like she was missing something obvious, but aloud she just said, "Well, Rachit apparently likes to use it. But it's probably because it was easy and low risk to give those enhancements. The worst that could possibly happen is someone ends up with a skin tone they didn't want, right?"

"Huh. Ok, so they're brothers that don't look like brothers." *It's always something, in Nissus!*

Jinjing paused momentarily as a slightly mischievous smile crept across her face. "Actually...they're twins who don't look like brothers. Identical twins, almost."

Impatient with constantly being off-balance, Agnes just stared at her and waited for her to go on. "Yeah. Rachit and Sahil are twins. They're both about seventeen years old in real time, but Rachit has another genetic enhancement to make him grow and develop a *lot* more slowly. That's why he's famous, at least to some of us, because it's experimental. Developmentally, he's about seven."

Agnes gave a look of disgust. "That's horrible." She didn't bother trying to keep the contempt out of her voice.

Jinjing appeared quite surprised. "What? No! He's going to grow up just fine. He just gets to enjoy a very long childhood, have plenty of time to learn lots and lots of stuff, but still play a ton, and hopefully have a longer lifespan. It's an experiment, sure, but it's supposed to be *better*."

Agnes looked back at Rachit, then around at the tables of people talking and eating. Mostly everyone seemed happy. But Agnes—she found that she was just *done*. She couldn't handle any more surprises today, and she knew what had pushed her over the edge. *It's the kids—I thought I'd found something normal and simple, and then I find out they're messing with the kids, too? Do they use mites on little kids— on babies? On embryos? If Jinjing is going to be a teacher, what does that even mean in a world where the kids have mites and genetic engineering?*

Agnes mumbled some kind of excuse, got up from the table, and headed back toward her apartment. *I was nearly done eating, anyway.* She changed direction when she caught sight of her mother and Faylen coming back through the ward's arched entryway, and she met up with them moments later.

Zusana began telling her about the Phoenix, but Agnes was feeling too distracted and impatient to listen very well. "Look, I'm going to go back to the apartment and rest there. I finished dinner already."

Zusana looked concerned. "What's wrong, Agnes? Are you feeling...."

With a bit of a start, Agnes realized what her mother was worried about. "Oh...no, I'm not having another episode or something. I've just had enough of Nissus for today.

Apparently, they do a bunch of their *modifications* on children, and I don't want to hear any more about it today."

"Oh. Ok."

"Just come up when you're done with dinner, ok? I'm tired of Bionics and I miss Dad and home." To Faylen, she said, "No offense."

Faylen just smiled sympathetically. Zusana promised she'd be up soon, and Agnes wearily climbed up to her apartment.

Chapter 11

# NSG

*Finally, this morning we get to see Dad.* It was an exciting thought—too exciting, as it turned out. Between that and an early bedtime, it appeared that Agnes was up before anyone else in Ward F-142. Showered and shod, she looked out at the dark commons and willed the fake sun to rise so they could go. *I'm still on the wrong schedule, I guess.*

Sitting on the couch to wait, she idly pulled out her handheld and started distractedly reading a little more about Nissus. The only thing in her reading that she really noticed was a discussion of some of the reasons for building the city in *Greenland* of all places. It turned out that the melting of the ice cap had created a *lot* of available land, land that had recently been under kilometers of ice. So, putting a heavy city in Greenland instead of elsewhere meant less trouble with the geology—the continental crust was already deformed by the weight of the ice, and wouldn't shift too much under the weight of the city that replaced it. Also, the relatively cold climate helped with cooling the city, which was apparently a perennial challenge.

Too restless to really read, she put the handheld away, and with a last glance at her mother's still-dark doorway, slipped out to walk around the ward for a fresh look at it.

The ward was just beginning to stir, hint of dawn in the East. Rounding a wall, she stopped, puzzled. Ahead of her through the archway, the street outside appeared to be bathed in sunlight, and was busy with people. She glanced back at the dark sky and quiet neighborhood behind her, then again at the light ahead.

Stepping up to the archway, she peered down the street and listened to the hubbub. The people she saw seemed, in her brief assessment, to be relaxed, like they were enjoying a lunch break, rather than the more subdued or focused crowd one might expect for a morning commute. *Ok, so it's nighttime in here, and it looks like the middle of the day out there. I wonder if they even scheduled any nighttime at all on the main street.* In no mood to get weirded out again, Agnes left the outside world behind and retreated to the quiet stillness of the ward where she was staying, where it was— barely—still night. For some reason, knowing of the busyness nearby made the ward feel peaceful. It might be Nissus-artificial, but it was still nice to enjoy the quiet dawn ahead of a big day.

Back inside the apartment, she found her mother up and getting ready to go—and before long, a knock at their door announced that Faylen had arrived. Agnes let her in.

Faylen looked rested and chipper. "Good morning!" she called out, and the others greeted her in return.

She turned to Agnes. "Feeling better?"

Agnes shrugged. "Yeah, for now. Faylen, do you know why the sun is up on the street out front? It's not nighttime like here in the ward?"

Faylen settled into a kitchen chair before answering. "Well, sure. New Canberra is like most districts in Nissus. The wards are on different schedules so that some are awake while others are asleep. You can let three times as many people use offices, classrooms, trolleys, streets, and things like that if they go in shifts. Helps make the city more compact. I'm not sure what the schedule is for that main street, but it would probably be unrelated to our schedule."

Zusana was skeptical. "Wouldn't that be inconvenient to have people on different schedules? Do people use housing in shifts, too, like, taking turns using the bedroom? That doesn't sound fun."

Faylen raised an eyebrow. "Well, it all depends on priorities, doesn't it? Some people choose to share housing that way. Canberra and probably most places don't. Some districts do have everyone on the same day schedule. There are a hundred other tradeoffs people can make, too, things that affect convenience or what amenities you have. I don't need a lot of private space, personally, so Canberra seems a bit opulent to me, to be honest. But I don't hold it against anyone here. I mean, this apartment isn't unreasonable, just more than I'd need."

"But who decides what's reasonable and what isn't? What if someone doesn't want to make those tradeoffs?"

"I guess it's kind of a collective community decision, about what's reasonable. Nissus is a pretty egalitarian place. If people don't want to fit in with that, they're not really on board with the Nissus project. There are other places they can go if they want a mansion or a private estate or whatever. In Nissus, we do have trillionaires living in smaller digs than this apartment."

Both Zusana and Agnes reacted with incredulity, but Faylen insisted, "It's true! Not many, but at least one I know of—Marek Svobda. I think he does it to make a point, actually."

The conversation shifted at that point as Zusana finished her quick breakfast, and then it was time for Faylen to escort them to the offices of the Nissus Security Group.

Agnes practically danced out the door with excitement, but Zusana seemed restrained by comparison, which at first surprised Agnes. *Am I the only one this excited to get Dad back?* And then she understood. *Oh. Mom's worried, because we still don't know why he's being held or when he can go home with us. This isn't the end. But hopefully, we can start to get some answers.*

Faylen led the others out of New Canberra to a spot where they could pick up an elevator. This time they went down— forever, or so it seemed. Really, it was just over two minutes, but for Agnes, it seemed longer. *I probably just covered more vertical distance than all the elevator rides in my life before today—put together,* she estimated. Petram hadn't been a big city, after all.

From the elevator, they got in a brief line for what turned out to be a gondola lift. Faylen explained, "To go to the NSG office, we may as well take the tourist route. It goes right that way, and you *are* sort of tourists anyway." Agnes had never ridden in such a contraption, but the cable car was rather large and seemed to have minimal sway, so she got over her apprehension quickly.

At any rate, once the gondola was underway, there was so much to see that she almost forgot she was heading to see her father. It was no wonder Faylen had called this the tourist route. Agnes lost count of the vistas and scenes they flew over as they toured a sampling of Nissus's districts: a quaint, snow-draped village nestled in pine-covered hills; soaring, impossible towers overlooking a shimmering bay; a city where the dusky sky was dominated by an enormous planet, complete with rings, making the small orange sun almost an afterthought. At one point, the gondola flew up the side of a sheer cliff, where a whole community had been built into the rock; later, they rose through a teeming coral reef, breaking the surface of the water and climbing into the air, passing a flock of seabirds as they went.

Agnes tried to figure out which parts of each setting were truly there and which were visual projections, but she was too busy looking around at them to check anything on her handheld. She was sure it was a fake when the cable car passed into a broadleaf forest and she glimpsed several brilliant white unicorns with golden, twisted horns, but Faylen swore they were real.

***

When the ride was over, they disembarked into a bustling urban district. Faylen led the group up to an official-looking office tower with "Nissus Security Group" in large but plain lettering over the entrance. *Dad's in here!* Agnes realized with a start. Here, with the NSG right in front of her, and with a reunion with her father imminent, she quickly pushed aside her thoughts of the spectacular scenic trip they had just taken. *Time for business.*

The lobby inside was spacious and rather elegant—surprising to Agnes, since she had assumed from the name that the NSG was small and almost informal. On the contrary, this looked like a serious place. For the first time that she had seen in Nissus, she was in a place that looked like it might be off-limits to public roaming.

A guard at the reception desk took their names and checked a schedule. "Yes, Mrs. Barker, your appointment is with Taia Jackson of the Neumann Investigative Division. You will go through those doors, down one flight of stairs, and you'll see a sign for Neumann at the end of the corridor." He handed Zusana three badges; Faylen and Agnes each took one from her, and they all followed the guard's directions.

The Neumann office seemed ordinary as they walked in; Agnes could almost imagine she was back in Petram. No one was at the reception desk here, but they barely had time to look around before a tall man came to greet them. It took a moment for Agnes to recognize the man from the video they had been sent at home.

"Good morning! Mrs. Barker, Agnes, I'm glad you made it here! My name is Erik Rud."

Zusana nodded. "Zusana, please. Yes, I remember you from the message you sent. This is Faylen; she's kindly offered to be our guide in Nissus."

"Yes, and we do appreciate you stepping in, Faylen. If you will all follow me?"

He led them down a short hallway, and through a door into an office—or, at least she assumed it was an office. They appeared to be in a room with walls made of rough wood. On the other side of the room were open windows and an open door looking out on a dusty Old West town, complete with a building labeled SALOON. A horse tied to a hitching rail just outside tossed its head and flicked at flies with its tail, while down the street some men were driving a wagon.

By now Agnes had seen enough odd things in Nissus to know that she could dismiss the view as a projection. The town was just a decoration no more than a few centimeters deep, even if it was so realistic that she could smell the horse and feel the hot breeze coming through the door. Agnes had a brief pang, wishing to go walk the street that wasn't really there and stroke the horse that didn't exist. It looked like life could have been simple and quiet out there, if it had been real. *Well, Nissus is diverse enough that there probably is a district like that somewhere.*

Turning her attention to the room she was in, she saw a sign proclaiming SHERIFF on the wall behind a desk. Surprisingly, there was a young girl sitting at the desk for some reason, watching the group file in. She appeared to be about ten years old and had dark black skin, her curly hair tied back. *Is this the daughter of one of the NSG employees?* Agnes wondered.

Surprisingly, Erik motioned toward the girl and introduced her, "This is Taia Jackson, Major, Director of the Neumann Investigative Division."

The girl stood up, greeting the group with a crisp, "Good morning." She looked amused at the confusion on Agnes's and Zusana's faces, and as she met her gaze, Agnes somehow knew that this wasn't really a ten-year-old girl—at least not mentally. "You can call me Taia," she said.

*Bionics...*

Faylen stepped forward and spoke to the Petram women: "Zusana, Agnes, the signifier 'Major' means that Taia is to be considered an adult, same as me or Erik." Turning toward Taia, she continued, "And apparently Sheriff, too?"

"Boy howdy!" Taia deadpanned, and they both laughed. Taia waved in the direction of the town outside. "Just having fun with it—you know, being an NSG director is one thing, but Sheriff, now that means I've arrived!" Faylen laughed again. The horse sighed and pulled at its rope. Listening to the not-girl talking this way was nearly as surreal as anything else Agnes had heard or seen—it was hard to think of her as an adult, regardless of what Faylen had said.

Taia turned serious. "Actually, this sheriff thing is just a way to lighten things up, given how busy and tense everything has been lately. A bit of self-care. I know you're not here for fun and games, and I'm not either. Please, everyone, take a seat." Erik took a chair next to Taia, and the others arranged themselves facing her. "So, you'd like some answers about Willym Barker, your husband and your father," she said, acknowledging Zusana and Agnes in turn.

Zusana tensed. "Yes. He's here?"

"Yes—well, in his lab nearby. We'll go over there momentarily, but first some background. You know he was researching mites?"

"I know he was investigating what the Factus do with mites. I think he was looking for ways to protect against them, to defeat them so that we can keep our city clean of the nanobots. We don't allow them in Petram at all, you know."

Taia replied, a touch sardonically, "Don't you, now." Despite being a head and a half shorter and decades younger in appearance, she leveled a piercing look at Zusana. "You would be surprised at how much I know about Petram. I know things that might make you question whether you want to be a part of it at all."

*There it is!* Agnes thought. *The Bionics really are pulling people away from Petram, just like Jonnan said!* Almost involuntarily, she blurted out, "You don't scare us! Do you know what the name 'Petram' means? It means it's a rock, a fortress to keep the Bionics out! We're keeping humans safe there, the original humans."

Taia's expression may have indicated a small measure of surprise, but she just stared at Agnes for a moment, long enough for Agnes to begin to feel self-conscious about her outburst. Finally, Taia answered quietly, "How can I explain when you don't know what you don't know? Agnes, most of Petram's funding comes from Factus sources outside the city. Much of it from Nissus, in fact. And I'm not talking about your agricultural exports. You may consider us Factus to be a threat to Petram, and I'm sure you are right—but we're not *trying* to fight you or undermine you. You have fans. It's just going to be very difficult to hold on to traditional ways, a hard life, when modernity beckons just outside."

Agnes was taken aback. *Factus are supporting Petram?* She had no idea how they could prove that, but one look at her mother told her that *she* believed Taia. Agnes flushed, embarrassed at her ignorance and angry at the whole situation.

Zusana refocused the discussion: "So, about Willym."

"Right. Willym was leading a group of researchers in Petram, studying mites and doing experiments with them. A little background about mites—you know what they are and what they do, right?"

"They are molecule-size robots that can change nearly anything inside a person's body."

"Pretty much, yes. It can be hard to generalize because mites have been built in many thousands of varieties and configurations. A mite for delivering a targeted DNA update needs to operate inside a cell, and it's obviously going to be pretty small. Some mites simply do some mechanical functions, like reshaping bone or delivering medicine, and they can be a lot bigger and simpler. Some are sensors or actually service other mites."

Agnes put in, "And some mites do things in the brain."

"Yes," Taia said. "And that's where things get interesting, so to speak. The brain is the single most complicated known thing in the universe. Mites can tap into neurons and synapses to observe or even to influence the signals, but there's a whole lot more to it than that. Let's see, what's a good analogy, Erik?"

Erik smiled. "I've got one. Observing neurons is like learning your letters. Using that as a tool to help understand or change a person's thinking or personality is like writing Shakespeare."

Taia gave a short nod. "Good one. So, Agnes, I know you are concerned about mites changing people's thoughts. And you're right—they can be a dangerous tool. With the right mites, I could make you hate your mother and love me instead. I could make you truly, deeply believe anything I wanted. You could forget Petram entirely and think you have been a soldier for the past twenty years, for example."

Agnes stiffened, but Taia quickly continued. "But if I wanted to do that or tried to do that, Erik here would pound my face in."

Erik looked at her with knitted brows. "I almost want to pound your face just because you suggested those things."

Taia looked satisfied and patted him patronizingly on his arm. "And that's why you're on my staff. Agnes, Zusana, the whole point of the Neumann Investigative Division of the NSG is to be on guard for misuse of mites. Mites are potentially dangerous, and not just because of 'evil people' who want to control your brain. You can really mess things up just by accident if you don't know what you're doing. Faylen, do you remember the Busan 'KnightsQuest' Tournament incident?"

Faylen thought for a moment. "Oh, that was, like, before I was born...I think there was a gaming event in Busan, Korea, and one of the teams was using some mites to give themselves an edge. But the mites were not very advanced, and they ended up killing most of the team."

Taia said, "But here's the scary part, Faylen—they started out with mites just to help them focus and get an edge in the tournament. But that focus and edge helped them justify turning up the dial some more on the mites. They had access to the mites' programming, and there weren't really any safeguards built in."

Erik continued the explanation. "Basically, the mites made them think, 'You must win this tournament,' and so they said, 'Ok, if we need to win, then why aren't we *really* using these things?' Pretty soon they were so obsessed with winning, they decided they didn't need to take bathroom breaks or listen to worried family members or anything. It snowballed out of control."

Taia summed up. "Yeah, start with 'focus' and end up with one murder, a police standoff, two gamers shot, and three more hospitalized with cerebral hemorrhages or heart attacks. *That's* what my team is for, to make sure that kind of thing doesn't happen again. So, if you're concerned about what mites can do, Agnes, you're preaching to the choir."

Erik interjected again, "I should point out that Busan is famous because that kind of incident isn't happening anymore. We do have safeguards and rules built into the mites now.

"However," he went on, "you can imagine that we at the NSG would be watching Willym's team in Petram closely. Especially if they were attempting to reprogram the mites, defeat the security protocols, et cetera."

Zusana frowned. "So, you invited them here to keep a closer eye on them?"

For once, Taia looked a bit discomfited. "I'm afraid we rather insisted that they come. It wasn't an invitation. And we were already watching closely—no, this was to contain any problems they caused, and to stop them once we had enough evidence that they were breaking the rules. Because it turns out we were right—Willym's team *did* defeat the mites' programming."

Zusana inhaled sharply. "What exactly did they do? And what did you do about it?"

Taia looked back grimly. "Let's go ask Willym, shall we?"

Chapter 12


# Willym


Taia got up from her sheriff's chair and headed for the door, motioning for everyone to follow. They began filing out of the room behind her.

It was an odd procession, to Agnes's view—a child leading, and the largest of them, Erik, at the rear. She walked nervously, Taia's warnings making her apprehensive of what she might learn next. They passed a few corridors, shared an elevator for a drop of a dozen floors, and exited into a sunlit atrium.

Evidently, this was Erik's domain, as he took up the point position in the atrium and explained where they were. "We set up the Petram team in a suite in this complex of laboratories," he began. "The whole team has been confined since shortly after they arrived—we substantiated our suspicions much more quickly than we had expected."

Taia put in, "Actually, that's because the Petram team was further along than we had thought. To be honest, we waited too long and gave too much deference to the Petram government. Willym's team was actively hiding what they were doing and misdirecting us the best they could."

Erik looked at her apologetically. "Yeah, not my group's finest hour. Nearly outsmarted by, well...." He looked at Zusana and Agnes. "People who we wouldn't expect to be so good at working with mites."

*He was probably going to say something like, "primitives,"* Agnes thought, not sure if she should be offended at that or proud of her father's savviness.

They walked on, to a locker room entrance. "Ladies," Erik asked, "please change into the scrubs you will find in there, and place your own clothes and belongings into a locker. You will find a scanning room just beyond, where you will stand like this—," he demonstrated the position, "—and then you will hear a command to proceed after the scan is complete. I'll meet you on the other side."

He disappeared into a separate locker room, and the remaining group entered the locker room as directed—even Faylen and Taia going through the same procedure. Agnes found that there was considerable privacy, and the scan was painless. She had no idea what they scanned or how, but she wasn't about to ask.

On the other side of the scanning room, the women rejoined Erik. The five of them walked to a large, sterile-looking room, where two other scrub-wearing men awaited.

These looked strong and large, the way Agnes expected employees of a "security" organization to look, in contrast to Taia's tiny frame. There was a glass wall and no furniture except for a few metal tables and chairs, which Agnes saw were bolted to the floor.

Zusana murmured at the austere environment, "Erik, in the video you sent last week, things looked a lot less, um, *extreme* than this."

Erik nodded once and agreed. "Yes. Things have changed a bit since then." He waved toward the glass wall, where, Agnes realized suddenly—

*There's Dad! He's—*

She looked more closely, eyes widening in alarm. The man walking toward their room was certainly her father, but— *what happened to him?*

***

Willym's face was haggard and his motions jerky and nervous. He looked like he hadn't shaved, and his clothes needed changing. Agnes heard her mother breathe in sharply.

Erik instructed, "Zusana, please come over here to the door where Willym will come in. Agnes, please stay right where you are until I say otherwise." Zusana did so, but shot a questioning look around at the Factus in the room. They all just waited expectantly, Taia quietly observing from the back of the room.

Apparently, the glass was only see-through in one direction, because Willym did not seem to notice anyone until he reached the door and stepped inside where everyone was waiting for him. As soon as he saw his wife, he broke into a big smile and quickly gave her a hug.

"Zusana, you're here! They said you'd be coming. Are you ok? You haven't let them do anything to you, have you?"

She hugged him back and caught her breath. "No, I'm fine, but what happened to you? You look tired and sick—what's going on? What have the Factus done?"

Agnes grinned, seeing her parents back together. *Why do I need to stay back here?* She was about to go join them, when one of the big men caught her eye and motioned for her to stay put.

Still focusing on Zusana, Willym began, "They haven't done anything to me except keep me cooped up here, and they confiscated nearly all of our equipment. Zusana, we need to get out of here, back to Petram, where it's safe. We—"

Willym stopped in mid-sentence, as he finally looked around and saw Agnes there. "What—What's *she* doing here? You brought Agnes?"

As he stared at her, the fear Agnes saw in his eyes was foreign and frightening. Something was very different about her father.

Zusana appeared taken aback at this. "Yes, I wanted her with me. I—"

"She's not supposed to be here!" He was almost shouting. "She's supposed to be safe in Petram!"

Zusana looked at him levelly. "She was getting too worked up about the Factus and your...situation. She was getting afraid of the mites and things."

"Good!" Willym exclaimed. "She should be. Excellent. Terrible. Can't trust the Factus." He trailed off into a mumble.

Zusana seemed to tremble with agitation. "Willym, what's going on with you? Why are you acting like this? Something happened! What was it?"

He looked at her. "You have to promise me that you'll take Agnes straight home to Petram."

Zusana looked at him, defiantly. "Not without answers, Willym. No. Don't you remember what we talked about a few weeks ago, before you started on this project?"

He deflated. "They got to you. They reprogrammed you."

Zusana began to protest, but suddenly Taia called out, "I think you owe it to your wife to tell her what you did, Willym. She's your wife. Tell her what we both know."

Willym looked around at everyone, finally locking on to Agnes. "Do you remember what I asked you before I left, Agnes? 'Would you do anything to protect Petram and keep it safe?' Do you still say yes?"

Surprised, Agnes remembered the conversation. "Y-y-yes?" Her answer faltered as she tried to think of what he might have had in mind, her confidence still shaken by the exchange with Taia earlier. *Would I really do* anything *to keep Petram safe? Does he think he can do something about the mites? Something dangerous?*

Looking disappointed, Willym squared his shoulders and announced, "I will not be taken over by the nanobots like you all must have been. I've made a defense."

Taia made an exasperated sigh and began walking up from the back of the room. "His defense against Factus mites is his own mites! The poor fool thought he could program them himself!"

"I *did* program them!"

Taia stopped in the middle of the room, some distance from Willym and Zusana. "Finally, an admission, or close enough." She looked at Agnes and her mother and explained, "You can see what his mites have done to him, physically and mentally. Busan all over again."

Willym mumbled to himself, staring into the distance. "Need the bots. Only way. Anything. Anything!"

Agnes looked at the others with shock. *He was supposed to be keeping the nanobots away, not using them on himself!* Her father was her biggest ally against the Bionics. Or he had been, before this happened. Was he like Taia said, just a sad, sick, misguided man?

Was he Bionic now, by his own actions?

Willym stared at his wife distrustfully. She, in turn, looked at Taia accusatorily. "Why did we bring Agnes to see him like this? She should not be here."

Taia softened her expression. "I'm sorry, Zusana, but she needed to see for herself, to really and truly believe that her father brought this problem on himself. Remember, just a few days ago she was terrified of the Factus. Now she's heard him admit what he did, at least part of it. And there are other reasons, too."

Willym looked around with a wild expression. "What are you all talking about? Zusana, don't you believe me? You can't trust them!"

Zusana crossed her arms. "Well, I think all of us need to have some hard conversations. And Agnes should go back to the apartment for now."

Taia put in quickly, "I completely agree. Faylen can take her back to New Canberra for us and keep an eye on her."

"*What?!*" Agnes protested, "I came all this way to see my dad! What did you do to him? Dad, it's me, Agnes!"

Willym turned his back on her and called out, "If you were still the Agnes I knew, you'd be in Petram." His coldness seemed to leave her reeling, and she could no longer hold back tears.

Zusana came over and conferred with Faylen, who gently took Agnes by the shoulder and started guiding her out of the room. "Agnes, I'm pretty sure the NSG didn't do this to him."

Unmoored by the revelations and her father's rejection, Agnes let herself be led back out the way she had come. She had been looking forward to seeing him again, holding on to that hope as if that would make everything ok again—and now that hope had come crashing down to reveal a worse nightmare.

He wasn't just a prisoner of the Factus—her father wasn't himself. Clearly, the mites were confusing him and making him sick. *Is he going to be all right? Are we going to be able to get rid of the bots he made—will he even let us?*

Faylen led her back to the scanning room, where this time a shower drenched Agnes, washing away any stray mites. She was glad for the streaming water, as it cleansed her face of her tears. It was a longer shower than protocol dictated, but Faylen let her take as much time as she wanted.

***

Once she was back at the apartment, Agnes suffered a combination of worry, powerlessness, and boredom that made each minute agonizing. She wanted to do something about the crisis with her father, but she had been sent away by the "grownups." *Argh! Just like at home, no one asks what I want.*

She tried calling her friends Emil and Jonnan in Petram, but the call was still blocked for some reason. She was much too restless to watch a show, let alone read something.

*I'm not sure if it's nice or condescending having Faylen here with me, but at least I have someone to vent to.* Faylen, for her part, was having no trouble focusing on some work, reading some materials and making some calls in the downtime. But she had promised to keep an eye on Agnes, so she stayed to keep her company.

Once Agnes had had some time to settle her emotions, she began to think about the events of the past few days more practically. *So, I've been really sure of myself, but also completely ignorant.* Her wild hostility toward people who turned out to be literally paying to keep Petram running, was, when she thought about it, kind of stupid. *And let's not even think about the incident on the vactrain coming here.*

True, the Factus did seem to be doing some disturbing things—like experimenting on children such as Sahil's brother. She had no idea why Taia Jackson had looked like a 4th-grader but was somehow an adult. *I'm going to need to understand this place better if I want to avoid embarrassing myself again.*

She pondered for a moment, and then reached for her handheld as an idea came to her. *Sahil is studying ethics, so I should be able to grill him about a lot of the things I think are wrong,* she realized. He also had connections to the NSG, so presumably he'd be aware if there were dissidents or people who didn't necessarily approve of all of the things she'd seen so far.

She sent off a quick message and got an automated reply immediately—he was in class, but would be free in about an hour, and an entry had been added to his calendar asking him to come by her apartment at that time.

Agnes spent most of the next hour making a list of questions and challenges for him to answer—she may have been too antsy to read, but the writing and rewriting turned out to be cathartic. It felt good putting into words all the reservations and resentments she had, and she began to think that she might even have a fighting chance of not coming across as hopelessly naive and ignorant this time.

When he arrived and they had exchanged greetings, Faylen moved to the kitchen table to give them a little space. Then, facing Sahil alone, Agnes felt a moment of shyness—arguing on paper seemed easy, but facing someone in the flesh, a boy who was slightly older and apparently brilliant, made her wilt a bit. *Maybe just don't think of him as a boy—he's a Bionic, and you're not afraid of Bionics. You'll always be better than them because you are* HUMAN!

She wasn't sure she was really that confident, but her little internal pep talk made her smile to herself, nonetheless.

Agnes explained to Sahil what had happened that morning with her father. It was painful to admit what he had done, that he had used his own mites with his custom programming, but she forced herself to say the words anyway. She *needed* to get some answers and a better understanding of the mites and the Factus.

Sahil understood right away and was sympathetic. "Yeah, unauthorized experiments like that will definitely get the

NSG involved. It sounds like he fabricated mites with completely custom programming—that's super dangerous. I'm sorry."

"Sahil, let's talk about the mites for a bit. I kind of get it if you want to, like, fix a broken bone or cure diabetes, but this whole thing about using them to mess with the brain—that just seems wrong on so many levels."

Sahil looked thoughtful. "Ok, so I'm not being flippant here, but why? Seriously, you need to articulate what specifically seems wrong about it or we might not be talking about the same thing."

"Ok, well, for starters, you could be messing with someone *else's* brain, changing what they think whether or not they want you to. That's just creepy. Next, you're changing who someone is, their identity. It's like you're playing God. People are supposed to grow and learn—are the mites taking that away? And like you said, they're dangerous!"

Sahil was unperturbed at this. "Ok, you're talking about everything from basic concerns to philosophical arguments." He grinned. "Agnes, I could give you a much longer list, especially practical questions. Who gets to decide exactly what control people should have over their brains? I mean, we're not going to let people do just anything even if it's only their own brain, but who makes those decisions and rules? How do you evaluate risk and benefit or do anything experimental? What do you do about social pressure, and how can you make sure the whole program is actually helping society—I mean, maybe something is popular, but not actually good for us. Mites are a *huge* problem."

Agnes raised her eyebrows at this. "You're not helping me feel better about the mites."

He kept going: "How do you establish consent? When is it ok to conduct surveillance on people's thinking?"

"Sahil...."

He laughed. "But you get it, right? We know. We take every one of those questions seriously. We've been doing this for a long time, trying to be careful and ethical in how we use the mites, the best we can. And the other thing is, you have to look at the benefit, the enormous payoff from using mites to change the brain."

"Enormous benefit?" Agnes was skeptical. "And what would that be?"

"I could sit here and tell you about what it does to the economy when you give the whole population a twenty- or thirty-point IQ bump, or eliminate crime, or make people's relationships so much better. But you are concerned it's changing a person's identity. Let's see...."

He pulled up a display on the coffee table surface and flicked through several screens. "Here, read this. You were telling me about how this morning at the NSG they mentioned the Busan disaster? This is the other side of the coin. This is from a real person, one of the early subjects to try brain-active mites when they were still experimental. Busan happened in a couple of different cases, but *this* one is something *millions* of people experienced."

Chapter 13

# Objections

Agnes pulled the document Sahil referenced over to her handheld and began to read.

**Early Nanite Trials - SQ35 - Ted Oliver
Interview with Subject About Trial and Results**
[Interviewer] Ok, we are here in St. Petersburg, Florida, with Ted Oliver. Today is October 18th, 2063. Ted, you were enrolled in the SQ35 clinical trial on April 10, correct?

[Ted Oliver] So they told me.

[Interviewer] Would you care to elaborate?

[Ted Oliver] Well, I was kind of messing with you there. Yeah, I enrolled in April. But I wasn't really keeping track of the days or paying too much attention to what was going on before the trial. Things were a bit confusing.

[Interviewer] Do you remember enrolling and how that came about?

[Ted Oliver] Pretty much, yeah, I do. I was homeless, see, living various places around the city. Parks, by the underpass, shelters sometimes. One day I was hanging out with this group of about four other guys, and a lady with an e-clipboard walked up and started talking to us. Asking us our names and stories. Nothing too unusual about that.

[Interviewer] That wasn't unusual?

[Ted Oliver] Nah, there are always people from the agencies and shelters trying to talk to you when you're homeless. Or police.

[Interviewer] What did you tell her?

[Ted Oliver] I told her my story. Ha, I had a pretty good story to tell, too. All about my bad luck and problems with my jobs. I had a hard time keeping a job, always had terrible bosses. I remember I was always so mad, and feeling sorry for myself, but at the clinic they told me a lot of my problems were because I had schizophrenia.

[Note: attached documents indicate that the subject was dismissed from multiple employers for insubordination, absenteeism, theft, and poor performance in the past five years. Medical and other records suggested a developing schizophrenia during this period, which was subsequently confirmed upon enrollment in the SQ35 trial.]

[Interviewer] And what happened then?

[Ted Oliver] So, she told me there was an experimental treatment that could maybe help me. To be honest, I didn't think much of what she was saying—just that she was offering me a nice place to stay for a week, free food, cash, all that. So, me and two of the guys went with her in this van to the clinic.

They talked all about the nanites, blah blah blah. I knew I should care, but it was mostly just words to me. I'd heard all sorts of stuff for years from people trying to help me, and none of it made much difference. So, I just signed all the papers they gave me. They hooked a needle in my arm for about half an hour, and that was it. They gave me a little room to stay in, really nice. It opened right on a courtyard, so I went out there to hang out with my friends.

[Interviewer] Ok, go on.

[Ted Oliver] They told me the nanites were going to take several hours to find the right places to go in my brain, and then they'd start watching what was going on. Kind of scouting it out in my head. When I went to bed that night, that's when they'd start tweaking things. So, there was nothing out of the ordinary that afternoon, other than being at this luxe resort-like place. Just went to bed, thinking how nice it was being in a real bed like that again, incredible luck. I was just going to enjoy it while it lasted, because I knew in a day or two, I'd be back at the underpass.

But, waking up the next morning....

[Here the subject paused until prompted by the interviewer.]

[Ted Oliver] That was the strangest feeling, waking up. I was in the deepest sleep of my life—I must have been just dead to everything for, like, twelve hours. And when I woke up, I just kept waking *up*, like I'd actually been asleep for the past ten years. I mean, all of the schizophrenia and stuff was real, and it sucked, but when I woke up that morning everything was way *more* real. Like my mind was clear and I was really aware for the first time in my life.

My life started right then and there. My life started with me just lying in a bed, saying, "Whoa, ok. Here I am. Whoever I am." I mean, I knew my name and stuff, but it was like I didn't really know who I *was*.

[Interviewer] So, what did you do?

[Ted Oliver] Well at first, I just looked around and tried to figure out my situation, how I got there. Not there in the room, I mean, because I knew I came to the clinic in the van. How I got in that homeless situation.

When I got up, I looked in the bathroom mirror and literally took a step back, I was so shocked at what I saw. I probably spent an hour showering, shaving, cleaning my ears, fixing my nails, it was the most wonderful feeling to get clean, put on something fresh. I had no idea I was such a mess. Or I kinda did, but just couldn't do anything about it before.

There was some food they'd dropped off, so I ate a bit. And then I went back to bed. I was really tired.

[Interviewer] How long did you sleep that time?

[Ted Oliver] Only a couple of hours. When I got up, I showered again, found another set of new clothes the clinic had left in the room for me, stripped the bed and put new sheets on it, really cleaned everything up. I started thinking about where I'd come from, and it didn't make any sense. I was like, "Ok, why did I get in that fight last week? Why did I blow that money I had?" I was a stranger, like I said. I had to figure out who I was going to be now.

I went out of the room and found some of the clinic people. They set me up with the social workers. It wasn't easy, getting all straightened out. There was a lot of recovering. I needed to get my health up, see a dentist like three times, get my eyes fixed. I think I gained ten kilos the first month. I went to see my parents and said sorry for all of the crap that I put them through. I had so much to learn. Things like how to hold on to a job, how to manage money, social skills, even redoing a bunch of high school classes. I'm still in school part-time, working part-time. The clinic found me a place to live and they're paying the first year of rent for me.

[Interviewer] So, your schizophrenia was cured just like that?

[Ted Oliver] Just like that. My life started that day. Whatever was going on before, most of it, that's just a nightmare. That wasn't me. It was, but it wasn't.

[Interviewer] What are you studying?

[Ted Oliver] Social work, for now. I think I can relate to the guys on the streets, 'cause I've been there. I've been helping out at the clinic, getting some experience. I want to get a girlfriend, but we'll see about that. I'll probably be in school for a couple of years still.

[Interviewer] Ted, this interview will be part of a report we are making to summarize the outcome of the SQ35 trial. I have to ask this. On a scale of one to five, how effective and helpful would you consider the treatment you received? One is not effective and helpful, five is very effective and helpful.

[Ted Oliver] Are you serious?

[Interviewer] Like I said, I was required to ask the question.

[Ted Oliver] You better hold on, because those nanite things are going to change the world. I don't know what else they can do besides fixing schizophrenia, but those things gave me a life. They took me out of hell itself. I might not be in heaven, exactly, but I have a life to live now. How much do *you* value *your* life on a scale of one to five?

[Interviewer] Point taken. Ted, thank you for your time today, and congratulations on your progress.

Agnes finished the document and thought about how to respond. "Hmm, well ok, he had a disease that they were able to treat. I guess you can't really blame him."

"Yeah, but that means you're agreeing that the mites can be helpful and beneficial. Once you're trying to draw distinctions between what's worthwhile and what isn't, well, you're just doing what the rest of us do. Rejecting mites is just a matter of degrees, then, not absolute."

Agnes got up and paced for a moment while thinking. "No, I think here's my take on it. There are people who probably need the mites. That's why if someone in Petram has schizophrenia, like this guy, we just send them on to the Factus. We—I—don't judge them. But most of us, the rest of us, can maintain the pure human race in Petram."

"You did say that a lot of what the Factus do is wrong, like you said, 'on so many levels.'"

"Well, look what they did to your brother! Keeping him a child year after year, not letting him grow up, that's not fixing a disease!"

Sahil shook his head. "No, he *is* growing up, just slowly. It's not fixing a disease, true, but remember what I said yesterday, there are supposed to be benefits. What if those benefits are at all like what this test subject experienced? A qualitatively better life?"

Agnes jabbed at the air with her finger. "You can't make that choice for someone else. It's not fair to *do things* to children who have no say in it. That's just...evil. It's unforgivable."

Sahil had sat back and put his hands behind his head to regard her as she said her piece. "Agnes, *not* acting is still choosing for them. That's what I think you're missing. Look around at Nissus." He stood and walked over to the big windows overlooking the commons. "We have the technology, the power, to choose any environment we like. I mean, we can make *this*"—his arm swept to indicate the view of the ward—"from what used to just be a whole bunch of rock in Greenland. Building the city was a choice, but not building it would have been a choice, too. The important thing is, it's not just our environment we have to choose—we have to choose who and what to be. Both for ourselves and our children."

He turned and sat back down. "We *have* to decide for children who have no say in it. When I have kids, I can choose their height, appearance, health, body dimensions, growth patterns, pretty much everything. There are real consequences to some of those. If I don't choose what I believe is best for them, isn't *that* evil? I don't get to avoid moral responsibility here by not selecting traits and just rolling the dice—I will absolutely own all of the attributes my kid has, because they were all in my power."

Agnes was waiting impatiently for him to finish. "What if the best thing for a child is for them to be a *Homo sapiens*?"

Sahil replied as if choosing his words carefully. "I think that would be a difficult argument to make."

Agnes was quick with a response. "Your brother—what benefit is he supposed to get by growing up at half the rate as everyone else? How is *that* choosing what's best for him?"

"Well, a couple of ways. It's a happy, fun childhood, and he's going to enjoy it for a long time, making memories. He's got plenty of time for things that he would be too busy to get to, otherwise. He can spread out his schooling, and still get more of it done."

"But all his friends are growing up faster than him! He's going to lose everyone his age, when they move on and he's left behind."

Here, Sahil seemed to concede a little. "Well, yes, there is some of that. He's developing at a bit less than half the normal rate, and some of his friends are more like three-quarters, so there's some more overlap where they're the same age developmentally...."

Agnes cut in, "And that's supposed to make it ok? That's probably worse—they have enough time to get really close, and then one of them just gets older and they can't be friends anymore."

Sahil thought for a moment. "I think that's actually kind of a common thing for kids, like, if the family moves. New friends."

"But relationships are what life is all about! You're being, I don't know, *cavalier* about what you're doing to him."

Sahil raised a finger to interject. "Actually, about relationships—our mom and dad can have more time with him as a child this way. I mean, there will be plenty of time as an adult, but you're only a kid once. Don't parents always say that kids grow up so fast? But they don't have to, anymore."

Agnes argued, "Kids are not *toys* for parents to play with. It's not like you order them off a menu as if you were at a restaurant, choosing whatever you want."

"And yet, here we are, presented with a menu."

"So, you admit your parents were selfish to do that to Rachit?"

Sahil seemed to be regaining his poise. "Not at all. I told you some of the benefits to him. I didn't mention that he'll probably end up smarter because of his long childhood, more talented and healthier mentally. Better than me, I'm sure."

"Well, then why don't you go do it, instead of him?"

"I do actually kind of wish I could have been the one to grow up slowly, but I'm the 'control' to his experiment. Rachit is the first to grow at this rate—in the future, probably everyone will be copying him. If they don't go even more slowly."

Agnes scoffed. "And what does *he* think about being an 'experiment'? He never agreed to it, not if he was a baby."

Sahil seemed a little defensive. "Well, no, you can't expect babies to be able to make important decisions. Parents always have to take that responsibility. You don't ask a small child if they want to be toilet trained or to brush their teeth or even get medical care, right? You just decide for them."

"But this is an experiment! How can you possibly justify making *that* decision for him?"

Sahil said simply, "Risk-benefit analysis."

The matter-of-fact way he said it unsettled Agnes. "Simple as that, huh? You're confident you aren't taking it too far?"

"Look, millions of years ago, a fish started crawling out of the sea. Its fish buddies probably thought *that* was going too far, too—but look what happened! That act unlocked the evolution of reptiles and birds and mammals. Who knows how humanity might evolve in the far future? Or what we would be missing if we don't let it happen?"

"Sahil, a lot of those birds and mammals started *eating* fish."

Sahil nodded thoughtfully. "That's true. And some day we may also carry fish to other worlds, too, spreading them out into the galaxy. So, crawling out of the sea might still prove to be the best, most important thing that ever happened to fish."

Reviewing her notes, she thought, *he's not really disagreeing that my objections are true, so much as saying they don't matter.* Aloud, she said, "Ok, so here's another problem. What you're doing is making a world where what matters is how good the technology is, not the value of human effort. People are supposed to struggle and work, have an inner drive, change themselves. What you're doing takes away the human accomplishment, the satisfaction, because all you need to do is just push a button to get what you want. It's too easy your way."

For once Sahil seemed genuinely surprised. "I...hmm. Maybe I should bring you to some of my classes and you can see us struggling and working. You remember what the name 'Nissus' means, right?"

"Yeah, you're all working toward something."

"Right. A lot of that comes down to working toward a better humanity. Building a better people. Better, richer lives. I'd say we're succeeding, too. Rachit is one step ahead of the rest of us."

"But what are you losing? At what point are you no longer human at all? What if there's no Petram, no people like me anymore? Surely you can see that something is missing if there's no one left who is truly human."

Sahil considered, seeming momentarily unsure how to respond. He rubbed his chin and answered, "I see what you're getting at, but to me it's like saying we're losing something if there's no more poverty or poor eyesight. I'm glad we fixed those things. I think any of us can be improved, even me. So, let's do it, right?"

"And what do you do when you reach your goal, when everyone is perfect? What's the purpose of life at that point?"

He smiled and acknowledged, "We'll probably have to figure that out at some point, won't we?"

Agnes looked at Sahil's earnest face, and affirmed for what seemed like the nth time, "I don't want to change humanity. I don't want super-humans or post-humans or 'Factus' engineered humans. I want people to just be people, loving each other as they are and as they always have been, forever."

Sahil nodded. "I can respect that, I think. I wouldn't want to make that trade-off myself, living a more primitive way, but it's fine—it's certainly a big enough world for your project in Petram. It's your right to live that way if you want. Self-determination. And it's probably worthwhile, what Petram is doing, to preserve ancient humanity. For its own sake."

Agnes smiled too, realizing her arguments didn't need to be enough to end the Factus experiment, just good enough to keep the Petram one going.

Sahil gave a little shrug, and continued, "I hope it works out for you, and for Petram. I really do. Just think about what I was saying. Please believe that we're not evil, can you?"

Agnes mumbled something noncommittal.

Before Sahil headed out, he invited Agnes to again sit with the group of friends that evening at dinner. She agreed she would and thanked him for coming by on short notice. Once he was gone, she realized how much tension she had been holding, and she consciously relaxed. *So*, she mentally gave herself a pat on the back, *I can hold my own in a debate with a genius Factus!*

Chapter 14

# Betrayal

"You're confident you're not taking this too far?"

Prime Minister Hale laughed, still looking from the window where his office looked out over Petram. He loved to see his city, never getting tired of the view. *My city*, he thought. *Soon, it truly* will *be mine.*

For the good of the people, of course. It wasn't *his* fault they needed a firmer hand to keep them away from the Bionics.

Finally turning, he regarded his old friend and occasional advisor. "How could I possibly take anything too far, Jakob? When did a leader ever fail because they were not strong and confident *enough*?"

Jakob nodded. *So refreshingly loyal.* "As long as the Bionics don't make too much trouble, sure."

Hale sat down to look his friend in the eye. "I think we've learned what will make trouble with the Bionics. Do you know what really happened with Willym Barker?"

Jakob looked uncertain, troubled. "You mean besides what you just said in that press conference?"

"Yes. The Bionics got involved because Willym had experimented with nanobots, and the bots were messing with his mind. It wasn't really the Bionics' doing. If that ever leaves this room, you're a dead man, by the way, and I'll deny it. But I think we've learned that as long as we don't touch any nanobots, the Bionics won't interfere, whatever I do." He didn't mention that Willym had been acting on his orders.

Jakob let out a breath. "Well, that's a relief, then."

Hale got back up to look out the window again at his city. Jakob would keep his mouth shut; he always did. It was nice being able to confide a little in his friend. He really did value his friends. If they were loyal.

***

Agnes ordered a lunch, and while waiting for it to arrive, called her mother for an update, which was frustratingly short on specifics: "Yes, I know you're worried about Dad. No, he's not willing to turn off his mites. He may not even have a way to do that. I'm going to be getting a crash course in biotechnology so the Factus will let me make informed decisions. They've pulled together teams of lawyers, doctors, and engineers to try to make a plan together. I'll be home in a few hours. Say thanks to Faylen for me."

*Right*, Agnes thought, *like I'm really going to say thank you to my babysitter.* But deep down, she was kind of glad Faylen was around. She had to admit this was a family crisis, and not one she could just blame Bionics alone for—and being completely alone in a crisis could only have been worse.

Her food arrived, and she munched on it thoughtfully for a minute, before she had an idea. "Faylen, I've got a question for you. Are there any groups of people in Nissus that don't agree with the whole 'becoming Factus' thing? Other people that don't want to use mites or genetic engineering?"

Faylen looked up from what she was working on. "Well, that's kind of a complicated question. Short answer is 'sort of'."

"Uh, ok. What's the longer answer?"

"Well, I'm not sure if you remember yesterday, back at the hospital, I said that the whole idea of calling us Factus was questionable and misleading. It's really just in the past few years that it's become popular to talk about all of these changes making people into a new species. The reality is that some people use a lot of the technology, and some don't. I think very few people say no to mites entirely. And most people have some genetic modifications. But for the ones who haven't, I suspect they generally aren't really *against* it; they just haven't seen a need to make big changes to themselves."

"I mean, people organized to say they don't agree with it. People who are against what they did to Sahil's brother, for example."

Faylen considered this. "Yes, I'm sure you could find some groups opposed. Some would just think it's not worthwhile, but others might have more of a rejection on principle, yes. In a population as big as this, there will be disagreements."

Agnes gave a short nod. "Good. I would be worried if hundreds of millions of people all thought the exact same thing."

"Here, I'll send you some resources so you can find out more about the social dynamics of Nissus and the larger world, about the debates and things that are going on. There are certainly fewer factions and disagreements within Nissus itself, because the whole city is kind of a big, shared project. But people do have different opinions about things."

"Cool, thanks."

Agnes reviewed the videos and documents for a few minutes, but soon grew restless.

"Faylen, I want to go out for a walk. I'll stay near the ward, don't worry."

***

Agnes crossed over the little stream she had found the day before at the back of the ward. A half hour of exploring and climbing the trails in the woods left her pleasantly winded, and she headed back to the apartment, refreshed.

For once her timing was good, as just then her mother sent a message that she was on her way. *Yay! Maybe they've decided what to do about Dad.*

When Zusana arrived at the apartment, Agnes was reminded that she wasn't the only one stressed about the situation—her mother looked exhausted and unhappy. She didn't look like she had had a refreshing walk in the woods, nor did she look like she had the energy for one. She thanked

Faylen genuinely for keeping Agnes company and let her go before giving her full attention to her daughter.

They sat at the table while Zusana sipped a drink. "Wow, you look tired, Mom. Did you figure out what's going to happen to Dad?"

Zusana equivocated. "We are making progress on a plan for what to do—it's the NSG's plan, to be honest. Most of what I've been doing today is trying to cram ten years of studying biotech engineering and legal precedents into one day. I guess I've made progress with it, even if it's an impossible job. They want me informed."

"You said that Dad won't agree to turn off the mites. So, we're going to have to do it by force, aren't we?"

Zusana looked sick at the thought. "Yes. And here's the thing. When he built these mites, he disabled their kill switch. The only way is to inject *other* mites to go fight his. It's going to be a full-blown war inside his body and brain, it's dangerous, and we don't know the rules. What if he made a different kind of kill switch that will kill him if the mites think they are under attack?"

Agnes looked stricken. "Oh...I...hadn't thought of that."

"We don't know their programming, where exactly they are, what their capabilities are, or anything. Agnes, it's a real possibility that we won't get Dad back, *even if* we can kill his mites and don't kill him in the process."

"Oh, no...."

Zusana reached out to comfort her daughter. "I don't want to make you more worried than you already were, but I just needed to be honest that this is serious, and we don't have any guarantees here. On the plus side, there are about a hundred world-class experts working on the problem. So, it's not hopeless."

"Mom, maybe it would be better to just leave the mites in him. It sounded like he's just really anti-Factus, and that's not really a problem anymore if we can just take him back to Petram. Then he won't need to be suspicious of you and me anymore, right? Because he got what he wanted then. Then eventually the mites will wear out and stop working, right?"

To Agnes's surprise, Zusana looked even more miserable at this suggestion. "Couple of problems. One, he probably has a big reserve of mites already inside him, enough to last years. So, they're not going away on their own. Second, he's not doing great, mentally or physically. It really is like the Busan thing, where it keeps getting more extreme and dangerous as time goes on. And third, there's one other thing I haven't told you yet. Taia Jackson suspected it, but I didn't learn about it until this afternoon."

She paused, and Agnes unconsciously held her breath. She couldn't help wondering what the revelation could be, what her mother could be afraid to say, after all the things she already knew. *What could be worse than knowing my father is infected by rogue mites and might die?*

"You remember how, when we were coming to Nissus, you were adamant that you didn't want to come? You were so scared of 'Bionics' that you tried to run away. You could barely look up from the window when we were on the train. You had a full-blown meltdown and practically went catatonic, and ended up in the hospital?"

*I don't want to think about it.* Agnes had been doing her best to shut out the memory of the incident on the train. It was the opposite of the 'strong Agnes' she wanted to be—an embarrassing distraction from trying to help her father. *Why is she bringing this up?*

Zusana continued, "Does that kind of reaction sound familiar? When someone is so obsessed with an idea that they kind of lose touch with the world? Their family is worried about them, but they won't listen?"

*I don't like where this is going....*

"It wasn't just a panic attack, Agnes. You were acting kind of like Dad at that point, weren't you? Kind of like the people at Busan." More delicately, she said, "Honey, we're pretty sure that you were under the influence of mites. Anti-Factus mites. Your father's mites—earlier versions of them."

Agnes froze with shock.

"That's why the NSG wanted you to come with me to see him. Based on how he reacted to you today, and some things he said later, we're pretty confident that's what happened."

The room seemed to spin around her as the implications of her mother's words began to hit her. *I would have been infected that whole time, before I even left Petram.* And the only way she would have gotten the rogue mites was if her father had somehow done it. *I sat there talking to Emil and Jonnan and Catteryn about how scared I was of going out among the Bionics, scared of being exposed to nanobots, when I already had them! They had already taken over my mind, the very thing they made me paranoid about!*

"*Dad* infected me with mites, before he left?! But why would he do that? He was *against* them!"

Zusana moved closer and put her arm around her. "He wasn't really afraid of mites—it was more like, he was determined to protect Petram. In studying the threat, he tried to learn about and experiment with mites, and he fell into the Busan trap. He eventually decided that the mites could help keep people from leaving. He justified it by asking you and me if we would be willing to do anything to protect the city. Do you remember? You said 'yes' when he asked that."

Agnes wanted to scream but couldn't seem to make the air move. Her own father had betrayed her. Over and over, everyone else kept making her decisions for her against her will—even the one person she thought had been her greatest ally.

Agnes tossed off her mother's arm and faced her. She felt dirtied, violated, outraged. "Both of you put those nanobots in me when you knew I didn't want them! You did it too, when I was on the train!"

Zusana didn't back down from her daughter's accusation. "Thank God I did, Agnes. The mites we used on the train hadn't been in you for ten minutes when I told the doctor to disable them all. When he zapped those mites, he also zapped the ones your father had put in. Those mites he gave you still had the kill switch, even though they had been reprogrammed and they were hiding. We got lucky that he used those early versions on you instead of the more dangerous mites he has now."

Anger welled up inside Agnes, frustration at being tricked and invaded—and she was glad of the anger, as it meant she wasn't crying. "But how do we know that's what happened? And how do we know they're gone, any of them? Your mites *or* his?"

"Remember how you said you felt different when you woke up at the hospital? You were worried that you felt different, that the mites, the legitimate ones, had done something to you because your fear was gone. You were right, sort of—you *were* different. It wasn't the new mites making you feel that way; it was because Dad's mites weren't there anymore. You were back to normal."

Agnes grumbled, "But I can never be sure if I'm really normal. Maybe your mites were only there for ten minutes, but his must have been messing with my brain for weeks. That had to leave an effect."

Zusana quietly said, "I'm sorry, Agnes. I wish I had realized what was happening back home. I'm sorry I had to let them give you mites you didn't want, even though it was the right thing to do. They might have saved your life. For what it's worth, you seem pretty much back to normal now that those mites are gone—at least you do to me."

*Back to normal....*

It was too much for Agnes—she'd been walking around, talking to her friends about everything, and she hadn't been in her right mind. She hadn't been *herself*, and she was chagrined to think back on what she might have said or done. *No wonder my grades were such a mess.*

Agnes mumbled something to her mother about being alone, and she hid herself in her room at the back of the apartment. She felt fully justified in wallowing in some self-pity for a while.

***

Music blaring in the background, Edmon whispered to his colleagues gathered at the table, "Why didn't you do it, Willym?"

"Change of plans. We'll use the girl."

Tomas frowned at this. "Your daughter? Why?"

"At first, I was upset they brought her here from Petram, but now I think she'd be better, actually. She will draw less attention, and she's more likely to take the message, anyway. We'll need to modify the message slightly, but it shouldn't take long."

Tomas shrugged. "I suppose you know your family. Fine. Edmon and I are ready with our diversion. Just don't forget us when you're famous, will you?"

Edmon said, "She'll be the famous one, I think. Everyone in Petram will know the name of Agnes Barker in a couple of days. If this works."

Willym said nothing.

# Chapter 15

# **Sympathy**

Agnes did her best to mope for the next few hours, hiding in her room as if to make a point by sulking. But, even as a teenager, there was only so long she could maintain that. Eventually, being cooped up became boring, and the anger she felt toward her parents morphed into a feeling of rebelliousness. *You want to give me mites to make me paranoid about the Factus, do you? Well, I'm not going to let you make me do anything.*

Sahil had invited her to sit with his group of friends at dinner. He hadn't done anything to her. Neither had Jinjing or even Pari. *In fact, they've been quite nice to me, come to think of it, showing me around the city yesterday.* She resolved she would meet them as promised, and maybe even relax a bit. *They* weren't the ones to worry about, apparently.

While waiting for dinner, Agnes idly attempted to call her friend Emil in Petram to vent. But, surprisingly, not only was the call still blocked, but she couldn't seem to get a message through. She couldn't reach Jonnan, either. *That's odd. It's like the whole Petram net is unavailable. Is something wrong back home?* She tried searching for news about Petram but found nothing significant.

Since Agnes was still mad at her mother, she didn't want to ask her about Petram, but just went to dinner without saying anything to her.

She found Sahil and the others and made a point of paying attention as she was introduced to some of their friends. Unlike yesterday, Sahil didn't seem to be distracted by the school project he'd been working on—everyone seemed to be laid-back this evening.

Agnes tried the Indian food. It was strange to her, and some of it was too spicy, but she found a lentil curry dish to be tasty. She'd probably be hungry later, but of course, she could always order some food as needed.

If the food was strange, at least the banter going on around her was refreshingly familiar. These teens—Sahil seemed to be the oldest—might be taking genius-level classes, but evidently, they could still entertain each other with the silly teasing and juvenile posturing she had seen at home. Often it was in a language she didn't know, but clearly, everyone knew English.

Jinjing sat next to Agnes—they had greeted each other warmly upon arrival—and they both talked to the girl across the table, who introduced herself as Devina. She seemed friendly enough, telling the others a little about herself.

While most of the people at the table had been born in Nissus, Devina had just moved from India in the past year. As she explained, "My family was drawn to Nissus by the connections it had to our temple in India, and we stayed when we saw the schools and the social networks here. You can imagine the opportunities for pursuing the purusharthas—the four life goals." Jinjing nodded knowingly, apparently having been around Indian culture long enough to understand the significance.

As Devina and Jinjing talked, they discovered that they shared an interest in a fantasy series that Agnes wasn't familiar with, but which sounded both interesting and refreshingly unrelated to the stresses of the past few weeks.

The rest of the girls at the table had a game going in which they made a joke about the boys down at the other end, and then the boys would do the same back, everybody laughing at it. Somewhat surprisingly, Sahil was letting some of the other boys dominate. She had assumed that he would be more in charge, given his confidence and outspokenness earlier.

At any rate, Agnes found herself feeling more at home than at any time in days. *Factus or not, they're letting me be a part of their group.* Given how she felt about her parents right now, she was grateful for some new friends, so that she could feel less alone—even if she still missed her friends back at her real home. And of course, Elaina, wherever she was.

Everyone was finishing eating when one of the other girls—Uchita—addressed Agnes's little group.

"Hey, we're all heading into the Network. You guys coming along?"

Devina and Jinjing looked at Agnes questioningly. Suddenly aware again of her unfamiliarity with Nissus, Agnes said, "Ok, you know I don't know what 'the Network' is."

Jinjing looked apologetic. She said, "Oh, that's right. So, the Network is basically a bunch of ways to get around the city, away from the normal roads and trains and stuff. Usually teens like us, if we want to get away from everybody for a while, we can use the Network. Pop out somewhere fun, hang out, relax, you know."

"Definitely, I'll come. Hang on—" Agnes said. She was starting to get a nagging sense that she was being a little too harsh with her mom. "Let me go tell my mom real quick."

Zusana looked a little hesitant when Agnes told her she wanted to go with the other youth. Faylen, who was sitting next to her, said, "Zusana, if you're concerned about the people she's going with, I wouldn't be. These are good kids. It's got to be better than moping in the apartment."

Zusana sighed. "Ok. But don't stay out late. We're going to see Dad in the morning."

Agnes dashed back over to where Jinjing and Devina were. The three of them followed the larger group, which was already heading toward an open space between some of the residential buildings. It turned out there was an unobtrusive staircase leading up to the roof of one of the buildings.

As they climbed and approached the roof, she wondered what they would find up on top, but then suddenly her perspective seemed to shift, the sky tilted above her, and she realized that they were climbing through an opening in the ceiling. Not only did it no longer look like a real sky once she was at eye level, but she could see some of the electronics that had created the illusion for those below. Above the ceiling was a jumble of ducts, pipes, and wires among thin support struts.

Half expecting to hear some sort of alarm or rebuke from the adults down below, she followed the group past the mechanical equipment and onto a sort of catwalk. She barely had time to get her footing before she found that the catwalk led out over the common area of the ward. Pausing a moment to hold onto the railing and look around, she fought vertigo—the eating area where she had been sitting a moment earlier was still visible directly below her through the grating of the catwalk, and she had a mental picture of herself floating in the air above it.

"Are we really allowed up here?" she whispered to Jinjing.

"Of course," Jinjing replied. "If they tried to make this off-limits, people would be curious and want to sneak in, wouldn't they? So, they just make it safe for us to walk around and explore up in here, and they don't have to fight it."

Agnes stepped carefully, following Jinjing as the group continued across the commons and eventually out to the main road of New Canberra. Their catwalk ended at a more solid-looking passageway, and Agnes breathed a sigh of relief that she no longer felt suspended above a long drop.

After a few minutes of hiking along a never-ending line of equipment, one of the boys stopped and slid under a large duct and out of sight.

The others began following. Agnes steeled herself and dropped to the hard floor. Lying flat, she scooted under the duct, expecting to find another industrial-looking space on the other side.

Instead, she blinked at the sight of a narrow but very long room, below her at the end of a short ladder attached to the ledge where she lay. Conversation, music, shouts, laughter, and other noises filled what could only be described as a party room—young people of all sorts were talking, eating, playing games both electronic and low-tech, and at the other end she even made out a band with a guitar and drums. The band playing seemed to be composed of amateurs practicing, rather than professionals giving a concert. Most of the walls of the room were windows looking down on the New Canberran main road, and even some of the flooring was transparent.

She sat up as Jinjing slid out from under the duct next to her. "This whole room is above the main road? And no one can hear or see all of this going on right over their heads?"

"There's no point in just leaving empty space above the road, so they built a hang-out room. The noise is all canceled so that it doesn't leak out of the room. From down there, you'd never know there's anything up here. Unless you got a really tall ladder or something and smacked your head on it, I guess."

"But you have to get to it by going under pipes and things? Why?!"

Jinjing laughed. "So the grown-ups won't want to come! If you were going to design a place to live and you could make it any way you want, wouldn't you want to have a hideout away from the adults? Something that seemed like it was supposed to be secret? Something that felt a little rebellious?"

Agnes didn't have an answer. The energy of the room seemed to fill her. She carefully climbed down the ladder to the hang-out room and looked around.

Devina, from her group at dinner, was there, apparently waiting for her. Jinjing joined them, and the two of them began showing Agnes around the room. The people they passed were of every race and color—some of which were clearly not natural—and the languages were nearly as varied.

Jinjing pointed out a spot where the room jutted out in a small extension, which contained what looked like a firehouse pole leading down through an opening in the floor. She explained, "If you slide down that pole, it takes you to another part of the Network. There are all sorts of places to see, if you know where to go and you have enough time."

Agnes looked through a transparent section of the floor to see where the firehouse pole led, and learned that, from the New Canberran main street, the party room firehouse pole exit was disguised as an enormous tree.

Devina put in, "Yeah, we probably don't want to stay here unless you're into one of these games. There's always a concert at Cristobal Park—want to try that? It's along a river walk; they even have boat rides."

Agnes considered for a moment. "There's a concert every night? What kind of music?"

Devina paused, a flash of amusement crossing her face. "No, I mean there's *always* a concert. Round the clock. One act finishes, another comes out. It's been going for years. There are a couple of different stages, actually, so you can probably find one playing music you like."

Agnes was a bit puzzled. "They keep playing all night and day? Who goes to a concert at seven o'clock in the morning?"

"We're not all on the same schedule in Nissus, remember. There's always someone finishing a long week of work or school or something, ready to go out."

Jinjing added, "Yeah, I think in Cristobal Park it's always 'evening'."

*I should have expected that in Nissus, by now, I guess.* Agnes remembered what she had learned earlier, that the name 'Nissus' meant effort or work. She commented, "You know, for a place called 'Nissus', you guys sure do *play* a lot."

The others chuckled, and Devina quipped, "All work and no play makes Jill a dull girl!"

Agnes thought about her friends from back home, wishing she could be with Catteryn, Emil, and especially Elaina. She made a decision. "The concert place sounds like a bit much for me right now, to be honest. I've had a pretty rough day and..."—here she pushed past her shyness—"I think I just need to talk to someone. Someone besides my parents."

The other girls looked at each other, thinking, and Devina suggested, "Let's take her to that overlook...what's it called...Hovedoya? That's a good, quiet place to talk." Jinjing nodded at this, and they started guiding Agnes toward another section of the party room.

Here was another exit from the room—this time, in what she decided looked like roller coaster cars. They all jumped into one of the cars, which promptly began rolling down a track. The track dipped, and their car dropped with it, accelerating, and then turning and rolling and banking as they zipped through the city. *I take that back—this isn't* like *a roller coaster, it* is *a roller coaster!* She was a bit windblown by the time they arrived at the overlook and got out.

A short series of steps took them up into what appeared to be the top of a dark observation tower, with views on every side looking out on a quiet nighttime scene; they were on an island in a bay. City lights twinkled across the waters, with mountains and stars behind. Ignoring the benches and the other sightseers, Devina found a hammock. They all crammed in.

"You weren't kidding about a good, quiet place for a talk," Agnes said. "It's almost like they made this just for us."

Jinjing replied, "Well, you're not the first one to need something like this."

The three sat for a moment, watching a ferry ply the waters. Agnes checked her handheld and confirmed that they were not actually looking out on a real bay and city—it was a recording. But, this being Nissus, the projection was so good that it was easy to just accept the gentle breezes and ocean scents, watch the stars, and relax.

Agnes took a deep breath. "Devina, I guess you've figured out that I'm not from Nissus. Actually, I'm not even Factus. I'm from a Traditionalist community called Petram. I'm here in Nissus because my father is being held by the Nissus Security Group. My mom and I visited him today, and it didn't go well...."

It didn't take long to fill them in on Taia's description of the Busan incident, Agnes's meeting with her father, and the revelation that he had infected her with unauthorized mites, putting her in the hospital. Apparently, the other girls hadn't had as much experience with security breaches as Sahil had, and they sounded surprised, and a bit shaken, by what Agnes described.

She summed up, "So basically my parents betrayed me. Even though I know at least my mom meant well, I still can't believe that *both* of them could do that to me—the one thing I was afraid of. How can I even get over it? I'm supposed to go see my dad again tomorrow, but I don't even know who he is, or who he was if he could betray me."

Jinjing just made a low whistle and looked at a loss for what to say, but Devina seemed to have something in mind. She asked, "Agnes, what was your father like before he got so deep into the stuff with the mites? I'm guessing 'betrayal' would be kind of out of character for him, right?"

"Well, yeah! He was great, really smart, really dedicated to us and his work. I always thought I had a good dad. I actually got along with him better than I did with my mom. So, it's like all of that is a lie now."

Devina shook her head. "No, I don't think so. Like you said about the Busan thing—people got caught in a trap and did things they wouldn't normally do. The only thing that was really their fault was that first mistake of playing with mites they didn't understand. The things they did after—that wasn't really them. I don't think you should give up on your dad just because of what he's like *now*."

Agnes was unconvinced. "I don't know.

Suddenly, Devina sat up a bit. "Hang on, I just thought of something. Let me see if I can find...." She stared blankly for a moment, apparently using her mites' interface to search for something. "Let's see, this one is good. Here, listen to this poem."

*Of all the wonders in God's green Earth,*
*To one above all she gives the most worth.*

*"Consider the lilies," it once was said.*
*Well, thoughts of flowers do fill her head.*

*Oh, how she loves these blossoms beautiful,*
*And gathers buds with tenderness dutiful.*

*She brightly submits her floral bouquet,*
*And I accept, not showing dismay.*

*She will continue, unaware,*
*That they will die despite her care.*

*It seems that love can sometimes lead*
*To outcomes which we never agreed.*

*Moreover, it makes me sometimes wonder,*
*What sins, unknowingly, I am under.*

Jinjing asked, "So, the girl picks flowers because she loves them, but she doesn't realize that picking them kills them?"

Devina agreed, "Yeah, it's like, there's nothing more innocent than a little kid picking flowers, but it's actually violent in a way. So, how can you know you're not like that little girl, doing something you think is good, but which you might regret if you really understood it? We all do things without knowing the full story, the full implications."

To Agnes, she continued, "I think when your dad realizes what he did, when he's back to normal, he's going to be really upset with himself. I think he never intended to 'betray' you, not until the crazy mites messed things up."

Jinjing laughed, "Hey, you just compared Agnes's dad to a little girl!"

Even Agnes had to laugh at that. Then they were all quiet for a moment, thinking while watching the scenery.

Finally, Jinjing spoke up. "I think you have to expect it to get worse before it gets better, though. Your dad isn't well, and it might take some time to fix his mites. He's probably still going to say hurtful things until he's better. Just be prepared for that."

Agnes agreed. "Yeah, that's probably good advice."

After a few more minutes, Agnes felt ready to head home and face her mother again. *Talking with friends can be therapeutic!* She was surprised to realize that these girls really were friends, Bionics or not.

Chapter 16

# Surprises

Agnes woke to the alarm she had set the night before, and realized how tired she must have been. *I don't think I moved a muscle from the moment I lay down!* She felt better, refreshed.

Then she remembered where they were headed today, and what dire straits her father was in.

For the trip back to the NSG facility, they took a more direct route than the scenic gondola ride of the previous day, as they were not so early leaving the apartment this time. Again, Faylen led them to the office of Taia Jackson, which she saw still had a Western theme. However, this time there was none of the joking or playfulness that had marked their introductions the day before.

They arrived in the middle of a meeting between Taia, Erik, and several people Agnes didn't recognize. One of the men seemed to be arguing with the others in the room—"No, the model includes those cases. Even if the dopaminergic S-type nanite population is not localized, there's over a ninety percent probability of an acceptable attrition rate in the simulations unless"—while Taia appeared to be losing patience.

She cut him off as Agnes, Zusana, and Faylen made their way into the room and found seats. "Yeah, we know what you're saying, but those cases aren't adequately modeled. They're in there, but they're only coarse-grained. There's still work to do on that. At any rate, I'm going to need to step out for a bit. Now that Willym's family is here, we're going to go pay him another visit."

She turned her attention to the newcomers as the man she had been talking to left with most of his colleagues. "Hi, welcome back, Zusana. As you can see, we've been working on the plans for combating the rogue mites. I dare say none of us got a lot of sleep last night. We're running out of time."

She continued, "Agnes, I understand that your mother has told you about the reprogrammed mites that your father used on you while you were in Petram. I hope when we treat him, it will be successful, you'll get your dad back, and he can make amends at some point. That," she shook her head sympathetically, "may be a long road for your family. I'm sorry you're going through all of this."

Zusana asked, "Do you still think we can give him the treatment tonight?"

"Yes, we need to. We've fabricated nearly all of the mites we need, and I don't think our strategy can get much better at this point. We want to salvage whatever we can of Willym and his associates, but every day they're accumulating more damage. So, tonight we act."

"Agnes wasn't here for the discussions yesterday. How about you go over the plans again—it's her father, so she should know."

Taia nodded in agreement. "Sure. Simply put, we'll wait until the subjects are asleep tonight, and we'll introduce our own mites via an airborne mist. Even with the lights on, I doubt they'd be able to see the mist coming through the vents, but we want to be sure they are unaware of it and don't take any actions to avoid the treatment or trigger anything with their rogue mites. The real battle will occur inside their bodies as a microscopic war. Our mites will need to infiltrate quickly and in large numbers, carry out reconnaissance, and neutralize the worst threats in a swift initial strike."

Erik continued, "The advantage we have is that we can add lots of mites as reinforcements, we've planned out all of the potential scenarios, and we'll have real-time communication and control of our mites. Plus, we have experience with this sort of thing. The disadvantage is that there's still a lot unknown about what Willym did with his mites, and they could easily cause any amount of damage to his body at any time." He let out a sigh. "We'll do the best we can."

Agnes digested this, then asked, "So, why are we visiting him now?"

Zusana answered, "We're kind of stalling for time. He's expecting us to visit, since we're here in Nissus. He's expecting us to try to talk to him and reason with him."

Taia added, "We'll suggest some concessions to come tomorrow, some additional freedoms. We're hoping that if he has something to look forward to, he'll hold off on anything rash. Anything further, I mean."

Agnes furrowed her brow. "I don't know what to say to him. I'm upset that he gave mites to me while we were in Petram. I don't think I can pretend it didn't happen."

Taia nodded thoughtfully. "That's fine. It's good, actually. If you confront him about it, that's perfectly natural, and it might give us more evidence and understanding of what he did. It eats up some time and stays away from the more dangerous topic of what comes next. Obviously, you have no idea what the plan is, right, Agnes?" She looked at her pointedly.

Agnes agreed glumly, "Yeah, I know."

"All right, then. Let's go."

Once again, Taia led the procession toward the changing and scanning rooms. Whereas yesterday Agnes had been eager and hopeful at the prospect of seeing her father again, today she was nervous, and honestly dreading the encounter. She knew she had every right to be angry at what he had done to her, but she had little hope that anything she said would get through to him. Not with his mites messing with his thinking. *This whole meeting is going to be a big, uncomfortable waste of time.*

Agnes, her mother, and several of the Factus sat at a table in the same room where they had met Willym the prior day, while one of the security personnel went to retrieve him.

Willym entered the room with the same gaunt look she had seen before, but he did seem more alert and aware this time. He came to their table, sat, and looked at each of them in turn as Taia began talking. He leveled an alarming look at Agnes, somehow calculating despite the eyes that were wide and crazed. She almost walked out of the room right then—and probably would have, if that hadn't been a certain way to draw more attention to herself.

He suddenly interrupted Taia. "You say you want to let me out of the lab tomorrow. A field trip. Why not now? Let's go right now."

She scoffed. "That's not how this works, Willym. You give something, we give something. Step by step. Show us we can work together."

He bowed his head and mumbled something that might have included the word "lying." *He's not buying it....*

His head snapped up, and she suddenly found those eyes on her once more. "What do you think, Agnes? Are they going to let me out of here tomorrow?"

"Umm...." She was caught off-guard, and before she had a chance to say anything, Taia cut in. "We told her what you did to her, Willym. She was pretty upset."

He didn't look away. "Yes, the Factus can be persuasive, can't they? Turn you against your father?" He fell silent, looking angry.

Taia was having none of that. "We didn't turn anyone against you! We cleared the mites out of her, and now it's just your daughter, clean, here in the flesh and you don't seem to care about her or how she feels. You're the one who's turning her away!"

Willym clutched his head for a moment, his rapid breathing gradually becoming calmer, before looking around again, and apparently coming to a decision. "Ok. I give something, you give something?" He stood and started walking toward the door. "I want to show you something, Agnes. I have something for you."

Apparently, she wasn't the only one surprised; the NSG people scrambled to get up from their seats and follow, with Erik and Taia looking at each other in evident confusion.

Willym led them down a corridor and stopped at a door, turning to face the crowd. "Agnes, come in and see my lab. This is where I've been staying. I have something for you."

At a hand signal from Taia, one of the large security men muscled his way forward and spoke. "She can come only if you agree to keep at least half a meter from her at all times. I will be watching. I don't have to tell you what will happen if you violate this rule."

Zusana piped up, "I'm coming too, Willym."

Willym didn't even answer; he just absently turned and walked into the lab, leaving the others to follow. The tour he gave was perfunctory and his explanations disjointed. There wasn't much to say, as most of his equipment had been confiscated earlier. Agnes saw his two Petram colleagues, men she didn't know, in one of the rooms appearing bored but also haggard, like her father.

He suddenly seemed to change, becoming less distracted, as he entered his personal quarters. Agnes stopped just inside the door, her mother beside her and Mr. Security on the other side.

"Agnes, this is what I wanted to give you." He opened a jewelry box, revealing a pendant with a flowing, stylized letter P. The letter was silvery, with diamond sparkles in a ring to frame it. The frame and the backing of the pendant displayed abstract patterns with fine detailing etched into the surface.

Willym looked at her with those wide eyes. "I want you to wear this pendant. The P is for Petram. If you wear this, you're still supporting Petram against the Factus. That's all that matters. Will you wear this, for me?"

*That's...beautiful,* she couldn't help thinking. *Not crazy at all....*

"Hold it!" The NSG man took the box and pendant, frowning at it. "Where did this come from?"

Willym stared at him innocently. "I designed it and fabricated it here in my lab. I've been working on it for days, just for Agnes. Well, I guess it was for Zusana until I found out Agnes was here. There's nothing dangerous about it. You can check, it's just diamond and silver alloy."

The other man considered this. "Huh. I guess it should be simple enough to scan it."

Agnes hadn't been expecting such a gesture. "Wow, it's really pretty, Dad. Thanks." *Maybe there's hope for us....* She caught his eye again, and then wasn't sure what to think.

With the tour concluded, Agnes, her mother, and the NSG personnel filed back out, leaving Willym in his quarters for the time being. Someone ran to take the jewelry box for analysis, while Agnes walked with her mother back to the meeting room. She found Taia and several others urgently conferring.

She heard Erik comment, "No plan survives contact with the enemy," and she frowned. *We did ask him to give something....*

But, of course, the pendant came from the man who had used the mites without her knowledge. She really didn't know if she should trust him or accept it.

At length, Taia came over to Agnes to speak with her. "We've looked at the present your father gave. It's as clean as can be. Perfectly safe. It'll be waiting for you when you go out of the lab. I think we're going to be here for a little while before we talk to Willym again. Why don't you and your mother go out, get some lunch, and you can come back later in the afternoon?"

"Ok," Agnes agreed. "I want to see that pendant up close. It's really pretty." And it was starting to get boring in the meeting room, with Willym gone and the NSG people all busy.

Zusana said, "You can go on ahead. I want to talk to some people, but I'll be out in a few minutes."

***

Agnes cycled through the scanning room shower, changed back into her regular clothes, and picked up the box with the pendant on the way out to the atrium, where she sat on a bench to open it. The pendant was indeed lustrous and beautiful, the tiny diamonds catching the "sunlight" streaming in through the tall windows.

*P for Petram....* She looped the necklace over her head and stood to see herself in a mirrored wall nearby. Something seemed odd about the situation—receiving such an ornate gift from her father, whom she hardly trusted right now. And it seemed extravagant compared with her ordinary clothes.

Agnes turned to look around the large, quiet atrium. It was nicely decorated with planters full of trees and flowers. It was peaceful and empty. A bee hummed among the flowers nearby.

There should be no reason to feel uneasy—everything seemed to be going as well as could be. In a few hours, the treatment for Willym should begin and they would have him back soon enough. And yet...she had always been a step behind, always off balance since prior to leaving Petram. There was always something she didn't know, and usually someone making decisions for her.

She looked at the flowers again. *That's strange...there's a bee in here? This isn't exactly "outside."* She barely had time to wonder about the presence of the bee, when it abruptly shot toward her and stung her on the arm.

With an involuntary yelp and a moment of flailing, Agnes knocked the bee off, heart racing from adrenaline and shock. *What was that for? How did that just happen? Everyone knows that bees will leave you alone if you leave them alone—they don't just attack out of nowhere. And since when do animals in Nissus attack anyone, anyway?*

She looked down at her arm, where the sharp pain was already fading. She had never had a bee sting. This didn't seem as bad as should be expected. She noticed that the bee had fallen to the ground when she had knocked it off. Peering at it, she found that it looked odd. *That's not an ordinary bee. That's...mechanical, isn't it? A flying drone disguised as a bee?*

Which meant that someone had intentionally created this bee and sent it to sting her. Why?

Agnes's shock at the bee sting began to be replaced by alarm at the idea of someone programming it to sting her for some reason. Breathing heavily, she sat on a bench as her legs became unsteady and a touch of vertigo began.

The only reason she could imagine that a disguised drone would sting her was to deliver something. Like a poison. Or mites. Not the NSG...*Dad.*

*I've just been reinfected.*

Chapter 17

# Breakout

Fresh panic blossomed. She fumbled to call for help with her handheld, but something was wrong with her fingers. Pulling out the device took an agonizing minute, until finally, she had it ready. But just as she was about to punch the button to raise an alarm, she paused, suddenly unsure.

*Wait, why am I calling the Bionics for help?* Somehow that didn't seem right. No, that was quite wrong, in fact.

She steadied her head with a hand for a moment, trying to think, trying to figure out what was going on. *I'm...in Nissus, the nerve center of the Bionics' world. Dad is being held prisoner here...and they're going to move against him tonight!* she realized with a start. *I have to help him! We can't let the Bionics turn him to their side!*

Dimly, Agnes was aware that she had been dosed with mites, that they were active in her mind. But that didn't feel like it was a problem. They were helpful, it seemed. Essential, even. *How else was I going to remember which side I'm on? We've got to use whatever tools we have, if we're going to fight the Bionics.*

Her head cleared, and Agnes looked around the atrium with new eyes. *In the heart of enemy territory. What can I do? How can we possibly fight when we're so outnumbered and far from home?*

At this point, Agnes should have been used to surprises, but still she was taken aback when knowledge and understanding began to flow into her mind. *These mites are so versatile! They can put ideas directly into my brain and talk right to me!* She smiled. She knew exactly what to do.

She had to move fast. Her mother would be coming to meet her any second now, and that would be a big problem—Zusana was still working for the Bionics.

Agnes briefly considered how she might slip some of the Petram nanobots into her food or something, to turn her away from the Bionics, but dismissed the idea. Even if she had the bots at hand, that would take too long, and it wouldn't really accomplish much. The main thing was to get herself and her father back to Petram, safe with their own custom mites. That way they could make sure the rest of Petram could use the mites—only if everyone in the city had the same defense could they hope to stay united against the Bionics.

*No time!* she reminded herself. She darted off down a hallway to hide from her mother. *Ok, mom, I'm going to lie, but it's for the greater good of Petram, trust me.* Hurriedly, she pulled out her handheld to dash off a message to her. "Hi, I'm heading back to our apartment to rest. Don't worry about me, I'm fine. You can just do your own thing for lunch. Oh, and don't worry if you don't hear from me right away because I might be taking a nap." She sent the message, then considered what to do about the handheld's location tracking. If the device wasn't back in New Canberra where they had been staying, her mom would know.

*Looks like I need to get a second handheld and send this one back on an automated carrier like the one that delivered our luggage. I just hope they're still used enough in Nissus that I can find one.* Agnes ducked around another corner and into a stairwell to put a little more distance between herself and her mother. Sitting at the top of the flight of stairs, she then worked to find a new handheld to "borrow," willing herself to move faster. *If I do a search to try to find a supply room or look through inventory records, there's probably a spare handheld sitting around nearby.* Idly, she wondered if the mites could help her to hurry or be more efficient. This was an emergency situation, after all. But she didn't know of any way to adjust their settings.

As with most things in Nissus, the door to a nearby empty office was not locked, and she found that she could simply walk in and take a handheld from a shelf. *This assumption that "nobody in Nissus steals" sure makes it easy to steal!* Within minutes, the old handheld was on its way back to the apartment, and its replacement was in her hands. *Next step, prepare to free Dad.*

She walked back to the stairwell where she'd been hiding, in case someone came past these offices. She was going to need a more secure base of operations. Time to study the enemy terrain. She quickly pulled up a projection of the area around the NSG lab and began studying. With the mites focusing her mind and giving her a goal, she dug into the information with a ferocity unlike anything she had felt before—except maybe during her bitter fight to stay in Petram.

Agnes made a note of where on the map she wanted to go, shut off the projection, and began running up the stairwell she'd been using. Taking the stairs two at a time, heart pounding from exertion and anxiety both, she cast aside any stray misgivings about her actions and just focused on what she had to do next. All that mattered was the fight against the Bionics.

She felt a touch of anger with herself for sleepwalking through the past few days in Nissus, palling around with the enemy and confiding in them. *How could I have thought any Bionics were friends?* But at the same time, she was glad for what she'd learned—it would help her to defeat them. *Into the Network—and thanks for that, by the way,* she thought sarcastically. *I can get anywhere climbing behind the walls, with no one to see me.*

She left the stairwell after several flights, jogged down another nondescript corridor, and found the door she was looking for. On the other side was a landing next to a ladder; climbing down the ladder, she soon found herself among mechanical systems like those above New Canberra. *The Network!* This could take her quite some distance, but in fact she wasn't going far.

Agnes found the spot she was looking for, merely a slightly open space behind a large piece of equipment, which formed an alcove for her purposes. This was close to a well-trafficked part of the Network, where she could easily slip into the public spaces or back to her hideout. It was secluded and had space to work. However, the hideout's real value was that it was close to a tunnel that automated carriers used.

All through Nissus, a network of tunnels provided routes for carriers like the one that had taken their luggage from the hospital to the apartment a few days prior. They may not have been exactly public areas, but she could get in, nonetheless. *No locks on doors.*

She plopped down on the bare floor in her temporary home, pulled out the new handheld again, and began to search. Talking to herself, she said, "Ok, Dad, I ditched Mom, found a safe place, and now I'm coming for you. Just as soon as I can find what I need…Wow, Nissus is so open. All of the data I need is just right here." With her mites' guidance, Agnes quickly filtered and sorted the shipping records to see which carriers were transporting the items she would steal. *Got it,* she thought a moment later, and hurried out toward the tunnel.

***

Past machines, around corners, up ladders—no question Agnes would have gotten turned around and would have lost valuable minutes if the new mites in her brain had not been focusing her attention on the task. *There isn't time—got to save Dad. Got to save Petram!*

At last, she opened an access hatch to find herself in a dim tunnel, standing on a small platform. On the other side of the metal railing, a narrow, irregular line of automated carriers whirred past, small vehicles laden with items or boxes of every variety. Some were enclosed, with a door or lid, but for the most part the items they were transporting were simply *carried*, making them easy to steal. The first one she needed would be passing in...she checked her handheld...ten minutes and fourteen seconds.

While she waited, Agnes placed an order for one tool that wasn't already scheduled to pass by her. She couldn't afford to wait all day for it, so there was no alternative. Using the handheld owner's account, she instructed that the tool be sent to an office nearby, but she planned to swipe it from the carrier just like the others, trying to give as much misdirection as possible to anyone tracking her actions.

At the end of the ten minutes, she ducked under the railing, holding it with one hand and getting ready to reach with the other. Right on schedule, the carrier came into view, and, as it passed, Agnes swiftly grasped the toolbox it was conveying and swung it onto the platform. *Wup!* The box was heavy, and she lost her balance and almost fell into the path of the carriers. Heart pounding after the near disaster, she steadied herself and got ready for the next carrier.

Two more carriers and an hour later, she had stashed a hoard of loot in her alcove. Breathing hard, she sat to rest for a moment, but almost immediately jumped back up. *No time to rest, with Dad about to be turned to the Bionics' side!* Instead of resting, she dug into the accumulated equipment and began organizing and putting things together. *Tools here, drones there. Let's add the payloads now....*

The vision of what to do seemed to form in her mind...not the specifics, usually, but general ideas. It all made so much sense, and the focus and drive might have been exhilarating if not for the fear and anxiety about the Bionics that remained beneath the surface.

Agnes had just launched two of the drones she had prepared, when she sensed an approaching deadline from the mites whispering to her mind. *Dad is waiting!* She picked up a heavy cutting tool, dropped it into a stolen backpack, and started off down the row of machinery while slinging the bag over her shoulder. For this trip, there was a long ladder to descend, followed by several places where she had to clamber over visual projection machinery. At one point, she caught a glimpse, through a grating, of the NSG atrium far below.

Eventually, as she neared her destination, she used her handheld to identify a specific spot, matching the coordinates the mites gave her mind.

The spot was along a smooth metal wall, among a jumble of ducts, pipes, and cables. She sat next to the wall—and finally, she could rest for a moment. She wouldn't act until the time that the mites appointed—clearly, there was a plan from her father at work here, and there was nothing left to do except worry. *I'm following your plan, Dad. I sure hope you have a plan for how to get us home, too, once I get you out of there.* The wait was agonizingly slow, but she used the time to study the Nissus maps again.

With one minute until the scheduled time, a sudden burst of loud music blared from the other side of the wall—and it must have been loud indeed, given what it sounded like out here. Agnes gave a grin as she realized, *and that must be to drown out the sound of my cutter!*

She positioned the cutter on the wall, counted down as the rendezvous time approached, and pulled the trigger at zero. It wasn't as loud as she had feared, but still she was glad for the music. At any rate, it only took a few quick slices to carve out a rectangle from the wall, which fell into the room beyond as she finished.

Her father Willym stood inside—and she saw that this was his quarters she had just broken into. "Hi, Dad," she said with a smile, loudly over the music, to which he replied incredulously, "I can't believe it worked!"

# Chapter 18

# **Sprint**

Triumphant, Agnes laughed and tossed the cutter aside as Willym dashed out through the hole she had made. "Come on, Dad, let's get back to the base I set up. I'm sure we don't have a lot of time."

"No, we don't," he replied as the two of them began climbing over machinery back toward the alcove. "The lab is under a negative air pressure to enforce a quarantine, so I sealed the vents and doors of my room. Hopefully, that way they won't detect that the wall's been breached. The others from Petram will try to stall the Bionics for time, but surely they'll break down the door at some point and see. They can't miss that hole, that's for sure!"

"What about the cameras? I don't think Nissus has a lot of cameras in most places, but that lab did," Agnes said as she began climbing a ladder, leading the way. Willym was struggling to keep up—apparently, captivity had not been kind to his health and stamina.

"We smashed them," he explained, as he huffed and pulled up the ladder, finally rolling himself onto the catwalk at the top. "Found the spy drones, too. Almost missed the one by the main door. That was a challenge without the right equipment."

She shot a look of unease at him—her father was still panting after the climb, and he was only slowly getting to his feet to follow her. "What's wrong, Dad? What happened to you? You don't seem very healthy."

He shrugged. "More important things to worry about. I'm only focusing on our mission here. All that matters is saving Petram—I'm not more important than that, you're not more important, nothing is."

Agnes considered that. "I understand, but if you're not in good shape, it's going to be harder to do what we need to do. You need your strength if we're going to escape successfully."

To her surprise, Willym suddenly seemed angry. "You're right, you're right. Can't believe I neglected something so important. All that time, focusing on the wrong things, ugh!"

His rant reminded her of the mumbling and weird behavior she had seen yesterday. "Come on," she ordered with an annoyed air. *He's right, of course—he may be in bad shape physically and mentally, but the important thing is to escape and get the mites to Petram so we can save the city. That's all that matters.*

Even with Willym slowing them down, reaching the alcove only took minutes. As he sat to rest and look over the materials Agnes had stolen, she began to pepper him with questions. *Enough with being in the dark!*

"Ok, Dad, fill me in a little on what's going on. You programmed a drone bee to sting me so I could use your nanobots, didn't you?" She began filling her backpack with some of the supplies.

He answered while taking her handheld and looking at some schematics and code. "I programmed it to sting whoever was wearing that pendant you have on, if they were alone."

"Oh!" She pondered that for a moment, inspecting the pendant that she still wore. "So, they were worried it was a trick, and it turned out it really was! It wasn't dangerous by itself, only as a signal."

"It was more than just a simple signal, actually. See this arrangement of diamonds?"—he pointed—"It looks random, but it actually encodes a message. That, along with all of the patterns and designs etched into the silver. Even the details of the styling and flourishes on the letter 'P' are part of it. It's called steganography. The message is hidden in plain sight, but there's no way to know about it or read the message unless you have the key to decoding it. The drone looked at the pattern to know how to program the mites it injected. That's how I could tell you when, where, and how to get me out."

"That's...really clever." *Wow, he may be a bit damaged, but he's what we need if we're going to win!* This led to a sobering thought. "Dad, you know we probably won't be able to escape, right? The Bionics, their technology...it's going to be really hard to outsmart them and get the nanobots back to Petram if they don't want us to."

He stopped working and looked at her. "Does that mean you're not fully committed? Do you want to turn yourself in?"

Agnes steeled herself. "Never. Petram always, even if we die trying. Even if we need to use mites ourselves to keep us focused." She giggled. "Even if we need to kill a bunch of Bionics, right?"

Willym went back to his work. "Right answer. At this point, now that I'm out of the lab, I'd have killed *you* if you were a threat to the plan."

*I'd like to see you try*, Agnes thought with a smirk, *given the shape you're in. Let's hope I don't see* you *as slowing us down!* Aloud she asked, "So, what *is* the plan?"

Willym picked up a drone, opened his hand, and watched as it flew away. "Well, for starters, that drone has some of our latest mites. Call that Plan C. It's an insurance policy, since like you said we probably won't make it back to Petram. But we'll try. If we can get on a vactrain with fake identities and at least get back to North America, we've got a much better chance. So, we've got to get moving and try to get on that train before they realize I'm gone from the lab and that you're with me."

"I take it we're not going to bring Mom along with us?"

Willym shook his head. "No real reason to. Let her distract the Bionics for now. She'll come back to Petram on her own, once we're there. They don't have any reason to hold her here. *She's* not doing anything with mites."

"Makes sense. So, what are we waiting for?"

Willym frowned at the handheld. "My communications were restricted when I was in the lab, so now that we're out I'm trying to send the latest code for my mites to the office in

Petram. Plan B. But I can't seem to get a message through." He picked up the handheld and peered at it, suddenly looking fearful. "Are they tracking this device?"

Agnes reassured him, "They shouldn't be, not yet. I've been having trouble communicating with Petram, too, the past few days, so that's not really new."

"Hmm." He muttered again indistinctly.

"So, can we go, then?"

"That depends. There were two diversionary drones you were supposed to launch earlier—did you?"

Agnes nodded impatiently. "Of course, Dad. And I set up alerts, so my handheld will let me know if the NSG has raised an alarm about you escaping. Now come *on!*" She picked up the backpack and started marching out of the alcove, glancing over her shoulder to confirm that he was coming.

He scrambled to catch up. "We need to get to the main train terminal. That's about thirty kilometers from here—so we need to find the fastest express route from this starting point."

She countered, "Not yet. First, we need to get out of this area near the NSG and make sure we don't leave a trail they can follow. I studied some maps and I've got an idea; come on."

Together they hurried down the catwalks and passageways of the Network for several minutes, occasionally hiding when they could hear other people passing nearby. Soon they arrived at a short ladder leading up to a hatch in the ceiling, beyond which was darkness. Night.

Agnes followed her father up into the dim space and shut the hatch behind her. She blinked and looked around, letting her eyes adjust—even though she knew what to expect, she still needed to get her bearings.

They stood on a small wooden platform, Willym gripping the railing tightly, fear in his eyes as he looked into the vast spaces above, around, and below where they stood. *He hasn't had as much experience with the fake Nissus environments as I have, has he?* Agnes thought.

"Oh, come on, Dad. Half of what you see in Nissus isn't real. It's not like you could actually fall to your death here. We just climbed up from below, so that means there's a floor right there." She peered over the railing into the night and, despite her dismissive words, had a touch of vertigo herself.

Somehow, the platform where they stood seemed to shift and sway with her movements, as if suspended by ropes. Indeed, now that she looked, it really *was* hanging from ropes. Impossibly far below, lightning silently flickered among fast-moving, shifting clouds. Above, a double moon shone, giving just enough light to see where they were going. A faint breeze wafted past them.

"Ugh, Nissus. Ok, as you can probably guess, this is a sky city, and it's the middle of the night, so hopefully no one will notice us. We need to get to that side over that way." Here she pointed, and they both looked at what lay before them.

Their platform was connected by a hanging footbridge to a mesh of other platforms, bridges, ladders, stairs, and rooms—everything suspended and hanging in the air. She followed one thick rope with her eyes to see where it led, and as far as she could see, it led up into the sky. *Skyhooks—fake ones, anyway.*

The community seemed to stretch a good thousand meters into the distance, but much of it was sprawling, both to the sides and upward and downward. The overall effect was of sparse and isolated structures—apparently, this was for a people who greatly valued their elbow room. The sky city reminded her of a children's playground, with towers and stairs and platforms on multiple levels, all connected—only, blown up to adult scale, vastly extended to be the size of a city, and then suspended in the air. And clearly, people lived here.

Willym seemed to be getting over his fears. He pointed out a cluster of some of the rooms. "It looks like that's probably where people are sleeping. Let's avoid that area, or at least try not to make any noise." Agnes agreed, and they set out across the swinging bridge. Their feet clumped against the wood despite their best efforts, but the open spaces seemed to swallow the sounds, anyway. Past the bridge, most of the walkways were rigid, and it became easier to hurry along.

At the other edge of the community, they found a short rope ladder and Agnes scrambled up, pausing at the top to impatiently help her father over the edge onto yet another platform. "So, the sky people, they like hanging in the air, right? So, they have this." She gestured.

Willym looked. "A zip line?"

"Yep. They've got several here, depending on which way you want to go. This one," she tapped it, "goes right to a transit hub. Couple of minutes on the line, then we can take an express train to the main terminal. Be there, ready to get out of Nissus, in about twenty-five minutes. I can't imagine most people normally take a zip line every day, but in Nissus they say they're all about giving people options."

Willym looked satisfied. "Good work. It's already been about half an hour that I've been gone from the lab. I don't know when they'll figure out I've escaped, but I want to be on that train in the first hour."

Agnes agreed, "Yeah, and it's been even longer since I disappeared. No idea if Mom bought my lie about being back at the apartment. Here, climb up onto this seat. I'll follow." She helped him up, and when he was strapped in, she pushed him off down the cable.

When she pushed off herself, she almost wished they had tried a different way of getting to the train terminal. She dropped *fast*, chasing her father, who was just barely visible ahead of her in the distance. The initial terror of the falling sensation didn't last long, though. While the whir of the pulley zipping down the cable and the rush of air past her face made the journey far from quiet, it almost seemed like it could be peaceful—she could imagine she was all alone, one girl flying through the clouds of a dark and empty sky.

*No. There are millions of Bionics all around me—I just can't see them.* Nissus didn't waste any of its volume—wherever it looked like there was a big open space, that must be a wall. They would just use a projector to make it look like the sky goes forever. *I see sky, but I'm probably zipping through a narrow tube with Bionics just meters away on the other side of the projectors.*

Her destination came into view—a grand, palatial balcony where the zip line terminated, empty in the night. Her father had arrived and was busy unbuckling himself from the seat and harness.

Her handheld chimed an alert. *Uh-oh.*

She quickly landed, undid the straps, and checked the message on the device. "No! We're too late. A general alert just went out."

Willym groaned. "So, they're looking for us, right? Can we still make it to the train? Use a fake identity?"

"Let me check...." Agnes looked up at him. "It's not going to work, Dad. This looks big. They're broadcasting both of our pictures to the whole city, it looks like. If we take one step out of here and go where anyone can see us, we're toast. That would mean any of the trains, any normal public areas. In fact," she looked at the doorway in front of them, "this whole zip line is part of the sky city. It's night here, and we got lucky that no one is awake right now. But through that doorway, just around a corner or two, it's a whole different district. It's going to be daytime, maybe, but it'll definitely be busy. We'll be spotted immediately. Right here, I don't think there's anything to give us away, for now."

Her father began pacing. "Except for that handheld, once they realize it's yours."

Agnes took a sharp breath of alarm, and quickly turned off its transmitter.

He continued, "Ok, so what do we have to our advantage?"

"Well, they don't know where we are yet, or they wouldn't need the alert. And the drones I launched should delay them a bit in figuring that out. Hopefully, they'll start searching in the wrong direction, and when the drones hit them with a cloud of mites, they'll be too worried about those to realize the mites won't actually do much."

"Divert, distract, delay. Good."

"But that's about all we've got."

He looked pensive. "We want to get out of Nissus, and we want to communicate with Petram, maybe ask them for a rescue or intervention. Can we climb out the top of the city? We could probably configure a shortwave radio from the handheld, maybe even send the designs for the latest mites via radio."

Agnes shot that down: "The top of the city is too high—if we actually got out that way, there probably wouldn't be enough air for us. They actually pressurize the living areas at the top because it's so high. But, maybe...maybe we could go the other way. Get out of the city from the bottom—or at least at ground level. We should only be a couple of kilometers from the edge of the city, from what I remember of the maps."

She caught his eye and made a decision. "It's crazy, I know, but we've got to try. We're out of options."

Willym gave a short nod, agreeing. "Let's do it."

Chapter 19

# Escape

Agnes peered over the side of the rock ledge she was crouching on, frustration welling inside. *We just need to get across this park area and we're nearly out of Nissus. I can practically* see *the exit from here!* But they had already spent nearly four hours climbing down from the sky city area to what should be nearly ground level of the city, heading westward as they did, only to be stuck here for twenty minutes so far. This park was just too busy—maybe as the local night fell, it would quiet down and they would be less recognizable to people, but she could sense that their time was running out.

The equipment they had found in an "emergency evacuation" supply cabinet had been a lifesaver, enabling them to basically rappel down some long distances quickly. Intellectually, Agnes knew it was practically a miracle they had escaped detection so far, not to mention the fact that they had managed to find passageways through the city that were sufficiently hidden from their pursuers' view. It may have involved climbing over equipment in areas behind walls and ceilings where they had absolutely no business going, but thank the Network and the open, trusting nature of Nissus for making it possible.

Unfortunately, they were certain that a manhunt was underway. Twice they had heard people discussing the "security breach" while the two of them were hiding and watching from behind scene projectors, and once, they were sure a search party had passed within shouting distance. Perhaps worse, Agnes could see that Willym was reaching the end of his strength—he'd been wobbly to start with, and hours of frantic scrambling to escape Nissus had left him gasping and near collapse, mites or no.

Time for some hard choices.

"Listen, Dad. We've got to get these designs to Petram, right? That means I need to get this handheld out of the city, try to raise Petram on shortwave radio, and transmit the data. I've been having you tag along because I didn't want to let the Bionics find you. That would tell them which way we're going. But now I'm going to leave you here. As long as you stay back behind those ducts, you should be able to stay hidden for a long time, unless someone actually walks back there. I'll make a break for it across this park and try to send the data from the outside."

She turned to gaze out at it. The park was really more of a wilderness—a steep canyon, with an enormous waterfall feeding a fast-flowing river, surrounded by mixed conifer-deciduous forest. She had been watching a steady stream of hikers and backpackers on the trail below her hiding spot, but as the daylight faded, the numbers seemed to be dwindling.

Willym actually looked relieved. "Yes," he agreed. "They're looking for both of us together, so you might be more likely to make it through on your own."

Agnes gave a sharp nod. "Right. You do what you have to. I'd say don't let them take you alive, but you might actually be able to delay or mislead the Bionics more if you're up and talking." She turned to watch for an opportunity to pop out onto the hiking trail. Mentally dismissing her father, she was glad for the mites in her head, for allowing her to focus on the task at hand. *Without the mites, I'd have been too worried about what's going to happen to Dad, too sentimental.* Instead, she could be completely dispassionate. No teary goodbye. The mission was the important thing, after all.

*Now!* She dropped off the ledge, landing roughly, and looked around to see if she had been spotted. Satisfied she was alone, she hurried down the trail, trying to listen to see if anyone was approaching. She took what appeared to be a long way around toward the falls up ahead, in the hopes of avoiding sightseers as much as possible.

One small group of people came around a bend in the other direction as she hiked. *This is probably the first time in hours anyone has actually seen me, other than Dad.* She tried to act natural, and apparently succeeded well enough because the others just talked among themselves and didn't pay much attention to her as they passed in the dusk. *At least here it's not out of place to be smudged and dirty and wearing a backpack*, she thought wryly.

As she approached the falls, the roar of the water became thunderous. Agnes paused among the trees to look around and get her bearings. Judging from the maps she had seen, this mighty waterfall was not just for show but was part of an actual river from real rain that fell in other parts of the island of Greenland. At least here, Nissus was built over the top of an actual forest and river on solid ground—and the canyon extended as far as the eye could see. If she had needed to hide instead of getting out of the city, she might have been able to get lost in the forest for days.

She spotted a footbridge that crossed the river and gave a view of the falls above and torrent below. *There! The exit should be up that slope on the other side of the river.* Eager to put her pursuers farther behind, she hurried over to the bridge before slowing to a walk, trying not to act like she was fleeing. *It's working! I'm walking right past a dozen people and none of them know who I am!* A moment later, she corrected herself. *No, not people—Bionics.*

Slipping among the trees on the other side, Agnes half expected to hear shouts or alarms, or any indication that someone had noticed she was not just another visitor out for a stroll. Elated and incredulous at her luck, she grinned as she began jogging up the terrain, stumbling a bit in the growing darkness as branches and roots tripped her up. And just as she had expected, in the trees at the top of the slope, she abruptly ran into a solid wall—the edge of the parkland.

Using the light from her handheld, Agnes inspected the barrier to look for a way through. Painted for a bit of camouflage, the wall was otherwise plain and unbroken—except that she could see some embedded projection equipment high above her head.

She took a step back to eye the distance between the trees and the wall. *If I can climb up that tree, I just might be able to sway it a bit and reach the wall. And if this is anything like what I've seen in other places, I should be able to squeeze through the spot where the projector is.*

Agnes was sure that without the mites pushing her, climbing the tree would have been too difficult—it wasn't like she normally shimmied up tree trunks back in Petram. But she was highly motivated now, and by wrapping a strap from her backpack around the trunk, she managed to figure out how to scoot up a bit at a time. The rough, furrowed bark helped.

In only a few minutes, she had made it to the middle branches of the tree and reached over to the wall-mounted equipment. By unfastening some of the projectors and moving them out of the way, she was able to slip through to the other side, where she roughly replaced the projectors before climbing down to ground level again, winded and sore. She found herself in a wide, dusty corridor.

In the far distance, an exit door beckoned, illuminated by a dim light. She sprinted over to the door.

After the hours of work, worry, and anticipation, finally leaving Nissus was simple. The exit door was solid and heavy, utilitarian and barely even labeled. She inspected it for alarms or sensors and was a bit surprised to find none that she could recognize. She pushed it open and stepped out into a frigid night.

*Ok,* now *I can believe I'm in Greenland. And this must be polar night, as well.* The wind was not strong, but it was bitterly cold, nonetheless. Stars shone through gaps in a substantial cloud layer, and low on the horizon the moon shone brightly as a cloud moved out of the way.

A snowy road led to either side of her, following the bulk of the Nissus city that rose out of sight at her back. On the other side of the road, the frozen ground was piled and littered with what looked like the detritus of construction, with another short wall just beyond. Shivering, Agnes walked across the road, and clambered up a dirt pile to peer over the wall. In the distance on the other side, a hamlet glowed with a few scattered lights. *I'm probably going to need to get some help from the locals or "borrow" a house to use for a few hours. I'll freeze out here before I can contact Petram, otherwise.*

Agnes looked around for something to stand on to help her over, and she noticed that the wall bore signs every ten meters or so. She illuminated the one nearest to her:

**Warning: Kalaallit-administered territory. Restricted area. Entry is forbidden without prior authorization.**

*Hmm,* Agnes thought, *does that mean there are no Bionics in the village, or just no NSG?* Either way, it had to be better than freezing or going back to Nissus. Maybe they'd even be sympathetic and help her. *No time.* She hopped up to swing a leg over the top of the wall, rolled, and dropped onto the other side.

She began jogging over the rocky terrain, quickly realizing that it was going to be a fair distance to cover, especially in the darkness. Looking back to see how far she had come, Agnes was shocked to see that the whole hulking mass of Nissus was gone—including the wall she'd just crossed. *No, she realized, it's just one final Nissus trick. They made the city invisible from the outside, hidden by projectors. Probably the idea is that if anyone in that village looks toward Nissus, they'll just see empty Greenland mountains and rocks and sky.*

Just as Agnes turned back to focus on the village in the distance, a noise reached her that sounded like...*is that a helicopter? NO!*

The helicopter came screaming up, searchlight picking her out as she tried to sprint away. *They found me and there's nowhere to hide out here! It's just rocks!*

Another helicopter came up behind the first and quickly continued past, slowing to hover just above the ground a few hundred meters ahead of her. Several men in military uniforms jumped out, training weapons of some sort on her, while a loudspeaker sounded.

Through her panic, Agnes barely heard whatever orders the men were giving. The mites in her brain screamed at her to run, to fight, to do whatever it took to get away. She dodged to avoid the soldiers running at her, then scooped up several rocks from the ground. *Bash them in the face!*

She was just winding up her throw when she saw one of the men stop and bring his weapon to bear. Immediately a wave of some unseen force threw her to the ground, and everything went black.

## Chapter 20

# Zombies

Waking up was, for Agnes, certainly an odd experience. In fact, she wasn't sure that "waking up" was what had just happened at all—it was more like she just steadily became *aware* of things. Come to think of it, she didn't remember opening her eyes, and, now that she noticed, she was sitting comfortably in a chair, not lying in a bed.

*Mom!* Agnes realized with a surge of pleasant awareness that her mother was crouching next to her chair, smiling and clasping her hand. "Hi, Agnes, welcome back." *Why does she look like she's holding back tears?* Agnes wondered. "Uh, hi? Mom?"

*Where am I?* Glancing around, she recognized what looked like a hospital room—her second in less than a week—and she also took in another, newer face belonging to a small person seated across the room near the foot of the bed that was next to her.

"You're Taia. From the Nissus Security Group. So, we're in Nissus."

"Yes, Agnes," Taia replied, her small, dark face betraying a surprising weariness. "You're going to have a lot of questions. Such as, why are we all here together and what's going on." Agnes gave a quick nod and looked at her mother questioningly.

Zusana began, "There's been an incident. A dangerous incident. For now, you don't remember what happened, because you have some mites—some of the safe nanites from the Factus—active in your brain right now. Kind of like how anesthetic blocks pain until your body can heal, the mites are blocking some of your memories while we get you oriented."

Agnes frowned, puzzled. "But I remember that I didn't want to use any mites. I told you that, both of you. I was pretty mad about it, actually. But," she gave a faraway look, "for some reason I don't feel upset about it right now. I should be, but I'm not. I guess the mites are doing that, aren't they?"

Taia spoke up again. "Indeed. Agnes, there are a couple of things you should know before we start bringing back your memories. First, we'll do our best to respect your wishes and deactivate the mites that are in you if that's what you want. But it won't be right away. I'll explain why in a minute."

Agnes felt oddly at peace with what Taia had said. "Hmm, ok then."

"Second, your mother here is on your side, and so am I. We're all on the same side, really. You may not trust me, but remember that *she* does. That should count for something.

And no, before you ask, she's never had any mites active in her body."

Agnes gazed at her mother, wondering how she'd feel about all of this once the mites were gone. *There's too much I don't know. I need my memories back to be certain of anything. I don't even remember what any of this is all about. But then can I even trust the memories when they're unblocked?*

"Lastly, about your father—he's alive."

Agnes gave a sharp gasp as she realized she'd forgotten all about him, that he was the reason they'd come to Nissus in the first place. *Of course, it's not my fault—I can blame the mites. They were probably blocking me from thinking about him.* Taia continued, "As the memories come back, keep that in mind. You both survived, in somewhat better shape than we feared. Are you ready to learn about the incident you've been through?"

Apprehensive, but eager to fill in the gaps, Agnes indicated yes.

"Good. Now, start mentally walking through what you can remember, and we'll unblock your memories in chronological order as we go. Feel free to talk about what you're remembering. That will help the process and make it easier to ask questions and discuss everything with your mother. I'm sure you'll want her to chime in."

Agnes nodded absently as she turned her attention inward, searching for any scrap of memory that would explain how she got where she was. *There's noth...oh! The lab....*

"Ok, I remember now, we were visiting Dad at the lab. He...he had experimented with mites, and they had sort of made him go crazy. You were going to try to use your own mites to battle the ones he made, to clean him out. I remember it was going to be dangerous...." She looked up from her introspection. "You said he's ok now?"

Taia countered, "I didn't say he's ok. I said he's alive and doing better than he could have been. We think he'll be mostly himself again, after some recovery, but he'll never be quite the same as he was before. Those mites had free rein inside him for a long time."

Deflated, Agnes glanced at Zusana again, and saw the anguish in her mother's face. Steeling herself, she replied, "I see. Ok, let's keep going. The last time we visited Dad, he gave me a necklace. It was really pretty, a pendant with diamonds around a silver letter 'P'...." The pendant was no longer around her neck, she saw.

Memory came rushing back. "The necklace was a trick! I...I got injected with some of Dad's custom mites from a drone disguised as a bee, after it saw the necklace...Wait, I got reinfected? He did it *twice*?" Agnes could feel the familiar outrage building again—either the mites were letting some of that emotion through, or they couldn't control everything. She doubted it was the latter.

Zusana squeezed her hand and quietly spoke. "I'm so sorry I couldn't keep you safer. Back at Petram, I had no idea he had even experimented with mites on himself, and here in Nissus, I thought we had everything under control."

Taia put in, "Yeah, we all did. None of us saw the drone attack coming. He pretty much just walked all over the world's premier security agency. No wonder he managed to keep it hidden from an unsuspecting family. You can't beat yourself up about that, Zusana."

Zusana gave a brief nod and a thin smile to Taia. She took a deep breath before continuing. "Willym and I have been married for a long time. I know him. I don't really feel like it's *him* that did these things—it's the mites that gave him this obsession."

"But he was the one who took that first step of experimenting with them in the first place," Agnes grumbled. "He's got a lot of responsibility for *that*."

"Yes, he does," Taia agreed, "but I hope your family can ultimately find some forgiveness. I wouldn't want the tragedy to be any worse than it already is. And Agnes, I think most of the damage he did was to himself, not you. You may also have some more sympathy for him when you remember what it was like to be under the rogue mites' influence yourself."

Agnes gave a pained expression. "Give me the next memories." A moment later, her eyes widened in surprise as the memories hit. She jumped out of her chair, tense.

"Is this real?" she blurted. "Just like that, I switched sides? I went from being against the mites and worried about Dad, to lying and fighting to *spread* the mites in Petram? But that doesn't make any sense!"

Taia shrugged a bit bemusedly. "Well, no, not to me. But it did to you. Can you remember why you wanted to take the mites to Petram?"

Agnes thought for a moment. "It was all about 'protecting the city'. Like, our community would die on its own. The only way to keep people from leaving was to let the mites convince them to stay. Actually, I'm not sure that's wrong. The city really might wither away, and the mites *would* have kept people from leaving."

Zusana interjected, "But why save Petram if it means we end up with mites? What's the *point* of Petram?"

Taia answered, "Well, playing devil's advocate here, you still wouldn't have any significant genetic engineering, right? So, you'd be maintaining the original *Homo sapiens* species, biologically. I could see choosing mites as a trade-off to achieve the other goal. If I were using your husband's mites, that is."

Agnes made a frustrated sound and plopped back down in the chair. "I can remember now believing in what I was doing, what Dad was doing. Mom…" Agnes dropped to almost a whisper, "you didn't matter to me. I don't know why, but nothing mattered to me—only my job, which was to get mites into Petram and save the city from itself."

She looked up at Zusana, her own face a mirror of the pain she saw in her mother. "I was ready to kill Dad if I thought it would help. I got him out of the lab, but really it was just part of fighting the Bionics. I remember. And I don't think I'm going to stay angry at Dad. I understand now what it was like for him."

***

For the next few minutes, memory and emotion seemed to pour out of Agnes as she told her mother about her experiences, about breaking her father out of detention and then attempting to evade capture and escape the city. Zusana, for her part, recounted what had happened from her own perspective—receiving the deceptive message from Agnes, her attempts to contact her once they realized that something was happening with Willym in the lab, her confusion turning to alarm as they discovered that Agnes wasn't at the apartment.

Taia had stepped out of the room to allow the others a private catharsis, but after a time Zusana went to the door and waved her back in. "I think we're ready to discuss what comes next, Taia."

She returned and took her seat again across the room. Agnes asked, "So, I still don't remember anything between when the people in the helicopters found me and being in this room. Are you still blocking some of my memories?"

"No. The mites are not doing anything to your memories or emotions right now—not since a couple of minutes after we woke you up. When the security teams found you, they used a knock-out gun, which does just what it sounds like— it knocked you out. Then we got mites into you immediately. Among other things, they put you into what you could call an induced coma."

Seeing Agnes's grimace, Zusana said, "The word 'coma' sounds bad, but it was the same kind of thing doctors do with medications back home in Petram. I've been badgering about a dozen neurologists trying to figure out the quickest and safest way to get you healed so we can stop using the mites. They've been trying to teach everything they know to me practically non-stop for the past few days." She looked exhausted, Agnes saw.

"Wait, how long was I asleep?"

Taia answered, "Only about a day and a half. Our mites made quick work of the rogue mites that were active in you, and there wasn't much damage to try to heal. The mites

Willym made were pretty simple. Very effective, obviously, but simple."

Zusana continued, "Agnes, the 'sleep' they gave you isn't really like what you might think." Hesitantly, she explained, "They can target everything down to the synapse level, so they could keep you asleep and work on patching you up, but also direct you to sit up, eat, walk, and stuff like that. They said it's not healthy or necessary to keep someone lying immobile in a bed while they work."

Agnes realized she was grimacing again. "Wait, you mean I was walking around like...like a zombie? As if *that's* not creepy!"

Taia said, "It's perfectly normal in a hospital environment, and safer than the alternative. It's not as though people would want to have a catheter and feeding tube and bed sores if they can avoid it. However, your mother did ask us to stop all of that and wake you as soon as we could, to try to respect your wishes. So, here we are."

Agnes gave the girl-woman a bit of a glare before her mother cut in, "I wanted you to know what to expect when we go see your father in a while. Just because he's up and dressed doesn't mean he's aware or awake. They said to give him another day or so before he'll be ready for that."

Agnes considered for a moment. "I want to go see him, but I'm not sure I can if that's how he still is. In the past few days, I've seen Dad when he was a crazy person, and then as my partner in a war when we were both kind of crazy. I don't want to see him as a zombie; I just want him *back*."

Zusana put her arm around her to commiserate.

After a pause, Agnes changed the subject. "So, you said your mites aren't messing with me anymore? So, we can get rid of them now, right? Zap them or whatever?"

For once, Taia looked a bit uncomfortable. "Not yet. Not for a while. It's gotten a bit more complicated than that."

"But...you said they're not doing anything."

"I said they're not doing anything to your memories and emotions right now. What they *are* doing is a bit of monitoring."

Agnes was about to protest, but Taia kept going. "Keep in mind that, whether or not it was your 'fault', you were a central figure in the most significant security breach we've had in years, maybe in Nissus's history. You managed to steal tools, break out a dangerous detainee by cutting a hole into a Level 4 containment facility, set off a massive manhunt, bomb your pursuers with clouds of unauthorized mites, *and* cause a major diplomatic incident with the incursion into the protected Kalaallit sector."

*Oh....*

She went on. "All of this happened because we invited and hosted you and your mother, as non-Factus, in the city, allowing you to wander around without any supervision. No mites or anything to act as a backstop to bad behavior, to allow us to know where you were or what you were doing."

"But it was only *because* of those mites that I did those things!"

"I know, I know. Personally, I'm not worried about you jumping up and stabbing someone, not now, but the simple reality is that these events have strengthened the argument of a certain faction in the city. Some people have long been skeptical of the idea of allowing residents or visitors who don't have mites, since there's no way to really know what they're up to, or if they're taking advantage of us. So, you're going to have those mites for a while longer.

"However," she gestured to Zusana, "Your mother went to bat for you. She insisted on some pretty strict protocols about the privacy of the data from your mites. All that the NSG will see is your location, and an alert if you are attacked again."

Exasperated, Agnes vented, "But I still have no say in any of it. I can't even keep track of how many people have injected me with nanobots at this point! 'Let's all stick needles in Agnes!' It's like I've had no control over anything for weeks!"

Taia said, flatly, "You're quite right. You have good reason to be upset. I'm sorry you were caught in the crossfire of this battle."

Zusana added, "Agnes, my goal this whole time has been to keep the family together and keep us all safe. For now, I'm asking for a bit of patience while your father heals, and, honestly, I think the two of us could use some rest and healing as well. It's going to take a little time, but I do think we're safe here in Nissus now. Safer than we've been in a while. Let's just focus on the healing and not worry too much about all of the Factus stuff."

Agnes sighed, realizing that arguing would be futile. She felt herself relax marginally. *Focus on the family.* "I guess I should go see Dad to see how he's doing. Maybe after I have some food and rest a bit. This is all a lot to process."

***

Taia led the way down the hall to Willym's room. As they entered, Agnes saw that it was much bigger than hers had been.

Her father was dressed in a simple set of scrubs, socks on his feet, sitting on what appeared to be a workout bench where he was lifting and stretching his arms. He looked better than the last time she'd seen him—not so ragged or neglected. He stared blankly, blinking occasionally. Nearby, a pair of white-coated technicians, a man and a woman, sat at a workstation with a complex web of holographic displays and controls. Taia motioned the little group to a halt by the door.

"We're not going to go try to talk to him or anything, obviously; we're just going to watch for a moment and get an update about how he's doing. It looks like it's exercise time?"

The man at the workstation turned and got up to greet the newcomers. "Hi, yes, we're giving him some upper-body movement to help him stretch out the new muscle we're building and keep those joints moving. By the time we're done, he'll probably feel a decade younger than he did before, despite all the damage he took."

"Can you give Zusana a neurological update, please?"

"Sure. We completely stopped the neurogenic signaling yesterday, as planned. Right now, the cortical...."

Agnes mostly stopped listening, not understanding any of the techno-speak. Instead, she just watched as her father mindlessly performed his light exercise.

It was unsettling to remember her state of mind from just two days ago, under the mites' influence. This was essentially the nightmare scenario they had feared then. Capture, involuntary conversion. Under the control of the Factus. Never mind the irrationality or questionable ethics of the mission to take the mites to Petram—Willym and Agnes had been right that, if captured, they would be changed. And here he was, a "zombie" for now.

It seemed somehow like a terrible thing to do to him, even though Agnes could plainly see that he was getting healthier. She knew that when they woke him up, he'd be "Dad" again, not the man who said he would willingly kill her if she got in his way. And yet, she had been that person, too. She felt sad for both of them, for their capture and failure, even though she was glad they had failed in their mission. *I'm not making any sense.* She shook her head, wishing things were simpler.

It was a relief when the visit was over, and they could head home to their apartment.

# Chapter 21

# Healing

After Taia bid them goodbye, Agnes and Zusana left the sterile-feeling hospital building and joined the crowds out on the street so they could catch a train back to New Canberra.

Halfway through the train ride, Agnes was finally able to put her finger on what was giving her a strange feeling: Standing there on the crowded train with her hand on the grab bar, it seemed like people were noticing her, looking at her. She realized with a start that, as the subject of a recent manhunt, her name and picture had been broadcast over the entire city. Literally *everyone* there knew who she was if they saw her at all.

Her face flushed with mortification as she thought about Jinjing, Pari, Devina, and especially Sahil. *They all know what I did. They probably have* video *of me attacking the people from the helicopter!* And what about Emil and Jonnan back in Petram? The news probably hadn't gone that far, she was thankful to realize.

Feeling suddenly exposed, Agnes could hardly wait for their train to pull up at the entrance to New Canberra, where their apartment was. Pulling her mother away from the main road and its trolleys, she pleaded, "Mom, let's go this way. Remember that forest area at the back of our ward? We can hike the trails to come out there instead of taking this road."

Zusana agreed, and it turned out to be a good decision. The weather was beautiful, and the "natural" environment was restorative—as was the exercise. Even the few people they encountered on the trails seemed friendly enough that Agnes didn't feel too self-conscious. In fact, given their lack of anywhere in particular they needed to be, they decided to order some lunch, and ate it at a secluded picnic table among the trees before heading to the apartment.

Once there, Agnes found herself relaxing some more, despite knowing about the mites still operating in her mind. *I guess knowing that Dad is safe now, and that this will all be over soon, takes a big load of worry off me.* And, settling in for a day or two of waiting was *such* a contrast to the worry and panic of the past few days.

As dinnertime approached, Agnes felt some anxiety increasing again. She might be expected to go down to join the rest of the ward in their communal dinner, and she wasn't sure she could face the other youths. *Yeah, I'll just be like, Hi everyone! Remember me, the one who hung out with you and then the next day completely flipped out and was all over the news?* And to think—she'd been embarrassed about her little meltdown on the vactrain coming to Nissus. This was several orders of magnitude worse.

As it turned out, though, Jinjing made the first move when, half an hour before dinner, she knocked on their door and Zusana let her in. She took a seat at the table where Agnes was sitting.

"Hi, Jinjing," Agnes said with uncharacteristic shyness.

The girl gave a look of sympathy. "Hi, Agnes, how are you doing?"

She started to give a noncommittal answer, but then something caught her eye. "Wait, did you just get a tattoo?" Peeking out above the collar of Jinjing's shirt and approaching the side of her neck was a representation of a thin tree branch, adorned with delicate pink flowers in sharp, clear detail.

Jinjing grinned, pulling her shirt back slightly to show more of the design. "Like it? It's cherry blossoms. It's actually copying a tree by my house, though that one isn't blooming right now."

"You just went and got that this week? While away from home visiting New Canberra? Don't you need to get your parents' permission or something to get a tattoo?"

Jinjing cocked her head in confusion for a moment, before realizing what Agnes was asking. "Are you thinking of a permanent ink tattoo? I don't think anyone does that kind of old-fashioned tattooing anymore. This is all done by mites. I can change it any time—in fact, this one *is* changing. Like I said, it's copying a tree back where I live. As the tree has been growing, so has this tattoo, for a couple of months now." She grinned again. "It's mostly on my side and my back, and I'm so excited it's getting big enough to reach my neck where everyone can see it. Maybe I'll have it grow the branches down my arms, too."

Agnes peered more closely at the fine branches, leaves, and flowers. "It's beautiful. And the colors look really good on you."

"Thanks!" Jinjing was clearly pleased. "Want to see how it grew?" An interactive display appeared on the tabletop in front of them, and she then selected several options in quick succession to show an abstract view of a person. "I started it with one branch here by my waist...." The tattoo was painted onto the figure, and then began growing, blossoming, and spreading up the person's torso. "If we go to the configuration here, we can guide it where to grow next."

Agnes perked up. "Wait, is this the interface for controlling the mites that are inside you?"

"Oh, right, you probably haven't seen any of the controls yet, have you?"

Agnes shook her head. "No, I haven't. And I don't know if you knew this, but I actually have mites in me now. They're not supposed to be messing with anything, but the NSG people said they won't turn them off until I leave Nissus."

Jinjing gave a pained look. "That's got to be upsetting. I know how you felt earlier about having the mites. How are you doing, after, you know...everything that's happened the past couple of days?"

Agnes decided to answer honestly. "Well, I'm not happy to have the mites *again*, but at least this will all be over soon, now that Dad's safe. And, of course, everyone knows what I did—it's like, how can I even go out where people are? It's humiliating."

"But it was the mites—"

"Yeah, I know. It was the mites that made me go on a crime spree. But you don't understand—I can remember how I really believed in what I was doing. It's like it was still *me* doing those things. It's like...."

Agnes struggled to put into words what she wanted to say, before suddenly it came to her. "I remember once, a couple of years ago, when I got mad at one of my friends at school. I made a big scene out of something. I think it was because of something she had said about me. I just totally blew up our friendship, but then afterward I was sorry about the whole thing. I knew we'd both kind of messed up, but what I did was way out of proportion."

She thought for a moment, and then continued. "I remember thinking, why did I say the terrible things I did? In the middle of the big fight, I had really meant it all. Even though later I was sorry, I knew I had done it on purpose. It was too late, and I don't think I ever talked to her again after that fight. It kind of feels like that now. Even though I know there were mites in my mind, it *feels* like it was really me being so...extreme. Don't go telling people, but...I was ready to kill someone if I thought it would help me."

"Whoa...." Jinjing looked disturbed, and Agnes was just beginning to regret her openness, when the other girl surprised her. "That's really hardcore. I mean, sorry, I know it's terrible you went through all that, but..."—Jinjing seemed to be looking at her with respect—"I think people aren't laughing at you, Agnes. They're more like 'That girl is serious business.' I mean, a death struggle with the NSG, breaking out your dad, crawling through the walls and the ceilings and going completely off-grid for hours? Yeah. Who could even do that?"

Agnes had to smile wryly at how differently Jinjing saw her experience—not as a humiliating loss of control, but quite the opposite. "So, what, I'm 'notorious' or something now?"

Jinjing giggled. "Maybe so! Anyway, want to see how to interact with the mites?" Agnes nodded and slid her handheld over to Jinjing. As soon as she did so, the screen blanked out, and Agnes had to take it back to confirm that her friend was allowed to access the controls.

The tabletop control panel updated to show Agnes's interface. "So, you have these groups of options...."

Jinjing ran through some of the high-level functions: reports on mental and emotional state and brain function, musculoskeletal systems, endocrinology, growth, genetics, and many more. There were options for directly tweaking certain aspects of Agnes's body—including a suggestion to even out her legs, which apparently differed in length by more than a millimeter.

For many features, though, there was simply an option to request enrollment. Jinjing explained the process, "Right, it's not like you select this icon and the mites immediately start teaching you Chinese, for example. You would say that's something you want to do, and you'd schedule a meeting with your coach, to see how it fits in with your long-term goals. If it's approved, there would be a whole plan for how you're going to learn it. The mites would begin prepping your brain for learning a language, and it would be a big process. Classes, immersion, all that stuff."

Agnes listened, flipping through the pages of reports and myriad of controls for what the mites could do. She found a display that indicated what data was being sent back to the NSG, and she marked it for reviewing later, and kept browsing.

"Check it out, it has a big list of 'genetic modifications' I can make. That's, wow, that's a long list."

Jinjing glanced at the list and gave a low whistle. "That *is* a long list. Well, I guess you've never had any genetic engineering or changes? Or your ancestors? That's why, then. *Homo sapiens* had...has, in your case I guess...lots of things that don't work quite right. It wasn't just diseases. Like, it used to be that every single person was walking around with a broken gene for making vitamin C. Now, of course, it's been fixed. For the Factus, I mean. And then there are all of the augmentations you can choose."

"I'm not choosing *any* of this, remember. If I'm going to be stuck with the mites for a little while, I'll want to learn what I can about all of this technology, but I'm not applying any of it, not if I can help it." She clicked a few options, then peered at the display as something caught her eye. "Wait, what's this? Reproductive system?"

Jinjing glanced at the display, which was showing a privacy notice. "Oh, right. Well, of course there are options around that, too. Most people can't imagine living without full control of their own bodies, so, obviously, people would want to be able to manage reproduction, libido and interests, sexual—"

Agnes cut her off, "Ok, I think I got the picture!"

"Well, you know a lot of people would say those functions are the biggest reason to use mites in the first place. The killer feature."

Agnes backed out of that section of the display. "Yeesh, I hope the people working on me in the hospital didn't poke around in that part of the controls!"

Jinjing stifled amusement. "Oh, I'm sure they wouldn't have needed to. And they would have talked to your mom if they thought they did. You can actually find a log in here of everything that happened at the hospital if you're worried about that. Anyway," she changed the subject, "we should make some plans."

Agnes was still concerned about the mites and what they'd told people about her, but she reluctantly closed the display and shifted her attention. "What do you mean? What plans?"

"You just went through a big ordeal with the NSG, the mites, and all that, right? And now you need to wait around for your dad to be released from the hospital. So, we should find some fun things to do—something to take your mind off what you've been through. You're not going to just hide up here all day! We already talked about it, Devina and me. She'll push back some of her school projects a couple of days, and I'm on break anyway."

Agnes felt a touch of embarrassment again that they had discussed her, but it was quickly replaced by gratitude—and pleasure at the thought of some fun times ahead. *She's right. I can't just avoid people.* And then a thought came—a reminder of what she had felt about the Factus while she was on the run.

*I was wrong when Dad's mites made me think Bionics could never be friends,* she decided firmly. *I'll save Petram if I can, but I won't push away someone who is being kind.*

***

Dinner that evening had little of the awkwardness that she had been fearing. Sahil said hello, and they talked briefly about the latest project he was working on. Uchita, one of the other girls, joined Devina and Jinjing in an extended discussion about some kind of drama involving a boy Agnes didn't know. They tried to fill her in on a few of the details, but overall, she was happy to just be among the group and not be the center of attention.

The one exception, of course, was Pari. She seemed to avoid looking at Agnes or acknowledging her, to the point where Sahil seemed annoyed that she wouldn't sit close to him, near where Agnes was. *Oh, well—can't win them all. At least she's not actively hostile.*

The following day, Jinjing and Devina came over to Agnes's apartment mid-morning. What followed was the most fun Agnes had had in weeks—they introduced her to some music from a band that she hadn't heard of before. Then, while a projection of the band played in the living room, the three of them did some baking and cooking in the kitchen: familiar chocolate-chip cookies, but also unfamiliar Indian samosas, which were filled with spicy potatoes and peas and served with a sauce.

Agnes knew that the noise and chaos of the music and the mess in the kitchen were probably too much for her mother—Zusana was in and out of the apartment for much of the time—but she was enjoying it all too much to feel bad about that. *Mom has been through a lot, but so have I.* At any rate, in the early afternoon, Zusana left to meet with the NSG, so the youths had the place to themselves for a while.

It was amusing how, while cooking, no one planned out what ingredients they would need. Instead, they just ordered everything as they went, and the needed supplies arrived within a few minutes—on flying drones for small packages, and wheeled carriers for large ones. This also cleared up a minor mystery for Agnes, when she saw that one of the larger carriers not only wheeled itself around Nissus, but also climbed the stairs outside by allowing a cable from the "sky" to lift it to their front door. *That* was a strange sight—it appeared to be an honest-to-goodness skyhook to her eyes, though she knew that the real ceiling of the "outside" was just at the top of their building's roof.

The girls hung out on the veranda in front of the apartment while the last of their creations baked, and then, after they had sampled everything, they wrapped up some of the food to drop off with their peers. Finally, with everyone tired out, Agnes bid her friends goodbye as they left for home.

***

When Zusana returned in the late afternoon, she brought good news. "It's confirmed—we're waking up Dad tomorrow! The doctors and scientists are getting more optimistic about how he's doing." Agnes beamed at her.

Agnes's feelings about her mother had still been quite muddled. Rationally, she knew that her mother and the NSG had saved both her life and her mind by clearing out the reprogrammed mites. But it was hard to get over the fact that it had been done using other mites against her wishes.

*Mom trusted Taia and the others. Maybe I can trust my mom a bit, too. She did say at the hospital that she hopes I can forgive her for doing what she thought was right. And she said that even if I can't forgive her, she would pay that price to save me anyway.*

Agnes felt very grown up as she worked to calm her residual anger and try to see the situation from her mother's viewpoint. *Maybe I don't have to be too hard on all of them about what they did for me.*

With the happy news about Willym received, and a free evening ahead of them, Zusana and Agnes decided to go out and see some more of the city. *After all we've been through, I'd say we deserve some time together to unwind,* Agnes thought. She could tell that an enormous burden was now lifted from her mother, with Willym safe and her daughter back in her right mind.

They didn't stay out late, but nevertheless managed to visit a couple of Nissus's more scenic districts, and they even took in a music performance. Agnes found herself really reconnecting with her mother—probably the closest she had felt to her in a month.

They sat in an outdoor café enjoying a treat, watching people pass by. Agnes talked about what her friends were planning for the next day—an outing that she would have wanted to attend, if she hadn't been so wrapped up with her own worries.

"Devina was saying that most of the group will be going to a water park. It's built so that it looks like you're in a jungle, and the slides look almost like water flowing on natural rock. But you can slide between pools in this long, branching network that goes on for *kilometers* ...."

Together they looked at some pictures of the park, and agreed that, someday, they'd have to visit it.

Thinking of her father, Agnes took her mother's hand in her own—allowing herself to be vulnerable for a moment—and together they stared at the cityscape before them as they thought of the future.

***

Agnes and Zusana were both tired out after a busy day, so neither stayed up late. However, despite her physical tiredness, Agnes couldn't sleep well—whether from anticipating getting her father back, or as a residual effect of her ordeal, she couldn't tell. Either way, a look at her mites' control interface confirmed that it would be a simple matter to fall asleep and rest soundly if she let the mites make some adjustments to a few internal signals. *Nope. Not going to use the mites to make any changes. I'm still human! A human doesn't push a button to fall asleep; we count sheep or something.*

She gave up and rolled out of bed and went out onto the veranda. Sitting in one of the outdoor chairs, watching the moonlit clouds drifting across the sky, it was peaceful for a time, and she allowed herself to forget that there was no actual moon or clouds or sky.

She was just starting to get sleepy when the clouds suddenly became heavier and a cool wind kicked up, swirling around the trees and buildings of her ward. She sniffed the air. *Did they actually just make it smell like rain? This feels like it does just before a storm....*

No sooner had she thought of the rain than a few scattered drops began falling nearby, quickly building toward a substantial rainstorm. While not exactly getting wet under the veranda's roof, she felt it was a good time to retreat inside and go back to bed. *They put on such a production, with the wind and the fresh air and rain, even in the middle of the night!* She shook her head, baffled. *Nissus!*

Chapter 22


# Sorrows


The next day was the big day, what they had come to Nissus for in the first place. *We're coming, Dad!* But to Agnes's surprise and annoyance, the rain was still falling lightly when she woke up, and the dawn was gray and gloomy—not the right feel for such an important day.

She remarked to her mother, "Ok, after being in Nissus for a week, I must've gotten spoiled. I wasn't expecting lousy weather. I thought they just kept it perfect all the time."

Zusana glanced out the front window as she got herself ready. "One of the other women mentioned they had scheduled some rain for today. They have a day like this a couple of times a month in this ward, apparently."

She glanced at Agnes and went on, "You should be glad, actually—in some places they have it rain several times a week, or even nonstop. I don't know why someone would want to live *there*, but they do."

"Ugh!"

As they left the apartment, Agnes couldn't help feeling like the gloom was a bad portent for the day—first she'd had the insomnia and resulting tiredness, and then this weather. But as they exited the ward to the main road, they found that out here it was again sunny and pleasant. *Maybe they give us lousy weather so that we appreciate the nice weather more*, she thought as her spirits began to climb.

***

The hospital room, when they arrived, had an orderly, calm busyness. Taia greeted them, looking rested and comparatively untroubled in contrast to the other day. *I guess we weren't the only ones who found some time to recuperate from the craziness.* Willym, dressed in comfortable street clothes, sat in a simple chair next to a bed, again expressionless.

Agnes looked around at the activity in the room as Taia talked briefly with a few technicians. After a moment, Taia waved Agnes and Zusana over. "Come on and take a seat here near Willym. We're pretty much ready to go."

Taia grew a bit more serious, addressing Agnes and Zusana. "So, we have a pretty good idea of how he's doing. His brain took quite a beating. We've tried to keep his personality mostly intact, but I'm sure you'll find some differences. We are making a point of allowing him to process this trauma in an appropriate way, since obviously it wouldn't be right to make him be all cavalier and dismissive about what he's been through or what he's done. The team has read through many of Willym's writings, watched hours of video and other recordings from his past in Petram, and of course consulted you, Zusana, to try to repair his mind as accurately as possible. But there's always an element of guesswork since we don't have a map of his neural connections from before his mites came on the scene."

Zusana looked stoic. "Yes, I realize that. I know everyone has been doing what they can. I really appreciate it."

Taia retreated to a chair farther from where the others sat. "Ok, here we go."

*This is it.* Heart pounding, Agnes watched her father for any sign of awareness, unconsciously perching at the edge of her seat. *There!* Willym's eyes suddenly came into focus as he began looking around, immediately alert and awake. He took in his wife and daughter in front of him, and Agnes felt warm inside as a hint of a smile crossed his face when he saw them.

Just as quickly though, he looked around at the rest of the room, and his expression turned toward confusion and worry. "Where are we? What's going on, Zusana?" She pulled her chair closer to him. "Hi, Willym."

Agnes's heart went out to him, seeing his confusion and remembering when she had to experience the same thing just days ago. "Hi, Dad."

Zusana explained briefly, "We're in a Factus city called Nissus. You've been here for a couple of weeks, and Agnes and I for just over one week."

His brows narrowed. "Why aren't we in Petram? Did the Factus do something against the city?"

Zusana looked regretful. "Not exactly."

Taia spoke up. "Mr. Barker, my name is Taia Jackson, Major. We've met, though you don't remember me right now. I am a representative of the Factus, more specifically of the Nissus Security Group. As your wife said, we did not do anything against Petram other than bring you and your workmates here to Nissus. Something did happen, though. Do you remember what you were doing at the lab? Your latest memories?"

"We...." He glanced warily at Taia and the technicians, then went on carefully. "We were studying the Factus nanites, trying to understand what's going on out there. I mean, out *here* I guess, since we're not in Petram right now. I can say that we were trying to reverse engineer them and test—"

Willym's face quickly registered alarm as he realized what must have happened. "Oh, no. No, no, no. The nanites got away from us?"

Zusana took his hand. "Or rather, they got *ahold* of you."

He gave a groan and covered his face with his other hand for a moment. Then he composed himself and looked around at the others grimly. "Ok, it must have been bad if my memory is a complete blank. Please tell me this wasn't...it wasn't like what happened at Busan that one time. We specifically—" Willym cut himself off, thinking, before continuing on a different track. "The others on the team, are they ok?"

Taia stood and took a step closer to answer him. "That remains to be seen. You didn't have quite the casualty list that Busan had, no. No one died, thankfully. In some other ways, though, this was a much more serious incident."

Willym looked perplexed. "Explain."

"I'll do even better than that—we'll start bringing back your memories of what you've been through. Right now, those memories are being blocked by some of our mites in your brain."

"Blocked?! By your mites? I think I need to talk to the ambassador before we do anything else. Or just let me talk to Prime Minister Hale. This is *way* outside—"

Agnes saw her mother squeeze his hand and interrupt him. "Honey, that's not going to work. I don't think anyone in the Petram government is going to want to talk about this. They've been stonewalling me for weeks now."

Willym was dumbfounded. "What? I report directly to Hale! This is his project I'm on!"

Taia chimed in. "They cut you loose, Mr. Barker, your whole team. Washed their hands of everything you'd been doing."

He swelled with indignation. "Prime Minister Hale told me that our work is critical to the future of Petram. We need to understand how the nanites operate and how to build defenses against any Factus interference. Our results—" He stared at Taia as he trailed off. "I can't quite remember the results of our research, but I know they are state secrets. I really should not say any more to you, I think."

She crossed her arms and looked at him with an air of confident authority, nearly at eye level even though she was standing and he was sitting. "Willym, you know the mites you were playing with got out of control. We've used our mites to neutralize them and try to rebuild your mind the best we could. Do you really think you are keeping any secrets from us in that brain of yours?"

Willym was speechless for a moment, then seemed to slowly deflate with resignation. "No." He gazed over at Zusana, hand in hers, and asked, "Did these Factus really save me? Do you trust them?"

She replied, "Yes, Willym, they did save you. And yes, I trust them. I've been with them every step of the way since we got here to Nissus. I trust Taia and the others more than I trust Hale, right now, and I'm starting to wonder what's going on back home." This seemed to satisfy him, as he relaxed marginally.

Taia was ready to continue. "Great, now, if you're ready, we'll start bringing back your memories." He motioned her to continue. She advised, "I suggest you talk about what you remember as it comes back to you. That will help you process it, and it will help your family understand what happened, as well."

Willym glanced at his wife, who nodded. Thoughtfully, he began, "So far, I remember we were a small team, running on a shoestring budget. We were figuring everything out as we went, trying to hack the nanite programming and see how to make them do what *we* wanted."

He continued, "The prime minister was really worried about Petram's vulnerability. I mean, *I* know that it's not like we could stop the Factus if they want to mess with Petram, but I'm not sure Hale really understands that. I agree more with Agnes"—he shot a look over toward her—"that the greater threat to Petram is that it kind of withers away. People go out on vacation, see the outside world, and eventually move away where there are more opportunities. Anyway, let's see...."

*He's not going to like the next memories that he gets*, Agnes knew.

"Oh...I think I see how it happened." He looked like he wanted to swear. He began explaining to Taia, "Look, we had to do all of the research without a lot of time or resources. Hale's orders. We experimented with the nanites on ourselves because that was the fastest and easiest way to test out the programming we were doing. 'For science,' you know? We'd just wipe their programming, load some new code, and report what it seemed to do. I remember now that...huh."

He looked sheepish as he glanced at Zusana. "See, the nanites had all sorts of weird effects when we were trying random things. One tweak made me think the room smelled like chocolate. A couple of times they made me feel angry, or sad, or whatever. But then someone tweaked the programming a certain way, and suddenly the nanites made me really excited about the idea of using nanites. So...."

Taia finished his thought. "So, then you convinced the others to leave the mites on for a while, and then reprogrammed their mites to match yours."

Willym nodded. "Well, yes, I told them to leave them on for some more adjustments to the code. I realized they were going to stop the nanites and I knew I didn't want them to, so I managed to distract them long enough to get into the control computer. We had been taking turns trying them out, so they already had some blank ones in their brains, ready to go. It only took about twenty seconds to get us all under the nanite influence."

"And you had to invent a justification for it—using the mites as a tool to protect Petram, to address Hale's concerns."

"Well, it wasn't that big a stretch. If the nanites could be programmed to encourage people to stay and build Petram, then—"

Willym suddenly sat up straight, struck by a look of horror. "Everyone would need to be given the nanites, then. Did we spread them around the city? Oh, no...."

Taia held her hand up. "No, you didn't manage to cause that kind of a mass incident. You were about to, but my team started figuring out something was wrong and intervened. We brought you here before you had really refined the mites. But there *was* one person outside your team that you did infect with your rogue mites."

He whispered, "Agnes," and looked over at her.

*Now,* that's *a proper look of shame,* Agnes thought. Her gratification at seeing his remorse was mixed with her relief that he was once again himself.

She reached out to take his hand. *I've finally got you back.*

***

At last, Agnes and Zusana were finally having the reunion with Willym they had been waiting for. Willym resolutely apologized for what he'd said and done, and the others began sharing what they'd been through from their own perspectives.

Willym was impressed with Agnes's story, even if it turned out to be relatively short. "You actually managed to get up a tree, through a wall, and out of the city! I pretty much lay quietly until a search party found me. And then I yelled at them like a maniac." He grimaced at the memory.

With the family together and safe, her husband back in his right mind, Zusana seemed to release the stress and worry and anger of the past month all at once as she talked, tears flowing, emotion racking her frame in a way that was a bit frightening for Agnes to witness.

*I gave her a lot of that stress, too,* Agnes knew, *though most of it wasn't* really *my fault.*

Just as when Agnes had been awakened a few days prior, Taia and most of the technicians had left the room to allow the family time to bond. Agnes appreciated that—not only was each of them emotional, but her father was clearly embarrassed by his original mistake and all that he had done since.

Willym was shaken by what he'd set in motion. "I never should have accepted the assignment or the terms that the prime minister gave me. I should have just resigned in protest. I ended up putting my family in danger and giving you a huge burden to fix it, Zusana."

When his memories of his time in Nissus returned—when he remembered tricking Agnes and then breaking out and going on the run—he was mortified, perhaps even more than she had been.

Agnes told him, "When I talked to my friend Jinjing, she said that people weren't laughing at me; she thought they were saying that all that stuff we did was 'hardcore.' She said they were impressed we managed to get you out and stay hidden for so long. She made it sound like a spy adventure or something."

He chuckled a little at that. "Mostly for me it was terrifying. And exhausting. Now, of course, I'm horrified at what might have happened to you, even though we're both safe now."

They shared a look. *We were both willing to kill during that time. I'll never forget that feeling, and I don't think Dad will, either.* Because of that dark past, Agnes was beginning to feel that she and her father were now comrades. There was a bond that they had earned by descending into such an abyss together, a connection that she hoped her mother would never be forced to share.

Chapter 23

# Complications

Once the family had spent some time reconnecting, Willym went to the door and called Taia back into the room to ask about his teammates. "I feel responsible for what happened. I need to see if they're ok."

She filled him in. "Both are ready to be 'awakened' later today. We brought their families here to Nissus shortly after yours arrived. Of the two, Tomas had the worse damage. It was about as bad as yours—a little more to the amygdala, but less to his cardiopulmonary system. I think the repairs and healing went pretty well, though."

Willym looked mollified. The group made plans for Willym to be on hand when his colleagues were awakened, and the family decided to go out and get some lunch in the meantime. As they were preparing to go, however, Taia motioned for them to wait.

"Zusana, Willym, there's one more thing we need to talk about. One more complication." That got Agnes's attention. *I'm ready to be done with problems, at this point.*

Taia retrieved a box from the technicians' desk, and pulled out three small, thin devices. "Willym, as I mentioned earlier, you are not keeping any secrets from us in your brain, right?"

"Right...."

"That doesn't preclude the possibility that you *had* a secret at one point, which you then deliberately erased from your memories. The mites you programmed did have a crude ability to do that."

He looked puzzled. "Well, if I don't know my own secret, then it should be irrelevant, right?"

Taia shook her head. "Just like that drone bee was prepared and waiting for Agnes, you could have prepared another surprise. One for yourself. A surprise you would have to deliberately forget, to scrub from your mind, because you knew that when we caught you, we would find out about it if you didn't."

Agnes felt her heart sink. *Can we never be free of those stupid mites?*

Taia distributed the three devices. "I know you are planning to deactivate the mites that we currently have active in you two. You would then be defenseless against more rogues, just as Zusana is now. I want you three to carry these with you at all times. If you ever have reason to believe that you may have been exposed to dangerous mites, you can use this to inject some of ours to counteract the dangerous ones."

Willym picked up one of the injectors reluctantly, peering at it. "This is hypothetical, right? Do you really think it's likely that we did something like that? Sent out another drone or something to reinfect ourselves?"

"Well, let me put it this way. We know from looking at Agnes's memories that you told her you had an 'insurance policy' in case you were captured. But you didn't tell her what it was, and we did not find the conversation in your memories—there are gaps. I'd say we can assume that there is something out there, waiting for you." She pointed at one of the injectors. "So, remember, if you decide to clear out your current mites, always have one of those ready!"

*Well, that puts a bit of a damper on the day!* Agnes thought.

***

Despite Taia's warning, Agnes found herself enjoying the next few hours. Getting out with her family, finding some food, and starting to see the sights with her father made for some carefree moments—certainly by her recent standards. This was what she had been waiting for ever since he had been taken from Petram, after all.

Agnes watched her father closely to see if there were any residual effects from the mites and the hospitalization, but all she noticed was that he had missed a few weeks of their lives and needed to catch up.

When it was time for Willym to go back to the hospital to see Tomas and Edmon, Agnes didn't want him to go. *We just got you back—stay!* she thought, but Zusana insisted on taking her back to New Canberra to wait for him to be done.

Agnes felt like they should have some kind of "Welcome Home" party for him when he arrived, but it didn't feel right since they weren't actually home yet. After consulting with her mother, they settled on ordering a cake for that evening that read, "Barker Family – Together Again" so they could at least celebrate. They also invited Faylen for the little party, since she had done so much for the family recently and had hit it off with Zusana so well.

When Willym arrived a few hours later, he was escorted by a man she didn't know—and, to Agnes's surprise, Sahil. Her friend greeted her and explained, "This is my dad. Since he works for the NSG and lives in New Canberra, it made sense for him to show your dad the way here."

Introductions were made all around—joyful ones, since Willym was just as happy to be back with his family as they were to have him.

While the conversation continued, Agnes caught Sahil's eye, motioned to him with her hand, and together they stepped outside to the veranda, where it was quieter. "I'm glad you've got your dad back, Agnes," he offered genuinely.

"Thanks. Me too. It's going to take some time to get over what happened, but at least we can finally go home as a family. We'll probably rest tomorrow, and then head out to Petram the next day."

He looked a bit disappointed at hearing about Petram. "We'll miss you. I know Jinjing will be sad when you leave. It's been interesting having you here, that's for sure!"

She grinned. He reminded her of her friend Emil back home—Sahil was just as earnest, she felt. "I've had enough excitement to last me a long time! I've retired from my criminal career—no more jailbreaks for me." She thought about what Jinjing had said. *I'll just have to find some other way to be "hardcore," I guess.*

He smiled wistfully. "Have you thought more about our conversation? Have you kind of made peace with the Factus world, with what we're doing? Do you still think that we're 'evil'?"

Agnes was taken aback. "I...guess I've been too busy dealing with the crisis to really think about it more. I am grateful that the Factus rescued me and my dad from his mites, but no, I don't think I can accept everything you do to people with the mites here. I'm eager to get back home. Life there is a lot simpler."

"Morally simpler?"

"*Everything* simpler."

Sahil hesitated, and then drew out a miniature book with a colorful cover. "I got this for you, as a goodbye gift. It's a pocket-size *Bhagavad Gita*. You don't have to think of it as a religious book—it's very philosophical and has life lessons. After our little debate, I was thinking you would appreciate this."

Agnes accepted the book, touched. "Thanks, Sahil. That means a lot to me."

"Will you visit sometime? I mean, Devina and Jinjing and all of us?"

For a moment, Agnes saw past the Factus in front of her, past the prodigy who studied advanced physics and ethics, past the mites and everything, and simply saw a boy. A friend. A youth who might be popular and successful, but who had vulnerabilities just as she had. *This can be simple, too.*

"Sure, Sahil. Absolutely, I'll come see you guys. You're my friends now."

***

Two days after getting Willym back, the family packed to leave. At first, it was a relaxing and comfortable morning—they were leaving in the early afternoon instead of before dawn, and of course this time the family was reunited and safe. But then at brunch, their last meal in the apartment, Zusana checked their schedule with her handheld and found something new.

"Willym, look at this. We're supposed to arrive in Petram on a sleeper tomorrow morning, but this says, 'Expect delays west of Billings. Situation at Petram is rapidly evolving; updates will be provided as they are available.'"

Agnes and Willym looked at her, surprised, and then at each other. He spoke up first. "What kind of situation could there be to cause travel delays?" He quickly dug out his own handheld to check.

"Is there a snowstorm?" Agnes asked.

Her mother, flicking among news reports on her handheld, replied, "No, it says here that there's a dispute with the Petram government. It doesn't really say what the dispute is *about*...."

Willym found some more. "It says here the Hale administration is refusing to talk to any Factus outsiders, and they tried to block the rail line through Petram overnight. Turned into a bit of a scuffle, getting it cleared, and they're still repairing some damage."

They all looked over at what he had found, projected onto the table, but there was little else to learn from the report.

Agnes said, "It couldn't be something about *us*, right? A complaint about how they took you from Petram? Because,

Mom, you said they've been ignoring you and Dad. They don't care about us."

Zusana nodded. "Yes, but why would Hale shut communications and the rail link? How are we supposed to sell our exports and get supplies without it?"

Willym looked worried. "Sounds like Hale has lost it. Almost as if he came across more mites like the ones I had, to be honest. Why don't you call some people at the NSG? They should be able to tell us more."

Agnes and Willym cleaned up the brunch and finished packing their last few possessions while she made the call. Agnes had been about to load their large luggage bag onto a carrier outside the door, when she paused, as if suddenly unsure. *We* will *be going home, won't we?*

"Hi, Erik," Zusana said as Taia's operative from the NSG appeared in a projection on the wall. "We were just about to head over to the vactrain on our way back home, but it looks like Hale's tried to shut down travel through Petram. Do you know what's going on? Is our train going to have trouble getting in? We're supposed to take a sleeper from Chicago tonight."

Erik sighed and looked tired. "I'm not sure what exactly is going on. I'd say go ahead and catch your train. Petram's neighbors won't let them block the line; they'd keep it open one way or another. Hale can close off Petram, but he can't bring the whole region to a halt."

"You don't think he...you know...found some of the mites Willym was experimenting with, do you?"

Erik scowled slightly. "I doubt it. But after everything that's happened recently, we're not taking any chances. I'm actually shipping out with a team now to do reconnaissance to ensure there's nothing of concern going on in Petram—nothing in our purview, anyway. It's part of a larger NSG mission. Up until now, we've given Petram all sorts of deference, lots of privacy, but that's over. Taia is fed up—the Neumann Division has been behind the curve one too many times."

Zusana nodded resignedly. "Will you be on our train, then?"

He shook his head. "Taia put my team on the first possible express vactrain. We even got a whole onboard business suite so we can work." He gestured around at the room he was in, apparently on the train already. "We're taking this all the way to Denver, then flying up to the Petram area this evening."

Zusana gave a low whistle, and Agnes shared her reaction—taking an express vactrain as close as Denver would certainly be quick, but using an aircraft for the final leg of the journey would add a new level of expense to that team's trip.

Erik continued, "Tell you what. I'm sure you're eager to get back home. If Hale or anyone has unauthorized mites, you can let us handle it—that *is* my job, after all. My team won't be allowed to wander around Petram—since we're Factus—so we'll be setting up a command center either at the train station or nearby. We'll be able to do our investigation from there."

Zusana agreed, and after a few more exchanges, the call was finished. Agnes went ahead and loaded the luggage onto the carrier and sent it off, and then the three of them left their brief New Canberran home for the last time, heading for Phoenix Square.

***

Each of them had seen the Phoenix within the past few days, so there was no need to stop by the statue again. Nevertheless, Agnes craned her neck to take another look at it as they all walked across the plaza to make their connection to the vactrain.

*The Phoenix*, it occurred to her, *may seem fierce and strong, dangerous, even. But it's not even looking at the Earth it's leaving behind. Earth is the past, for the Phoenix. Just like the Factus aren't really focused on Petram if they can help it— not unless we're cooking up illegal mites or blocking the rail line. They're moving on, leaving us behind.*

She thought about her class discussion at school a few weeks back, when she had called the Factus the enemy.

Her thoughts were interrupted as she had to keep an eye on her parents to avoid getting lost in the crowd, and then they began to draw near the vactrain they would ride.

She allowed herself a smile, as she realized that this time, she could enjoy the trip. *I might be worried about what is going on back home in Petram, but there's no way I'm going to have a meltdown like the last time I took the vactrain,* she thought as she glanced at yet another person across the platform sporting a set of horns; she felt none of the panic that she remembered.

For their return trip, they were making more stops than they had made coming to Nissus—six hours to Chicago, a long layover, and finally a sleeper train back to Petram. The vactrain was uneventful, other than the parts where the vacuum tube was transparent, when they got to watch the landscape pass in a blur at several thousand kilometers per hour—something she had not properly watched on the way to Nissus.

*I've got my dad back, I'm not freaking out about Bionics with "augmented" bodies, and we're heading home!* Things were definitely looking up.

They boarded their sleeper car in Chicago, finding the accommodations comfortable and well laid out. After exploring the train and finding it too dark outside to view any scenery, the family turned in fairly early, since they hadn't yet adjusted from New Canberra time. The ride was smooth, the sway of the train quite subtle, and Agnes slept well despite the unfamiliar surroundings.

In the morning, Agnes and her parents just had time to grab some breakfast before they began slowing on the approach to the Petram station. It didn't appear they were delayed after all—the sun was just peeking over the hills behind them as the farmland began to give way to houses and then to larger buildings. As they were eating, though, the train slowed abruptly, and they began to see the first evidence there might be something wrong.

Chapter 24

# Revelations

"What's going on up there?" Zusana pointed to a spot ahead of them in the distance. Everyone tried to get a better look, but the angle made it difficult to see until they had rolled closer. Once they did....

"Oh... are those soldiers?" Willym asked. Outside the right-hand windows, a few people milled about on a road near the tracks—men and women with rifles slung over their shoulders, and unfriendly glares at the train as it passed. The windows on the left side of the train, by contrast, showed the city seemingly deserted.

Agnes realized that the soldiers, if that was what they were, appeared to be guarding two bulldozers nearby, which were busy scraping up the street and pushing dirt and asphalt into mounds alongside the tracks. *What the...?*

The spectacle got stranger. A little farther on, the dirt mound was larger and steeper. And when they approached the train station, they could see a flurry of activity outside: Machines were tearing down a building right in the heart of the city next to the tracks, and then, moments later, as they rolled into the station, a rough block wall was blocking their view completely on that side.

By this point, the whole train was abuzz as nearly all of the passengers tried to look out the windows and talk about what they were seeing. It seemed they had little better idea of what was going on than Agnes's family did.

As the train came to a stop, she gathered her things and followed her parents to the end of the car, where the conductor met them. "Barker family?" he asked. "Come on this way. We'll need to disembark on the left. Bit of a situation here, obviously." He helped them down to the track bed, where they stepped over the eastbound tracks, then climbed up onto the south platform. The conductor handed Willym the luggage bag they had sent off from their apartment the day before.

To Agnes's surprise, waiting for them there was Erik, the NSG employee they had just talked to the day before. She also saw several other men and a woman scattered around the station platform, all carrying weapons of one sort or another. They seemed to be standing guard, watching the new wall on the other side of the tracks or peering up and down the rail line. To Agnes, who had never seen lethal weapons until moments ago, they looked quite frightening.

Erik came to greet them, looking nervous. "Hello, Willym, Zusana. Come on over into this station building. We need to talk." He led them to a cramped office inside the station.

"It's strange to think just how isolated Petram is," he began, "considering there's a train line running right through the city, but as you know they've always been withdrawn. Now they've completely cut off their net. Of course, with the NSG now on site, we have ways around that. We've been tapped in since last night, and what we're learning isn't pretty. They've shut down ties to the outside even further than before."

"Prime Minister Hale is doing it?" Zusana asked.

"Yes, his whole administration. He's always been anti-Factus as you know, but now that means he's cut all connections. He's saying that Petram has to go it completely alone: no more trade, no more travel, no more communications. No one in or out."

"But," Willym protested, "the people surely won't accept that! That would be a huge hit to the economy, for one thing!"

"I know. And I would think he'd have to cheat and quietly do some trading, eventually. But this move is all about PR. He's getting people on board with this by demonizing all of the Factus, saying that we're all dangerous. He's managed to evacuate the southern part of the city, and now he's working to wall off the whole train line, starting here with the station. He's pretty serious about this."

Agnes spoke up. "So, he really is under the control of Dad's mites. That's what I was like when I had them. He's trying to keep people in the city and away from the outside world."

Erik equivocated. "We don't have any evidence yet that this has anything to do with mites. But I agree that he's trying to do the same thing with propaganda that you tried to do with mites, back when you were under their influence."

Agnes groaned. "You know, a few weeks back I probably would have agreed with him. But now, I don't like the idea of completely shutting the city off from the world. I actually made friends with some people in Nissus. I told them I'd visit sometime. Now you're saying I won't be able to do that, or even talk to them, unless Hale is voted out in the next election?"

Erik paused, looking very uncomfortable. Zusana spoke up. "What is it, Erik? What do you know?"

"Hale is blaming our incident with Willym's mites on the Factus. He made up a completely different story about what happened. That's how he's stirring people up. He says that we kidnapped or lured you away, and then brainwashed all three of you. That you're one of us now—worse, even. A tool to try to infiltrate Petram and undermine it. He's hinted that, if you try to get into Petram, you should all be shot without warning."

"*WHAT?!*" all three Barkers vented shock and outrage.

"You can see the videos for yourself. And you've seen that he's managed to acquire some weapons."

"But we're citizens!" Zusana cried. "You can't just go shooting innocent people!"

Willym scowled angrily. "If that's true, he's backstabbing his own people."

Agnes was still trying to process what she was hearing. "Wait...we can't go home? What are we supposed to do?"

Erik spread his hands helplessly. "Look, we've just barely learned about any of this. We're still trying to understand what exactly is going on and where this will all end up. If there are mites involved, we'll stop them, I can tell you that. But, otherwise, we're probably going to let Petram run itself the way it wants to. That's not official yet, but I think it's pretty likely, to be honest with you."

"But he's lying to everyone! And threatening us. You can't just let him get away with that."

"He's lying in the service of an ideology that may be of little threat to the world. As long as we keep you from trying to climb over or around that wall, there should be little threat to you, too."

Agnes felt numb. Her life was across that wall, in Petram. *How long is this going to last? What about school? What about my friends, Emil and Jonnan and Catteryn?* Her whole identity was wrapped up in Petram.

***

Their waking nightmare continued throughout that day, as the Barker family had to try to find a place to settle for a day or two while the situation played out. There were quite a few buildings to choose from, since the people of Petram had abandoned the small part of the city that lay south of the tracks.

However, Erik's words about potential violence had spooked them, especially Zusana—at her suggestion, the family eventually settled on using a small house nearby that seemed to be out of any likely line of fire from the north. Meanwhile, the newly arrived NSG personnel had joined some other Factus representatives from the region in establishing a joint command center, using the train station and an adjacent office building.

Agnes couldn't help comparing the sparse and unfamiliar house with her real house, out of reach beyond the wall. Staring at an empty bedroom, she thought of her own bedroom on the other side of the tracks, waiting there for her to resume her life, possessions still scattered about. *Here I've been the most vocal advocate for Petram, and it's turned on me,* she couldn't help thinking bitterly.

Fortunately, the Factus at the command center brought in some food supplies, and the house still had water and electricity service, so the family was able to meet their immediate needs and prepare a simple lunch after a chaotic morning.

While the house provided a place to eat and rest, Agnes soon found that she was drawn to the command center near the station—that afternoon, and each of the following days as their exile wore on, she made her way over to where the NSG were conducting their investigation. She craved information, and sitting around the house was far too boring.

On the first afternoon, Agnes and her parents watched intercepted video of the unrest in Petram. The prime minister's speeches were every bit as bad as Erik had said—bombastic, inflammatory, untruthful, and quite often focused on the Barkers. It made Agnes feel sick to hear her name invoked in his cause, both as a martyr of the Bionics and as a dangerous saboteur to be put down. The truth of what had happened to her, her real story of the nanobots, had been completely twisted and turned around. She ached to talk to her friends, to tell them *it's not true!*

The following day, Agnes managed to get a look at the NSG spy operation—she was persistent in asking questions, and whether from their sympathy for her or just because of her constant presence, she ended up seeing a lot of how it worked.

Agnes watched a live video feed of Hale's empty office—he wasn't in it at the moment—and asked one of the technicians about it. "Don't Hale and his people have equipment to detect if their office is bugged?"

The woman looked up from the batch of bugs—miniature, disguised flying drones—that she was preparing. "Of course. But who made that equipment and sold it to them?"

Agnes raised her eyebrows. "The NSG?"

"Not technically, but let's just say we have a lot of friends."

A memory came back to her, of a dragonfly in the November cold. "Did you use those things to spy on *me*, back before I left for Nissus?"

The woman gave her a considering look before replying. "Well, it wasn't like this. We didn't send these into your house, or anything. We were mostly scouting out the city."

"You know, this kind of plays into Hale's hands. He's paranoid, and you really are spying on him."

The technician waved dismissively. "I think we're seeing that he's not nearly as paranoid as he sounds. This is his way of getting what he wants—to close the city off completely."

Erik, listening from across the room, chimed in. "That's what you wanted, too, not long ago, Agnes. I think you were right, in a way. Isolation really could keep Petram going longer. We've just got to make sure they aren't tampering with mites to make it happen."

Agnes just watched silently for a moment. *When I told Dad that I would do anything to help Petram, I didn't have lies and banishment in mind. Is it even worth saving Petram if it's full of people who are only kept there by fear? You don't need mites to turn people into sheep, apparently.*

The thought of her friends believing her to be a monster was unbearable. An idea came to her.

"Erik, you know I have friends in there, over in Petram. I don't know if they believe what they're hearing about me, but they should know the truth. Maybe, if this situation…you know…doesn't get better, we could use one of those spy drones to send a message. Maybe I could communicate, let them know it's safe to get out if they don't want to live the lies that Hale is trying to give them."

He turned and considered her for a moment. "I'd have to pass that idea up to my boss. It would probably need to be approved at the top levels of the NSG, but they might go for it. I don't know."

Agnes mentally crossed her fingers.

***

"Ok, go," Willym said as he tapped the 'record' button. Across the room, Agnes smiled to the camera and began what felt like the weightiest recording she might ever make. What she said here could certainly change lives.

"Hi, Emil. It's me. I'm back from Nissus, and I've found out what Prime Minister Hale has been saying about me and my family. I need you to know the truth."

Agnes had a lot to say: about her father's misadventures with nanobots and her own infection by them, intrigue and danger in Nissus, and recovery. She told about the new friends she had found and her appreciation for what they had done for her. She was open about how overwhelmingly powerful the Factus were compared to Petram, and about the troubling choices the Factus made for their children.

"Emil, it's been a few days now since we arrived here at Petram—outside the new borders, anyway. It doesn't look like Hale is going to back down. I'm...I'm losing hope that I'll ever be able to get home. I was the biggest fan of Petram, but now I'm basically a refugee."

She looked intently at the camera. "I think you should leave Petram. Sneak out before the wall gets finished. Your family, Catteryn's family, whoever doesn't want to live in a closed-off Petram with the lies. I guess Elaina had the right idea when she left, months ago.

"We're in the south part of the city, just over the wall. My family is, for now. But we may end up heading back to Nissus. No one knows yet. But I know you, and I think you're better than this. You can do more with your life, more than live with whatever Petram has to offer, now. It's only going to get harder to leave as that wall goes up, so you need to decide soon. I miss you all and hope I see you again sometime. Bye for now."

When she finished, Agnes's parents came over to her to give her a hug; she certainly needed it. The unwilling transition from Petram advocate to dissident, from rooted to rootless, was heartbreaking for her.

Agnes looked up at Zusana. "Well, if we do need to go back to Nissus or something, at least now we know what to expect."

Willym wasn't so sanguine. "For now, yes. It's a big world out there, and it's getting stranger every day."

Agnes frowned as the three of them walked over to the kitchen to sit at the table. "What do you mean?"

"I had some long talks with Erik and the others the past few days. It's not just those of us from Petram that feel like the world is changing on them. The Factus feel it too."

Zusana asked, "How? They're the ones *making* the changes."

"It's what comes next. You know how Erik is pretty tall? Taller than most people in Nissus? He's not very happy about it. Being tall is not considered an advantage. Apparently, there's a consensus that smaller is better, and there's going to be a new generation of Factus at something like half of our size. They're going to build a whole new section of Nissus and redesign all sorts of transportation and infrastructure around that."

Both Zusana and Agnes were incredulous. Agnes asked, "Why on Earth would they want to do that? What's so much better about being smaller?"

He explained, "Erik said that someone one-half his height could weigh a small fraction of what he does. They'd require less food, less space, less energy for transportation and things, and would be proportionally stronger and more agile. And that's not even the biggest change that's coming."

"Do I dare ask?" Zusana said dryly.

Willym grimaced. "I'm not sure, to be honest. He said that once they can replicate all of the brain circuits in silicon and software, people don't even have to be tied to one body. They could literally be like Tinker Bell and fly around with wings one day, and then be mermaids the next, if they want. Just move around as bits and bytes and you can inhabit whatever form they can make."

*Even the* Factus *are having trouble adapting?*

Agnes started laughing. *I don't know what the world is coming to, but if even the Bionics are scared of the future, I sure can't stop it.*

Her parents looked at her, concerned, but she just shook her head, grinning. "And I was so worried about those horns Faylen grew."

Somehow, Agnes felt that everything would be ok. People like Faylen, Taia, Erik, Sahil, and Jinjing were building the future. Maybe she didn't need to hide from it. She certainly didn't want to hide in Petram with Hale. *I want to see the future,* she realized. *It's going to be an adventure.*

Epilogue

# Warao

"Elaina, I'd like you to meet my friend, Vaishnavi. She's the one who told me I should visit Warao. Here it's been three months and we're finally doing it."

Elaina greeted the small girl cheerfully. "Nice to meet you!" She smiled at Vaishnavi's parents, who were standing to the side talking to Agnes's parents.

Vaishnavi waved hello, but quickly became distracted by something in the forest where they were standing, and she wandered off instead of chatting.

Elaina turned to Agnes. "I'm glad you invited me here to Nissus. In all my time on the 'outside', since I left Petram, I've just been busy getting established down in Mexico and didn't do any traveling. While you've been having adventures, I've mostly been going to school and writing papers. At least my Spanish is pretty good now."

Agnes chuckled, and replied, "Some of those 'adventures' I wish I could erase. And don't feel bad; my new classes start next week, so I'll be in the same boat. Actually, worse, since I haven't started using the mites yet." Elaina just smiled in response.

Warao, like most places in Nissus, hadn't taken Agnes long to get to from her family's new, temporary home. After two ten-minute train rides and then a long drop on one of the ubiquitous elevators, they found themselves a world away from the metropolis above.

The elevator had opened onto a small waystation in the middle of a shady forest, trees towering around them and muddy ground below. A rough building offered some basic water and restroom services and had log benches where a dozen other visitors were sitting or milling about.

Agnes breathed in the warm, water-saturated air, listened to the birdsong around her, and felt her mind begin to clear and her muscles start to relax as she set aside her thoughts and worries for a moment. Not to mention, being with her friend again, after so long, provided a measure of long-sought peace.

A dark-haired, shirtless Amerindian young man approached from the building to greet the group. "Hello, do we have everyone?" He quickly counted. "Looks like it. Does anyone need some more time before the tour?"

They all indicated no, and so he continued, "We can start a couple of minutes early then, so—" he called out more loudly as he turned, "—if you'll all follow me, let's head to the canoes."

He led the tourists down a short path to a riverbank, where he stopped to face the group, everyone gathering around. "All right, here we go. This—" he turned and cast his arm around to indicate the river and forest, "—is Warao. More precisely, this is a replica or similitude of the Warao homeland in the Orinoco Delta of Venezuela. As you probably know, our homeland was mostly destroyed when the level of the oceans rose and inundated much of the delta with salty water. Before that, though, our culture was largely lost—through contact with other groups and due to conflict. Our people were ultimately scattered and absorbed into the surrounding populations or entirely marginalized."

He smiled. "I am a result of one of the first initiatives of the larger Nissus project: to recreate the Warao. My parents had genetic engineering to bring them as close to the ancestral Warao people as possible. Along with many others, they relearned the Warao language and culture, and reestablished our people and the delta ecosystem here at the lowest, oldest level of Nissus."

Agnes quickly found herself growing interested as he told the story of the resurrection of his people. *Back from the dead!* Her history with Petram made her empathize with the Warao, who had been similarly besieged by outsiders.

The young man continued. "I was born into this community. I am fully Warao. I can—and will—show you how to make bread from the *moriche* tree and how to catch fish in the river. I spend months at a time living here on the water.

"I am also fully Factus. I have been pursuing anthropology studies and served an internship in applied ethnology at the

Algerian Makan. Most Warao are similar, in that we embrace the traditional lifestyle as a part of our modern identity. We live in multiple worlds.

"Now, what will you call me? Since we're in my homeland right now, we'll follow Warao tradition. Those of you who are male can call me Dahé, and females can call me Dakóbo. Both mean 'brother'. If you are significantly older than me, male or female, you can call me Auka, if you wish. That means 'son'. We'll just keep it simple since you are visitors."

Elaina nudged Agnes and whispered, "Is that a joke? How is that keeping it simple?"

Agnes whispered back, "Well, he doesn't look like he's joking." Indeed, the guide—Dakóbo—had kept a straight face.

He began assigning people to canoes, and she soon found herself sharing one with Elaina, glad that they had known enough to dress appropriately for getting wet.

She worked a paddle from her seat at the front of the canoe, while her friend did the same from the rear, moving them out away from the dock and into the river proper. Then, while waiting for the other boats to launch, they looked around at the scenery.

From a nearby canoe, Zusana pointed out a sloth in the trees above them, and soon several tourists in canoes were watching it and commenting to each other. When Dakóbo finished getting the boats launched and saw what was going on, he said, "Everybody wave to our sloth Nakuakua. This one lives in the trees here by our dock, so he usually can come out to greet the tours. Ok, everyone ready to paddle?"

***

Their guide talked as the group began paddling down the river, his voice magnified by some unseen speakers to make it sound as though he were next to them. "Here in Warao, we have recreated not just the human culture, but as much of the original Orinoco ecosystem as practical. This district totals over five hundred hectares of river delta, threaded into more than forty kilometers of waterways and forest paths."

He explained some of the traditional culture: how they lived in family-based villages where they built stilt houses with no walls, made canoes, hung hammocks, and planted gardens. How he expected to move to his wife's village when he married and live with her family there (during the times they were staying in Warao, at least). How the house, canoe, and nearly every other possession in his village was considered temporary and could theoretically be abandoned as the families moved around with changes in the seasons.

Several times, Dakóbo halted the flotilla of canoes to point out particular animals or plants and discuss how they were important. At one of these stops, he laughed at the alarm caused by a crocodile suddenly swimming past, nearly close enough for Agnes to touch. *No animals would eat me here in Nissus,* she reminded herself.

They all docked at an island and climbed out of the canoes, and then filed up a muddy path. A short distance beyond, they found the gardens and the small group of houses that comprised Dakóbo's village, built next to another river channel. Children and a few adults came out to greet them, some of the youngest being entirely naked.

At this point, the group split up. Some of the visitors followed the guide down a path to see how he collected food from the forest, but Agnes's parents wanted to stay at the village, and she and Elaina ultimately decided to stick with them. An older woman began showing and discussing the houses and gardens. Agnes noticed some Warao youths piloting a canoe that drifted past and continued down the river.

After a few minutes, the woman directed everyone to another of the open-sided houses, where she demonstrated how rough palm fiber twine could be woven into a variety of items, such as mats, ropes, and nets. She then distributed some of the materials to her guests, and they each attempted to follow her instructions and weave a simple souvenir bracelet.

Agnes checked to see how the others were doing. "Nice, Mom, Elaina! Dad, don't quit your day job." They laughed, but Agnes immediately flushed as she realized that wasn't a good joke—both of her parents had lost their jobs, and, while the Factus were patient with them, as refugees, it was taking some time for them to decide what to do with the rest of their lives.

Neither seemed upset, though. Conversation flowed while they all worked.

"Elaina," Zusana asked, "have you talked to your other Petram friends yet?"

"Emil and Catteryn? Yes, thanks to Agnes tracking them down after they escaped from Petram, we've been able to have some group calls. I can't wait for tomorrow when they get here."

Agnes said, "And you will all get to meet my New Canberran friends. I know you don't know them yet, but they mean a lot to me, and I hope everyone can hit it off. They were there for me during some of the worst days of my life. Remind me to tell you sometime about how Sahil, two months ago, managed to singlehandedly find and defeat our 'Plan C' drone, possibly saving me from getting reinfected with rogue nanobots yet again."

"Seriously? Is he single?" Elaina asked, at which Agnes laughed.

"Elaina, can I ask you a question? Why did you leave Petram? Why so suddenly?"

The other girl grew quieter. "Petram had gotten to be pretty homogenous, you know. Racially and culturally, I didn't fit in, and people were starting to remind me of that. I didn't feel welcome. When I learned enough to know that I would be welcome on the outside, it was an easy decision. I didn't tell you because I knew how you felt about Hale and the Factus. I'm sorry I just abandoned you like that."

"Well, you probably judged it right. I wouldn't have been supportive, would I? I'm glad I found you again out here."

∗ ⅄ ⅄

Before long, their guide, Dakóbo, returned with the other tourists, and they all had a snack: vegetables from the gardens and from the forest, palm juice, and roasted fish. This last item caused a bit of a stir and a few expressions of consternation from the visiting group.

Several people hesitated to accept the meat, asking if it was from a living animal—indeed, something Agnes was wondering as well. *This is still a modern Factus city, even here in this "primitive" district. They wouldn't actually kill animals, would they?*

Dakóbo addressed them while holding a tray of the food. "I understand your concern about eating other creatures. You ask, is the desire for a traditional lifestyle reason enough to kill? To predate animals, or, even worse, to raise them as livestock for consumption? We can't accept all traditions, right? If a culture practiced human sacrifice or slavery, obviously we wouldn't want to bring those customs back.

"So, here is how we draw the line in this community—we do eat some animals, such as insect larvae. We also allow animal predators to kill and eat here in Warao, although we protect certain prey species for conservation purposes.

"Now, fishing has long been a part of the Warao lifestyle. For this question of whether we should eat fish, we have a technological solution. This fish meat—" he held up the tray, "—was grown as part of a hybrid. The fish that we catch from this river are partly mechanical and partly made of living fish tissue—notably, they have computerized controls instead of a brain. That way, we can catch fish and eat the flesh, without killing any creature with awareness."

This seemed to mollify most of the visitors. Agnes still wasn't sure she could stomach eating something that had been swimming around recently, but her parents seemed to be ok with it. Eventually, at her father's encouragement—"It's really not much different from the cultured meats we ate in Petram, Agnes. Same idea"—she tried some.

As people ate, some of them talked to the guide, her parents among them. Zusana asked, "Auka, isn't it hard to keep one foot in each world, in Warao and the outside, since they are so different?"

He considered the question while he finished chewing his honeycomb. "What do you think would be hard about it?"

"Well, is it hard to stay here and be satisfied with simple technologies when you know what's out there in the world? In Warao, you could spend hours catching fish, and then preparing them and cooking them, but out in the rest of Nissus, you can have food delivered any time in just a few minutes."

He nodded. "I understand what you mean. But for me, living this lifestyle is a relief, a joyous coming home again. I like the conveniences of the outside when I am out there. But sometimes it's good to feel the satisfaction of living with my hands and my muscles, finding food, building things. Being close to family and community, close to the river."

The young man looked pensive for a moment, before speaking again. "You know, it's really an old idea, that there is something noble and virtuous about living a simple life like I just described. Something magical about being close to nature. But I don't want to romanticize the past more than it deserves—maybe the Warao from long ago felt that way at times, but I think they were mostly just trying to get by. They had to worry about food, diseases, dangers, and wars.

"But I think we are making the fantasy come true, now, more than it ever was for the ancient Warao. I can have the joys of this lifestyle, but I know I won't really go hungry, and my children won't be eaten by crocodiles or anything. I can get a scientific Factus education as well as learn the ways of the Warao. I have all the joys of a modern lifestyle, and this is simply one of those joys." He waved his arms around at the surroundings. "In its way, *this* is the most modern part of society."

Someone asked, skeptical, "Warao is the most modern part of society? Living on a river?"

Agnes glanced around her, at the hand-built canoes lashed to a pole holding up the thatched roof, the basket of vegetables next to her, the naked children a few houses over. Water was visible between the slats of the floor where she sat. *Well, obviously they need an incredible amount of technology and machinery to keep this ecosystem running inside a city, but that is a strange way for him to describe living in a primitive village, saying that it is the most modern part of society....*

Dakóbo answered enigmatically, "Ok, this may sound odd, but bear with me. Tell me, what do you think a tree wants? Imagine a redwood sequoia standing in a forest. If it had a mind and voice, what would it say it wants to accomplish?"

Nobody answered right away, so he went on. "If it were a palm tree in this forest, it would be an easy answer. A palm tree wants to live and grow and make seeds for more palm trees. There is space taken up by other kinds of trees that it could try to claim. But a redwood, that could be a harder question. I'll tell you why.

"Any organism wants to survive, to reproduce and spread. But what happens when it succeeds? What then? A redwood is probably surrounded by a whole forest of redwoods, where each mature tree might send out millions of seeds every year. And mostly it's pointless for them because they're already in a redwood forest. There's only so much space. None of the seeds will grow up unless another tree falls and makes an opening. Those seeds aren't necessary. If the tree had a brain, it might try to figure out what else it should do instead of making millions of them, year after year.

"We, humans, are redwoods in a forest. We're no longer being eaten by tigers, killing each other in wars, dying of cholera or cancer, or struggling in poverty. So, what's next? Once we don't need to worry about our children surviving, when we don't need to struggle just to live, we need to find other purposes. Hence, Nissus. Warao. I'm not sure what I would decide is worthwhile if I were a redwood, but since I'm a *Homo factus*, I choose to find it rewarding to fish on the river with my brother, to swim and play in the sun, to use my skills to make things with my hands, and to teach others such as all of you. At least, I do that some of the time, as one part of my life. And the Warao district of Nissus makes that possible. This lifestyle is therefore *supremely* modern."

For some reason, Agnes felt emotional listening to Dakóbo's little speech. She thought for a moment about why that was. *He is saying that he is free—from danger, yes, but also free to rebuild and enjoy the life that had been taken from his people. He can choose what he wants to make of his life. Something meaningful to him.*

*What would be meaningful to me?* she wondered. Her life had been turned upside down—she had lost her home, been expelled from her community, and even been rejected by the people she had been trying to advocate for.

*Petram was unsustainable, at least without forcing people to stay. Dad and I tried to do that with the mites, and Hale's doing it with propaganda and walls. Petram is now the opposite of what Nissus stands for.*

Her smile was bittersweet as she thought about the upcoming reunion and meeting with her friends. She was beginning to understand why she felt some happiness amid her pain, despite what she had lost.

The life in Petram that she had expected was gone. But she had found her fellow outcasts—Elaina, Emil, and Catteryn. Together they would build a community, of friends old and new. The trauma of her losses and experiences might always be there, but there was a glimmer of hope, nonetheless. She felt that she was starting to lay the foundation of a new life— brick by brick, intentionally, like the people of Warao had done.

*For a long time, I felt like everyone was making choices for me—giving me no say in anything. But not anymore. My family is safe, my friends are safe, and I can do anything I want with my life.*

*Finally, I am free.*

Thank you for reading and exploring the world of Nissus with me. I hope you have enjoyed the journey as much as I have.

Please consider leaving a review on Goodreads, Amazon, or another retailer.

More information about me, links to my websites and additional writing, as well as fan art, can be found at nissusnovel.com.

Carl Sorenson